Rel   Mabry, Richard L,
Fic   Medical judgment
Mab

MAR 1 5 2018

ARCHBOLD COMMUNITY LIBRARY
ARCHBOLD, OH 43502

More praise for Richard Mabry

Stress Test
"It is easy to understand why Mabry's popularity has been skyrocketing. He is a fine, fine writer."
—Michael Palmer, New York Times best-selling author

Fatal Trauma
"Asks big questions of faith, priorities, and meaning, all within the context of a tightly crafted medical drama."
—Steven James, best-selling author of *Placebo* and *Checkmate*

Critical Condition
"Mabry has the uncommon ability to take medical details and make them understandable while still maintaining accuracy and intrigue."
—*Romantic Times Book Reviews*

Other Abingdon Press books by Richard L. Mabry, MD

Prescription for Trouble series
Code Blue
Medical Error
Diagnosis Death
Lethal Remedy

Fatal Trauma
Miracle Drug

MEDICAL
JUDGMENT

RICHARD L. MABRY, M.D.

Author of the Prescription for Trouble Series

Abingdon Press

Nashville

Medical Judgment

Copyright © 2016 by Richard L. Mabry

All rights reserved.

No part of this work may be reproduced or transmitted in any form or by any means, electronic or mechanical, including photocopying and recording, or by any information storage or retrieval system, except as may be expressly permitted by the 1976 Copyright Act or in writing from the publisher. Requests for permission can be addressed to Permissions, The United Methodist Publishing House, 2222 Rosa L. Parks Blvd., PO Box 280988, Nashville, TN, 37228-0988 or e-mailed to permissions@umpublishing.org.

Macro Editor: Teri Wilhelms

Published in association with Books & Such Literary Agency

The persons and events portrayed in this work of fiction are the creations of the author, and any resemblance to persons living or dead is purely coincidental.

Library of Congress Cataloging-in-Publication Data

Names: Mabry, Richard L., author.
Title: Medical judgment / Richard L. Mabry, MD.
Description: First edition. | Nashville : Abingdon Press, [2016]
Identifiers: LCCN 2015048015 (print) | LCCN 2016001264 (ebook) | ISBN 9781630881207 (softcover : acid-free paper) | ISBN 9781630881214 (e-book)
Subjects: LCSH: Women physicians--Fiction. | Women--Violence against--Fiction. | Man-woman relationships--Fiction. | GSAFD: Christian
fiction. | Romantic suspense fiction. | Mystery fiction.
Classification: LCC PS3613.A2 M435 2016 (print) | LCC PS3613.A2 (ebook) | DDC
813/.6--dc23
LC record available at http://lccn.loc.gov/2015048015

16 17 18 19 20 21 22 23 24—10 9 8 7 6 5 4 3 2 1

Manufactured in the United States of America

For my family, with thanks for believing in me

Acknowledgments

When I began to write novels, I had no idea I'd get this far, and it wouldn't have been possible without the help and encouragement of a lot of people along the way. At the start, two great writers and teachers, Alton Gansky and James Scott Bell, suggested I try my hand at fiction. Along the way I learned from numerous others—too many to name. Agent Rachelle Gardner saw something in my writing she liked and has helped guide my course for years. The folks at Abingdon Press, first under the direction of Barbara Scott and now Ramona Richards, have been a pleasure to work with. Cat Hoort and her team have made sure word gets out about the book. Teri Wilhelms supplied the finishing touches with her edits. My wife, Kay, in addition to being an encourager, has served as my first reader for all my novels, always pointing me in the right direction when I get off course. I appreciate every one of you. I couldn't have done it without your help.

My retirement from medicine has not gone according to my plan, but rather that of God. But that's okay, because His plan, as always, has turned out to be much better than mine. I can hardly wait to see what He has in mind next for me.

1

THE SMELL OF SMOKE GRADUALLY NUDGED DR. SARAH Gordon from a troubled sleep into semi-wakefulness. Hours earlier she'd finally given in and taken a sleeping pill. Now it made her feel fuzzy and uncertain, as though she were moving through cobwebs. At first, she couldn't separate the odor of smoke from the dream in which she'd been mired. Sarah struggled to bring herself more fully awake. Had she really smelled smoke? Or was it a nightmare? She eased up in bed, resting on one elbow, and sniffed the air around her. There it was again. The smoke was real.

Her brain, still numbed by sleep and Ambien, took a few seconds to make the connection. Smoke meant fire. Something in her house was burning—perhaps the whole house was about to go up in flames. She had to wake Harry. He'd take charge. After she awakened him, they'd hurry down the hall together and get Jenny. Then Harry would lead them to safety.

Sarah reached to her left across the king-size bed, but when her hand touched a bare pillow, the reality hit her, forcing her fully awake more effectively than a bucket of ice water. Her husband wasn't there. He'd never be there again. He was dead. He'd been dead for eight months now. So had Jenny, their two-year-old daughter. Sarah was alone... in a burning house.

But was she alone? She had a vague recollection of hearing a noise about the same time she became aware of the smoke smell. Was someone out there, waiting for her? Or was that part of a dream as well? Should she stay here in the bedroom until she was sure? No, she needed to get to safety. The "someone" might or might not be real, but the fire wasn't the product of her imagination. She had to get out, and quickly.

She threw on her robe and shoved her feet into slippers. Sarah dropped her cell phone and keys into the pocket of the robe. She took two steps away from the bed before turning back to pick up the flashlight from the bedside table. Sarah flicked it on and checked the beam. It was dim—the batteries probably hadn't been changed since before Jenny died—but it gave off enough illumination to let her see a few feet in front of her. She hoped that would be enough. In several strides that displayed more confidence than she felt, Sarah covered the distance to the door leading to the hall. *Feel the door. If it's hot, find some other way out.*

Cautiously, she pressed her palm against the door. When she felt no heat, Sarah let out a breath she didn't know she was holding. She opened the door and looked around. No flames. Then she sniffed, and there it was again—a faint aroma of smoke wafting up the stairway—not enough to choke her, not an amount capable of blocking her vision, but sufficient nonetheless to send her hurrying toward what she hoped was a safe exit.

Guided by the faint glow from the flashlight, she descended to the first floor. As she got lower, she coughed a little, her eyes watered a bit, but she could breathe, could see through the tears. The smoke still wasn't bad. Maybe that was a good sign.

At the bottom of the stairs, she stopped to listen. Was that a noise? She strained her ears but heard nothing more. Maybe there was no intruder. Maybe that was all in her imagination. Maybe.

But the smoke wasn't something she'd imagined. It was real, and where there was smoke, there was fire. But where was it? She heard no crackle of flames. She felt no pulse of heat on her face. She blinked away a few tears and sniffed again. The smoke was still there, and now it seemed to be increasing.

The light from the flashlight had become so dim as to be almost useless. *I need to see. Why haven't I tried to turn on lights?* Wasn't there something about electricity failing if the fire got too near the supply line? Sarah flipped the switch at the foot of the stairs, and the overhead fixtures blazed into light. The power was still on. Good. She turned off the flashlight but held onto it. *It might be a useful weapon.*

Sarah started to exit the house the way she habitually did, through the kitchen and into the garage. She turned to her right to go that way but stopped when she saw tendrils of dark smoke drifting under the door from the garage and into the kitchen. The garage. That's where the fire was. She couldn't get out this way.

She turned back and scanned the area straight ahead of her, the living room. No smoke. No heat. No noise of flames. Best of all, there was no movement or sound that signaled someone there...at least, no one she could see. She could hurry through to the front door and make her escape.

Should she stop and call the fire department now? Was there any reason to further delay that call? Wasn't it important to call them immediately? *Get out of the house first. Call for help when you're safe.*

Sarah hurried to the front door, threw it open, and felt the fresh night breeze on her face. Her instinct was to run, to get out of the house as quickly as possible, but she stopped as yet another rule heard long ago surfaced in her mind. *Keep doors and windows closed. Air can feed the flames and make the fire grow.* She shut the door behind her.

Sarah hurried to the end of the sidewalk, her slippers making a soft shushing on the concrete. When she got there, she paused and turned back toward her house. At first she saw no one there. Wait! Had there been a flicker of movement in the shadows at the corner of the house? Or was it her imagination, fueled by the adrenaline of the situation, turning wisps of smoke into the shape of a prowler?

She watched for perhaps half a minute more, trying not to blink, looking with unfocused eyes into the middle distance. *Let your peripheral vision pick up faint images.* She saw no figures, no movement.

Enough. Get help. She pulled her cell phone from the pocket of her robe and stabbed out 911 before hitting send.

"911. What is your emergency?"

"This is Dr. Sarah Gordon. My house is on fire. The address is 5613 Maple Shade Drive."

There was the briefest of pauses, during which Sarah heard keys tapping. "I've dispatched first responders. Is anyone injured? Are you in the house?"

"No injuries. And I'm outside, on the lawn."

"Is anyone else there? Or are you alone?"

Sarah hesitated before she answered.

"I'm alone." *At least, I hope so.*

The call awakened Detective Bill Larson. He brought his wrist close to his face and squinted at his watch. Two fifteen a.m. The phone had interrupted a dream—not a pleasant one, but that wasn't unusual. Troubled sleep and disturbing dreams were part of the pattern his life had taken on during his struggle for lasting sobriety.

"We've got a fire at a private dwelling," the dispatcher said. "The fire chief on the scene thinks it might be arson, so I wanted to notify you. If you like, I'll send a patrol car by there now to do a preliminary. Then you can hook up with the fire marshal tomorrow. Would you like me to do that?"

Larson yawned. "Probably. Where's the fire?"

"The location is 5613 Maple Shade, the residence of Dr. Sarah Gordon."

The name brought him awake. Larson had met Sarah Gordon and her husband shortly after the detective moved to town. He'd been introduced to them at church. Realizing that being part of a church family would be important as he tried to get his life back together, he'd joined the First Community Church shortly after moving to Jameson. It was one of the larger churches in town, and Larson figured he could lose himself in a congregation that size. He needed to be just a taker for a while. Maybe after he had a few more months of sobriety under his belt he could find a place to serve. Maybe.

Larson called up his mental picture of Harry Gordon: a nice-looking man in his 30s, his blond hair always a bit tousled, a perpetual grin on his face. But the person his memory could more easily recall was Sarah. She had dark hair cut short, flawless olive skin, and always seemed to be laughing. Each time he saw the two of them together with their two-year-old daughter, Larson realized again what he'd lost when his own family was torn asunder.

After his initial meeting, he'd seen Sarah a few times at church, always at a distance and generally with her husband. Then she'd suffered the tragic loss of both husband and daughter, a loss that seemed to devastate Sarah. After that happened, Larson figured he should express his sympathy to her, but the time never seemed right. Then it wasn't long before she stopped coming to church altogether. He hadn't seen her since.

"Larson, are you there?"

"Sorry. Just thinking," Larson replied.

"So what do you want me to do?" the dispatcher asked.

"Tell you what," Larson said. "I know her from church. I think I'll head over there now." He ended the call and began to dress.

Sarah sat huddled under a Mylar blanket in the fire chief's SUV, her teeth occasionally chattering despite the warmth of the summer evening. One hand held an empty china mug, courtesy of her neighbor who'd brought coffee and offered to let Sarah spend the night—what remained of it—at her house. Sarah had declined with thanks. She wanted to be in her own home.

Her home. The phrase resonated in her mind. It was the house she and Harry bought when they were married. It was the home into which they brought Jenny over two years ago. It was full of memories. And now, although both Harry and Jenny were gone, she wasn't going to turn loose of those memories—or the house.

Sarah wasn't about to be driven from her home by fire or anything else. But was the house habitable? Just how bad was the damage inside? She'd soon know, because here came the chief. She decided that, no matter what he told her, she wasn't going to easily abandon her home. Sarah wasn't certain whether her attitude was based on pure stubbornness or a sentimental attachment, but whatever the cause, she was adamant.

The chief climbed into the driver's seat of his vehicle and half-turned to face her. Sarah had a vague recollection of meeting him at some point in the past, although she couldn't recall his name. In her present condition, she wasn't sure she could even remember her own.

"Doctor, I'm Stan Lambert, the deputy fire chief," he said, answering Sarah's unasked question. "I know this is unsettling. Are you okay? The EMTs are here. I know you told one of my firemen earlier that you didn't need any attention, but maybe you should let them check you over."

Sarah made a conscious effort to still the shaking she felt inside her, shaking due not just to her ordeal but to the emotions it set churning within her. She put the empty coffee mug on the floor of the SUV. "I'm fine, Chief. What I need to know is whether I'll be able to get back into my house tonight."

"That's the good news," he said. "The fire was centered in a pile of oily rags burning in the garage near the door to the kitchen. It produced a lot of smoke, sort of like a smudge pot. Despite depositing soot around the area of the fire and leaving the smell of smoke in some parts of the house, the fire didn't do any real structural damage."

"Even in the garage?"

"There might be a little scorching of the wood in a place or two, but nothing that would make the house unsafe. By the time my men got to it, most of the rags were consumed. As soon as we arrived, some of the firemen unrolled the hose and hooked it to the fire plug down the street in case it was needed, but as it turned out, all we had to use was a hand-held fire extinguisher."

"So I can go back into the house?" Sarah said.

"Yes, that's the good news," the chief said. "But I think there's some bad news to go with it." He looked up. "And I think I'll let this man tell you about it."

The back door of the SUV opened. A man edged in and took a seat behind Sarah. In the illumination provided by the dome light, she could tell he wore a suit and tie. However, the suit was wrinkled and the tie askew. He closed the door, brushed his dark hair out of his eyes, and rubbed his unshaven chin. "I'm so sorry this happened," he said.

Sarah searched her memory. She knew this man. That is to say, she felt like she should know who he was. Then it came to her. She'd seen him at church, heard his name there. His name danced on the edge of her memory, and she found it at about the same time he held up a badge wallet and identified himself.

"You may not remember me, but we go to the same church. I'm Detective Bill Larson."

"Why are you here? Are you part of some group at the church that ministers to people who've had a fire?" She did a double take. "Surely you're not here as a policeman. This was just a fire in some oily rags in my garage," Sarah said.

"No, I'm not here as a church member, although I'll do anything I can to help," Larson said. "And I'm very definitely here as a policeman. I'm sure the chief has already told you this was no ordinary fire."

"No, it was just some oily rags burning," she said.

"And where did those oily rags come from? They didn't just materialize and set themselves ablaze." Larson said. "Do you even keep such things in your garage?"

"No," she said. "I'm careful about that. They could catch on...Oh!"

"That's right," Larson said. "That fire was set. This is arson."

Bill Larson watched from the back seat of the fire chief's SUV as firemen loaded their gear onto the truck. Sarah Gordon sat huddled in the front seat of the vehicle. Her dark hair was mussed, she wore no makeup, her eyes were red-rimmed. This was quite a different Sarah than the picture Larson had carried in his mind. Although she looked so miserable that he wanted to comfort her, the detective reminded himself that tonight he was here in his official capacity. To do his job properly he'd need to put aside any personal feelings.

He pulled a notebook from the inside pocket of his summer-weight suit coat, clicked a ballpoint pen into life, and said, "Sarah...Dr. Gordon, can you think of any reason someone would want to do this?"

She pulled the blanket tighter around her shoulders. "No."

Larson waited for her to expand on that answer, but she just sat silent, unmoving. He figured she was probably in shock, and it was unlikely he'd get any useful information from her right now. But he had to try. However, his assumption proved correct, as the answer to every question he put to her was the same—"I don't know."

Finally, Larson put his notebook back in his pocket. "Tell you what." He looked at his watch. "Tomorrow—or rather, today—is Saturday. Why don't I give you a call about mid-morning, and you can give me your statement then? Meanwhile, let the chief and me get you settled in with a friend or neighbor so you can get a few hours of sleep."

The chief said, "Doctor, where would you—"

She turned to face him, and her expression—the set of her jaw—stopped him in mid-sentence. "I'm perfectly fine to be alone," Sarah Gordon said. "I'm planning to spend the night—at least, what's left of it—right here. You've told me there's no structural damage to the house. Well, I can stand the smell of a little smoke. I've lived through much worse." She swiveled to look at her home through the windshield of the vehicle. "Nothing and no one will force me out of that house."

Despite what she'd said about her willingness to be alone in her house, when the front door closed behind the fire chief and the detective, Sarah felt depression and loneliness descend on her. She dragged herself up the stairs, entered her bedroom, and—still wearing her robe and slippers—threw herself across the bed and buried her face in a pillow. She spent the next half hour sobbing into that pillow. She'd managed to hold it together in front of the fire chief and Detective Larson, but now she let it all out, not just the emotions caused by the fire, but her sorrow at the loss of her husband and daughter, the struggle she'd had since their deaths. She thought she'd be over it by now, that she'd have moved on. But that's not what had happened.

Come on, Sarah. You're a grown woman. You're a physician. Every day in the emergency room you make critical decisions. Why can't you hold your personal life together?

That question had occupied Sarah for the past eight months, and she was pretty certain she had the answer. Before Harry's death, she'd gotten into the habit of shedding her professional persona at the door. At home she and Harry shared responsibility. They had been a team. If she didn't have an answer, Harry did. If one of them was unable to do something, the other one would. They could talk about things, make decisions jointly, lean on each other. But that changed with his death. Now she was alone, in every respect.

There was no more respite from responsibility when she came home from her work at the hospital. She simply moved into a different set of circumstances, another situation in which she had to make decisions. Wherever she was, whatever she was doing, it was all up to her. There were a few times when she thought she heard Harry's voice whispering, "Go ahead, Sarah. You can do it. You're strong." *But I don't feel strong, especially when things keep coming at me.*

And in addition to the burden she felt, Sarah was still subject to episodes of grief, interspersed with anger—at God and (although she hated to admit it) at Harry for leaving her so alone.

The hardest times, times that seemed to tear her apart, came in the middle of the night. That's when she'd think she heard the sound of Jenny's voice. Sarah would roll out of bed, still half-asleep, and head for the room where Jenny slept before realizing that room was empty—just like all the other rooms in the house. Sarah was no longer needed as a mother. Jenny was dead.

Tonight the smell of smoke was pervasive throughout the house, but she could tolerate that. Her depression at the loss of her family nipped at the edges of her consciousness, but with an effort of will she put that aside to consider something of more immediate importance. What she couldn't get past was her fear that whoever set the fire would return. Every noise she heard seemed to represent footsteps on the stairs or movement in the next room.

Sarah wished she still had the pistol Harry kept in his bedside table. Right after they were married, she'd told him she felt uncomfortable with a gun in the house.

"I'm a nut about firearm safety," he'd said. "I want to have it to protect us, but I'm careful. Believe me."

After Jenny was born, Sarah renewed her objections. It wasn't safe to have a pistol in the house where there was a child. She'd read about gun owners who shot a family member or were wounded or killed themselves. Finally, Harry had given in to her entreaties to get rid of the weapon. But now she wished she had it with her. More important, she wished she had Harry beside her.

They'd worked together—she, an ER doctor, and he, a surgeon—to mesh their schedules so they'd have time with each other and with Jenny. Things were going well. They'd even talked about trying for a little brother or sister for their daughter. But one afternoon, as Harry drove home from the day-care center with Jenny in the car seat, another driver crashed into them and snuffed out both their lives, as well as her own. And, so far as Sarah was concerned, her life ended at that moment as well.

Sarah told herself for the hundredth time there was no need to go over the past. Harry and Jenny were gone. She was still here, although she wasn't sure just why, and she had to concentrate on moving ahead. That had been her priority since her loss: moving ahead, one day at a time, one step at a time, even if she had to force herself. This fire was simply another roadblock she had to get past. *Harry, I'm trying. Really, I'm trying.*

The firemen had thrown the main electrical breaker to the house until they determined the location and severity of the fire. Now, although the electricity was back on, the clock at Sarah's bedside continued to flash 1:13, the time when all this took place. She'd fallen into bed without resetting the clock, so that now when she opened her eyes and looked in that direction, she saw a constant reminder of what had happened tonight. She knew she should get up and reset the clock, but the effort was beyond her at this point.

It seemed to Sarah she'd done nothing but toss and turn since dropping onto the bed in a state of exhaustion at almost four a.m. She untangled herself from the covers and punched the button to light up the dial of her watch. It was ten after five. Sleep wasn't going to come.

She slid her feet into the scuffs that had fallen at the bedside. She shrugged out of her robe, then went to the closet and wrapped herself in Harry's robe, one she'd kept because even after eight months she thought she could smell his after-shave lotion in it. Even now, it felt like she'd put on a suit of armor. It was a little like Harry was there with her. And she needed that.

Sarah padded down the stairs. In the kitchen, she flipped on the coffee maker and waited, hoping the scent of the freshly brewed coffee would overcome some of the smell of smoke that seemed to follow her wherever she went in the house.

She looked at her watch and wondered how long it would be before she could begin making phone calls. Sarah moved to one of the kitchen cabinets, opened a drawer, and withdrew a notepad and pencil. Then, armed with a fresh cup of coffee, she sat down at the kitchen table and began to make a list of the tasks that faced her.

The last emergency vehicle had gone. Clouds covered the moon and stars, and there were no streetlights nearby. He couldn't have planned better circumstances for watching unobserved. With the car windows partially open to let in the night breeze, he was comfortable leaning back behind the steering wheel. Other than a cou-

ple of officers driving by earlier, apparently the police had decided that regular patrols in the area weren't necessary for the rest of the night. That suited him just fine.

The house had been dark since he drove up, but he knew that didn't mean its occupant was sleeping. Sure enough, at that moment the light in an upstairs room came on. In a few minutes another window, this one downstairs, was lit, the illumination faint as though from a light in an adjoining room. He figured she'd been unable to sleep, had tossed and turned before eventually getting out of bed. Now she was probably sitting in the kitchen, perhaps drinking coffee or tea, wondering why this had happened.

Well, that was the point of the whole exercise, wasn't it? He didn't want to kill her—not yet. First, she had to suffer—not necessarily physically—but she had to suffer. That's what this was about—the waiting, the wondering, the fear. The dying would come later.

2

KYLE ANDREWS SAT HUNCHED OVER HIS LAPTOP COMPUTER at his kitchen table, his second cup of coffee at his elbow, skimming the news headlines. He looked up from the computer, took a sip of coffee, and wondered if it would be a good idea to call Sarah.

He'd first met Harry and Sarah Gordon when he came to town to set up his law practice. He'd actually met them where a lot of people in Jameson met—at the First Community Church. It wasn't long before he and Harry became good friends, and Sarah appeared to be happy about that. Soon thereafter, Kyle met someone else at church, someone who changed his life. It wasn't too many months later that he was engaged to Nicole, and the two couples double-dated frequently after that.

Nicole's sudden death had left Kyle with a hole in his heart, but he'd tried not to show it. After all, that was what Christians did. But when Harry and Jenny were killed, Kyle figured he, more than most, had a sense of how the tragic death of a loved one might affect Sarah. And that was even more reason for him to offer support to her now.

Harry had never said, "If something happens to me, take care of Sarah." Kyle figured he didn't have to. That sort of thing was understood between friends. In the eight months since Harry's death, Kyle had worked hard not to press Sarah, while still making sure she knew he was there for her. He'd like to do more, but there never seemed to be the right opening. For now he'd best simply stay close and be available.

Would this be a good time to call? He looked at his watch. Not quite eight. It was Saturday, and she might be sleeping in. On the one hand—

The ring of his cell phone made him look up from his computer. When he saw the caller ID he realized his decision had been made for him. Sarah was calling.

"Good morning," he said. "I was about to call and see how you're doing."

"That's why I'm phoning. I...I need your help this morning."

"As a friend or as a lawyer?" Kyle reached for his coffee cup. "Did you get a speeding ticket yesterday, Sarah?" He smiled at the thought. Sarah was the epitome of the term, "straight arrow."

"I'm meeting with the police this morning, Kyle, and I'd like you to be there with me."

Kyle set the cup on the table without drinking. "Of course I'll be there, but what's going on? This sounds serious."

The silence that followed went on longer than Kyle would like. Finally, Sarah said, "Someone tried to set fire to my house last night. That is, someone started a fire in my garage. It didn't do much damage except for the smoke, but the police called it arson and want to talk with me this morning. I'm sure they're going to ask me who might want to do such a thing, but—"

"But they have to consider whether a homeowner might do something like this to collect insurance," Kyle said, finishing her thought. "Who are you meeting and what time?"

"Bill Larson said he'd call and set it up."

Kyle's mental file whirred and spit out data on Detective Larson. Late thirties, dark hair that always seemed to need a trim, not really handsome but possessor of just the type of rugged good looks some women liked. Larson had a reputation for persistence among the lawyers in town. When he was working a case, he was like a dog with a bone, never turning loose until he finished. That didn't bother Kyle, but the presence of another man in Sarah's life at this point was a bit disconcerting.

Of course, there were also whispers circulating around the courthouse that Larson's excessive drinking was the reason for his divorce. The man's ex-wife and son had moved to Montana, while Larson was starting over here in Texas. Evidently the detective had it more or less together thus far in his new situation—at least, it seemed that way. But Kyle knew that with alcoholics the struggle was lifelong and neverending. An alcoholic was never "recovered," just "recovering." Larson would bear watching—on several levels.

"Did you see Larson after all this took place?" Kyle asked.

"Yes, we sat in the fire chief's SUV and talked a bit. I didn't really answer all his questions, but I think he could tell how upset I was. He suggested we meet today." She cleared her throat. "Will you go with me?"

"Sarah, just tell me where and when. I'll be with you as a friend, not simply as a lawyer."

"Thank you," she said. "But if I need a lawyer, I want you."

You've always had me, Sarah . . . and not just as a lawyer.

Bill Larson heard her footsteps before he saw her. He got up from his desk in the otherwise deserted police squad room. "Sarah . . ." he started to say. But he stopped the word before it left his mouth. *Keep it professional.* "Dr. Gordon, thank you for coming down here," he said.

She took the chair he indicated. "I . . . I didn't think I had much choice."

"Last night you didn't seem up to answering too many questions. Coming here this morning seemed more convenient for both of us," Larson said. "It saved me some time and effort. That's all."

"I hope I haven't missed too much." The words were accompanied by the sound of leather heels hitting the linoleum of the squad room in a rapid rat-tat-tat.

Larson frowned when he saw attorney Kyle Andrews hurrying toward his desk. "Nothing of significance, counselor." The detective stood and offered his hand, then said, "Pull up a chair from one of those other desks. I was just starting to interview the doctor."

Andrews reached down and hugged Sarah Gordon, perhaps a bit more enthusiastically than mere friendship would dictate, something that didn't escape Larson's attention. Then the lawyer grabbed a chair from the next desk, pulled it over beside Dr. Gordon, and sat.

"Well, I'm glad I made it in time," the lawyer said. "I always advise my clients not to talk to the police without their attorney present."

Larson wasn't certain why he didn't trust Kyle Andrews. Perhaps it was just his nature as a policeman to look askance at people. His wife—that is, his ex-wife—had mentioned that tendency on more than one occasion. Today, Andrews was in full lawyer mode: gray glen plaid suit, red and gray tie, rust-colored hair carefully styled, rimless glasses giving him a serious look. Even his briefcase was perfect for the part, scuffed just enough to show it wasn't just for show.

The detective directed his attention to Sarah. "Dr. Gordon," Larson said, "Let me make it clear that we don't suspect you of anything. I don't think you'll need a lawyer." He looked pointedly at Andrews for a moment before turning back to Dr. Gordon. "I'll say up front that all I'm looking for from you is information."

"And I'll say up front that I'm here to lend some support to a friend," Andrews said with a half-smile.

Larson nodded. He sensed that he and Kyle Andrews might not end up exchanging Christmas cards. On the other hand, it seemed they both had Sarah Gordon's best interest in mind. He'd accept that for now. The detective pulled a note pad toward him. "Let's start with the names of anyone who might be angry with you—not necessarily someone who'd want to kill you, but people who might carry a grudge, be unhappy with something you've done. Disappointed patients. Frustrated colleagues. People from your personal life who might wish to harm you. Anyone."

The doctor's immediate response was, "I don't know of anyone who fits that description."

"You may change your mind as you think about that," Larson said. "Let's consider patients. How about them?"

"As an emergency room physician I treat dozens of people every day. Some of the cases are simple. Some are literally life-and-death situations. I exercise my medical judgment all the time, and if I make a mistake, the consequences could be minor or they could be catastrophic. Most of the time I don't even remember the names of the patients I treat, much less which ones could be carrying a grudge."

"Okay, I may want to go through some ER records with you to get some names, but we'll come back to that," Larson said. "Anything from your personal life? I'm sorry that I have to ask, but any ex-boyfriends, former lovers, men you disappointed?"

Before Sarah could open her mouth, Kyle Andrews said, "Are you implying—"

"I'm not implying anything," Larson said. "I have to ask these questions, and if you think about it, you'll see that." He looked at Dr. Gordon. "Anyone?"

"No," she said, and shook her head.

"Did you hear or see anything last night before the fire started? Was there anything that suggested there might be someone in your house or garage?"

She chewed on her lower lip. Larson knew from experience there was something there—if he could just keep quiet long enough.

"I didn't hear anything until I awoke to the smell of smoke. There might have been a noise downstairs at about that time—I wasn't sure. Then, after I got out of the house, I thought I saw a shadow hurrying around the corner of the house."

"Which side?"

"Where the garage is," she said.

"That would be the west side." Larson made a note. "I know you didn't mention this to me at the time, but did you tell the chief or any of the firefighters about it?"

"No, I guess I was too rattled," she said. "And, honestly, I wasn't even sure I hadn't imagined it."

"Do you have any idea how an intruder got into the garage to set the fire?" Larson asked.

"I've wondered about that," Dr. Gordon said. "I have an electric garage door opener, and the remote is supposed to have what they call a rolling code so someone can't just open the door with his or her own remote."

"There are at least a couple of ways, actually," Larson replied. "First, I noticed your car was parked at the curb last night. Most people keep their garage door opener remote clipped to their auto's sun visor. Is that what you do?"

She nodded.

"Thieves now have sophisticated ways to get into cars without leaving a trace. If he did that, a press of the button on the remote and the garage door would open for him."

"Is that what he did?" she asked.

"No, he used a very low-tech method to get into the garage, and he didn't need a remote control for it."

Andrews leaned forward in his chair and asked, "And you know this how?"

"Two things," Larson said. "First, when we looked inside, the fire marshal and I both noticed the emergency release for the garage door opener had been tripped. And second..." He reached under his desk and produced a straightened wire coat hanger and a small triangular piece of wood. "I found these on the floor of the garage near the door." He shoved them forward. "You can touch them. They didn't have any useful fingerprints on them."

"How—" Dr. Gordon started to ask.

"Whoever broke in inserted the wooden wedge under the weather-stripping at the top of the garage door. Then he used the opening he created to insinuate this coat hanger along the track. When the coat hanger was far enough in, he hooked the emergency release lever and pulled it."

"Then—" Andrews said.

"Then he set the fire, closed the garage door manually, and waited to see what happened," Larson said.

"And maybe that's the noise I heard," she said.

"Which brings up the question of why all he did was pile some oily rags on the garage floor and set them afire. It would have been easy for the intruder to go through your garage into your kitchen and…"

"And take what he wanted, assault me, or even murder me in my sleep," Dr. Gordon said. "I wonder why he didn't."

Larson's gaze went to Kyle Andrews and he realized the attorney had made the same assumption he had. Maybe whoever did this didn't want to kill Dr. Sarah Gordon. Maybe he wanted to frighten her. And judging from what Larson had seen last night and this morning, he'd succeeded.

Early summer days in Texas could be pleasant or they could be very hot. It was almost noon, and today the sun on the concrete in downtown Jameson produced heat that was withering. Sarah stood in the shade of the blue awning that covered the entrance to the Jameson Police Department's headquarters and listened as Kyle Andrews offered advice she didn't want to hear.

"If you don't want to stay with a friend or neighbor, why don't you let me get you settled into a hotel for a few days? I know the owner of a company that does remediation—that is, they restore damage after fires. If I call him right now, I can meet his crew over at your house with a key. If they start cleaning the smoke and soot from your place this morning—let's see, this is Saturday—you'll probably be able to move back in by Monday. Maybe even earlier."

"Kyle," Sarah said, trying to be patient, "First of all, I don't want some stranger to have a key to my house. And besides that, I'm not going to leave there... not even for one night."

"Why?"

"Because that house was our home—mine and Harry's and Jenny's. It may be silly, but I don't want to leave it." She paused. "In a way, being there helps me feel close to the family I lost. And moving out, even for a day, might break that bond."

This went on for a few more minutes, with Sarah repeating her reasons, until finally Kyle gave in.

"Okay, how's this?" Kyle said. "Let me call the guy. You can meet him there and go over the damage. He can start his crew working this afternoon, but I'll ask him to quit by seven or eight this evening, so you'll have the house to yourself tonight. They'll work around you. You won't have to move out. They should be finished in a day or two, and when they do, your home will be good as new."

No, it won't. It will have been invaded. It will never be the same. But it will still be our home—mine and Harry's and Jenny's. "I guess that would work," Sarah said. Then she had another thought. "I need to call my insurance agent and report this."

"Tell you what," Kyle said. "Let's get out of this heat. We'll go to my office. You can contact your insurance agent and let him get started. He'll probably want to schedule a visit from an adjustor to inspect the damage. While you're on the phone, I'll use my cell to call Tom Oliver so he can get started. After that I'll buy you some lunch."

Sarah hesitated. "Kyle, you don't have to do all this. I know I called you, but that was because I thought I might need a lawyer. If Detective Larson is to be believed, I didn't really need legal representation."

"You may not need me as a lawyer, but I'm pretty sure you could use a friend to help you through this. Remember, I was Harry's friend. Now that he's gone, I think I owe it to him to be around when you need me."

As the two walked away, Sarah wondered if the call to Kyle had been unnecessary. When she reached out to him, she thought she might need an attorney, but judging from what Larson said this morning, that wasn't the case. Now it seemed that Kyle wanted to take charge and help her through this trial. Sort of like what Harry would have done.

Bill Larson sat at his desk with his tie loosened and his shirtsleeves rolled above his elbows. He probably ought to get some short-sleeved dress shirts to wear during the summer. He'd thought about it recently, but he kept putting it off. Maybe it was because there were times when he thought this stop in Texas was just temporary. He had dreams of winning back his ex-wife, and of his family reuniting and moving back to Minnesota. Then again, maybe it was just inertia, the same thing that kept him living in a furnished apartment rather than looking for a house although he'd been in Jameson for almost a year.

He looked at his watch and did a rapid calculation. It would be an hour earlier in Montana. Annie and Billy would be up by now. She'd be having her second cup of coffee at the kitchen table and his son would be watching cartoons. He pulled out his cell phone and made a call.

"Annie, this is Bill."

"Good morning." He couldn't tell from her words or the tone in which they'd been spoken what her mood was.

He wanted to tell her he was working to get his life back together. He wished he could ask her if she was seeing anyone. He had lots of things he wanted to talk about, but any one of them might set off an argument. It was like trying to navigate through a minefield.

He talked for a few minutes with her—desultory conversation, nothing of consequence. He did manage to mention that he was staying sober, but Annie didn't seem to want to pursue the subject. Finally he said, "Can I talk with Billy for a minute?"

But if trying to talk with his ex-wife was difficult, talking with Billy was like pulling teeth. It was obvious that the preschooler would rather watch Saturday morning television than talk with his dad. His answers were mainly monosyllables. Larson could picture him, one eye on the TV set, shifting from one foot to the other as he tried to talk with his father while not missing any of his favorite cartoons.

Finally, Larson ended the conversation, promising to call again in a few days. Just before she hung up, Annie said one thing that encouraged him. "It's good that you're sober. I hope you stay that way."

Larson sat for a few minutes afterward, wondering how he let his family get away from him. Actually, he knew very well how he did it. The same way he wound up being given the choice of resigning from the Minneapolis police force or being fired. He'd drunk himself off the force and out of the life of his wife and son. And he was still working to repair that damage. He wondered if he ever could.

He sighed and picked up his notebook from where it lay on his desk. Larson riffled through the pages where he'd jotted down information about the fire at Sarah Gordon's house. He was about to start reading when he heard someone come up behind his desk.

"Working on a Saturday! Are you trying to get promoted to Chief of Detectives? If so, let me remind you that the

Jameson police force doesn't have that position. We're too small."

"Just doing my job, Cal," Larson said. He swiveled around to face Cal Johnson, who was standing next to his own desk, right behind Larson's.

"I waited for you, but you didn't show. I thought we were going to run together this morning at the high school track," Cal said. He half drained the bottle of water he held.

Cal's skin, the color of old mahogany, glistened with sweat, evidence of his recent exercise. Cal wore a University of North Texas tee shirt, grey shorts, and well-broken-in Nikes. In the hand opposite the one holding the water, he grasped a ragged towel with which he mopped his forehead. His dark hair was plastered to his skull by perspiration.

"Sorry. I should have called you," Larson said. "I had to come in and take a statement this morning. Someone set a fire in Dr. Sarah Gordon's garage in the middle of the night."

Cal's eyebrows went up, which for him was a significant display of emotion. "Why would someone do that?"

"That's the question I'm trying to answer." Larson gave Cal the information he had thus far. "Now I'm getting ready to do what police work boils down to—knock on doors, run things up on the computer, nose around. Want to help?"

"I will if I'm needed," Cal said. "Otherwise, I'd better get back to the house. Since it's my day off, I promised Ruth I'd take care of a pretty significant honey-do list." He took another swipe at his forehead with his towel, then finished the water he held. "Of course, if anything breaks and you really need some help, give me a call."

Larson was already shaking his head. "Cal, you've already had one marriage end because your wife couldn't stand your being gone so much. I'll call you if I have to, but I'm not going to contribute to your second divorce."

"It'll happen or it won't," Cal said. "Ruth seems to be a little more understanding than Betty was."

"That's good, but don't test her." Larson was silent for a moment. "You'd better do your best to make your marriage work."

Cal moved to Larson's side and laid a hand on his friend's shoulder. "I'm sorry. I know that's a sensitive subject for you. How long's it been?"

Larson didn't have to think about it. "It's been a little over a year since Annie left."

"She still in Montana?"

"She and Billy. I call them about once a week." He held up his cell phone. "I just finished talking with them."

"Any chance you and your wife will get back together?" Cal asked.

"She hasn't remarried, so that's good. Even though she divorced me, I keep hoping if I stay sober she'll agree to try it again." Larson looked at the ceiling and counted. "I've got eleven months of sobriety now."

"That's great," Cal said.

"Time will tell whether it's good enough," Larson said. "Meanwhile, I guess I'd better get to work. Getting fired from this job wouldn't help my situation."

After lunch, Kyle offered to follow Sarah home to make sure she arrived safely, but she declined with thanks. He'd persisted, but she finally convinced him that she'd rather be alone. "I'll be safe. Don't worry about me."

"Well, call me if you need anything. I've talked with Tom Oliver, and he and his crew should be at your house when you arrive."

When Sarah parked at the curb beside her house, a white van and a red pickup truck were already there. Three men in work clothes leaned on the van, talking and laughing together. As she exited her car, a middle-aged man in jeans and a tee shirt emerged from the pickup and walked toward her. He was clean-shaven. Brown hair in a brush cut. His face was pleasant but unremarkable. Average build. Sarah decided that an hour from now she'd be hard-pressed to describe him.

He stopped in front of her and held out his hand. "Tom Oliver."

She took the proffered hand. "Sarah Gordon. Thank you for coming out on a weekend, Mr. Oliver," she said.

"It's Tom. And when people need us, they need us right then. Besides, Kyle's pretty persuasive, and I owe him something," he said. Then he pointed to the three men by the van. "Darrell, Carl, and Louie are ready to get started. Why don't we see how much work we have to do?"

Sarah led Oliver inside. She was curious about the apparent debt Oliver owed Kyle, but decided not to pursue it right now. Instead, she briefly told him about the fire, where it had been located, and the fireman's description of the damage as mainly cosmetic. "So, can you take care of this?" she said, waving her hand in the general direction of the soot-blackened wall in the kitchen.

"If the fire chief's right and there's no structural damage, we start by dealing with the residual smoke stains and soot. Ridding the house of most of the smell will take at least a day. We'll shampoo the carpets, use fans and vacuum extractors, probably apply some air freshener, whatever it takes."

"What will it take to get everything back like it was before the fire?"

"Just a little more work and expense. We'll get rid of the smoke smell first. We may need to replace some of the carpets—I'll have to see what they're like after we shampoo them. We wash down the affected walls and treat them with a chemical that further neutralizes the smoke smell. Finally, we apply fresh paint. Of course, you'll be trading the smell of smoke for the smell of paint, but that won't last long, and pretty soon everything should be back like it was."

No, the house will never again be like it was when Harry and I bought it, but at least I can remove the traces of this invasion.
"What's 'pretty soon'?"
"Three days at the outside, probably less, certainly no more," Oliver said.
"Do it."
"Well, it's going to cost—" he started to say.
"Never mind. I've already talked with my insurance agent. He told me that, beyond my deductible, everything is covered. Just do the best you can, and do it as quickly as possible."
"I'll get right on it," Oliver said. "Should we start now, or wait until you get stuff together to move out? I presume you'll be staying with a friend or at a hotel."
Sarah repeated what she'd said before—no one was going to drive her out of her home. But even while she was saying it, she wondered if she wasn't being stubborn without any valid reason. Well, whatever her motivation, she was staying put.
Oliver frowned. "Suit yourself," he said. "If there's anything you need from the kitchen, I suggest you get it now. We'll probably be working in there for a while."
Sarah didn't have much appetite when she and Kyle went to lunch, and she still wasn't hungry, but maybe she should eat something anyway. She stood in front of the refrigerator, but nothing caught her fancy. After about five minutes, she picked up an orange and wandered into the living room.
She had just started to peel the fruit when her cell phone rang. Sarah put the orange on an end table before she answered.
"I just heard," a familiar voice said. "Are you all right?"
Sarah felt a twinge of conscience because she hadn't thought to call Connie Douglas, who was both a friend and colleague. Connie had been an ER nurse for a number of years. Her hair was white, and Sarah initially took Connie to be much older than her late-forties. Later Connie revealed that her hair color had turned from blonde to silver-gray

almost twenty years ago. Maybe it was because the prematurely white hair gave her an air of wisdom, it could have been the common-sense advice Connie gave, but Sarah treasured their friendship. The nurse had been a rock during the days and weeks after Harry's death, and Sarah regretted that she hadn't contacted her friend with news of this latest event.

"I'm fine, Connie. I'm sorry I didn't call you," Sarah said. "I'm not sure I was ever in any danger. It was just a fire among some oily rags in my garage."

Connie leaped right to the point Sarah had ignored last night. "You don't ever keep stuff like that around. Do you think the fire was deliberately set?"

Sarah wished she could go back, hit the "reset" button, rewind the tape, do something to make all this go away. She didn't want to talk about it. She wished it had never happened. But Connie's question was cloaked in genuine concern, and she deserved a straight answer. "Yes, the fire chief told me that last night. I was at the police department this morning giving a detective my statement about the fire."

"Did you tell them about the harassment that went on before this?"

"Connie, I'm still not thinking straight, I guess, but what harassment are you talking about?"

"Sarah, you told me about these things when they happened. You just haven't put it together. Think back to the phone calls after midnight. And what about the time someone was sneaking around outside your house?"

Sarah realized Connie was right. Maybe the events her friend had mentioned were connected to the fire. She'd ignored these things, pushed them out of her mind when they happened. They'd started after the deaths of her husband and daughter, and she guessed she was still too much in shock at her loss to realize they might all be tied together. At that time Sarah had tried to put an innocent face on each incident, but now she wondered if maybe the fire last night was simply the latest gesture in a series aimed at her.

She had poured a glass of water while looking for something to eat and brought it to the living room with her. Now she reached for the glass that sat beside the unpeeled orange on the end table. Sarah took a couple of swallows, but the dryness didn't leave her throat. "I guess you're right. And I suppose that means I need to call Bill Larson back."

"Well, I won't keep you from making the call. But don't forget to stay in touch," Connie said.

Sarah promised to do that, and quickly ended her call. Then she took a couple of deep breaths, pulled out the card Bill Larson had given her, and punched in the number. "Bill...Detective Larson? This is Sarah Gordon again. A friend has reminded me of some other things that might be helpful in your investigation." *Some things that may mean there's someone trying to frighten me...or worse.*

3

Bill Larson hadn't been home since he received the phone call twelve hours ago. Since then, other than his time at Sarah Gordon's house, he'd felt almost chained to his desk and the surrounding parts of the squad room. It was time to repair the damage. *That's enough. If I look like I feel, I'll frighten anyone who sees me.*

He turned away from his computer, rose from his desk, and headed for the locker room. There, he pulled out the toiletry kit he kept in his locker. He did a quick above-the-belt wash with a wet cloth, then applied some Axe body spray. He wet a comb and ran it through his hair, although experience told him that five minutes later it would probably look unkempt again. As he observed himself in the mirror, he wondered idly when he'd have a chance to get a haircut. Finally, he changed into the clean shirt he kept in his locker. The same tie he'd been wearing would have to do. He felt better, but he still wished he had time to go home for a shower and a complete change of clothes.

Back at his desk, he ran his hand over his jaw and felt the rasp of day-old growth. *I could swear I had a razor in that kit. Got to put one in there.* Then again, maybe he'd just let his beard grow. Not shaving would give him another five minutes of sleep in the morning. Of course, this was Texas, not Minnesota, and summer was about to start in earnest.

Perhaps a beard wasn't a good idea. Besides, five more minutes in bed would most likely be spent staring at the ceiling, struggling with his always-present desire to start the day with a drink. Maybe a Bloody Mary, or... No! Enough of that.

He gathered the pages he'd filled with notes while talking with Sarah Gordon, butted them together, and stowed them in a manila file folder. He was about to shove everything into a locked drawer in his desk and get out to start chasing down leads when the phone on his desk rang. *Please don't let it be another case.* "Police department, Larson."

"Bill... Detective Larson? This is Sarah Gordon again. A friend has reminded me of some other things that might be helpful in your investigation."

He opened the file folder that was still on his desk, found the last sheet of his notes, and pulled out his pen. As Dr. Gordon talked, questions arose in his mind, but he didn't stop her. He'd flesh out the information later. For now, he wanted her to keep talking.

When she finished, he said, "Yes, you should have told me this when we talked earlier, but I'm glad you decided to call me now."

"I'm sorry," she said. "I guess I tried to ignore these episodes. After Harry and Jenny were killed, it was all I could do to keep going each day. I focused on the patients I saw, tried to move forward a day at a time, and if there was a bump in the road, I swerved around it and kept going."

Larson knew the feeling. After his wife left him, taking Billy with her, his whole world felt like it left the tracks. Even the simplest decisions were hard to make. He'd found it difficult to concentrate on anything beyond what it took to get through the day. Matter of fact, the only time he seemed to be able to keep everything together was when he was dealing with police matters. Focusing his attention on cases was almost therapeutic. Maybe that had been the case with

Sarah Gordon. Maybe that's how everyone handled a traumatic event.

"Look, why don't I call you later and get more details?" he said. "Meanwhile, it would help if you check your calendar, see if you can pin down the dates of these calls."

"I will. And I'm sorry—"

"No need to be sorry. You've been under a lot of stress." He knew how she felt. Larson wondered if she realized just how long that feeling might last. In his case... well, it was a slow process.

After he hung up, Larson's thoughts remained on Sarah Gordon, although not as the victim of a crime. As he'd told Cal, he still hoped his family could be reunited, but there were times when it seemed to him even his continued sobriety wasn't enough to mend the rift. As a result, Larson sometimes had dreams of starting over with a woman who loved and accepted him, one who would stand beside him as he fought the battle of continuing sobriety. And at times, especially now, those thoughts involved someone like Sarah Gordon.

Tom Oliver's crew was hard at work, and a cacophony of sound made by fans, motors, hammers, and occasional shouts seemed to surround Sarah. There was no peace to be found in her living room, so she retreated to her bedroom upstairs. She lay there, propped in bed trying to read, but rather than being focused on the book that lay open in her lap, her thoughts flitted here and there like a restless butterfly.

Because of the noise of the fans, extractors, and cleaning machines, Sarah wasn't sure if someone was really knocking at her door. She closed her book, not bothering to mark her place, and hurried down the stairs. As she approached the front door, she heard the sound more clearly. It had increased in intensity to a banging such as she'd seen on TV when the policeman hit the door with the flat of his hand and called out, "Open up. Police." Although no words accompanied this knocking, there was no mistaking the intention of the person behind it.

Sarah looked out the clear diamond of glass in the center of the front door and saw a determined Bill Larson, slamming his hand against the wood. She called, "Hang on. I'm opening it."

"Sorry," Larson said once she had the door open. "I tried the bell several times. I wasn't sure if the noise inside kept you from hearing it, or that it just didn't work."

Sarah averted her eyes. "The bell was one of the things Harry was going to fix. But he never...he never..." She fought for control of her emotions.

"That's okay," Larson said. "I wonder if you have time to go over a few things."

He came in and Sarah closed the door behind him. "I thought you were going to phone," she said. As she spoke, she led him into the living room.

"I decided to come by, instead. Is it okay if we talk there?" He pointed to the sofa and chairs in the room.

"I'm afraid the quietest rooms in the house are upstairs," Sarah said. Immediately, she wondered about the propriety of leading a man upstairs to her bedroom. What other rooms were upstairs, away from the noise? She thought of and discarded the choices immediately. Jenny's bedroom and the large room where her daughter played hadn't been used since the accident, and Sarah couldn't bear to think of going into them now, especially to talk with a detective.

"I think down here is fine," Larson said. "Or, if you like, we can get out of the house for a bit."

That was the last thing Sarah expected, and she let her puzzlement show on her face. "Look, you show up unexpectedly, you don't have another detective with you, and then you ask if I'd like to go out somewhere." She looked directly at him. "Is this an official visit, or are you trying to make it personal?"

"I'm sorry. That didn't come out right." Larson shook his head. "Let me explain. I'm in kind of an awkward position here. To begin with, one of our detectives is out after surgery, where they found cancer. This is a small department, and that leaves two of us staffing the detective bureau. The other man, Cal Johnson, has the weekend off and needs to spend some time with his wife. So this investigation is up to me. That's why I showed up alone."

She opened her mouth to respond, but he held up his hand to stop her.

"Then there's this that makes it sort of personal with me. You and I go to the same church—or, at least, you used to go there. We..." He took a deep breath. "We've both had losses in our life—we don't need to talk about mine, but I imagine you're having some of the same feelings I had after my ex-wife, Annie, left with Billy." He grimaced. "So it's hard for me not to identify with what you're going through. I mean, you lost both your husband and your baby. That must have hit you hard."

Sarah averted her eyes. *Harry. And Jenny. I'm not a wife anymore. I'm not a mother. And I may never be.* She fought to keep from crying, but the tears came anyway. When she turned back, Larson was holding out a clean handkerchief.

She took the handkerchief and blotted her face. "Sorry. My emotions are still pretty fragile sometimes."

"No problem," Larson said. "There've been times I wanted to cry myself."

Sarah turned away for a moment, took some deep breaths, and fought for control. Finally, she turned back and said, "I'm okay now." She handed him the handkerchief. "Let's get back to what you came for. I suppose you want more details about the episodes I told you about." She pointed to the sofa. "If you can stand the noise, maybe it's best that we sit in here."

Larson took a seat, but before he could get out his notebook, Sarah cocked her ear toward the front door.

"I think someone's knocking," she said. "I'd better get it."

She headed for the front door. Given the tension associated with her interaction with Larson, she was glad for the interruption. Sarah appreciated the detective's obvious empathy for her, but it seemed to her there was more to it than that. Could the detective be hitting on her?

First Kyle and now Larson. She'd have to be careful about the signals she was sending. Of course, Sarah had heard tales about the vulnerability of young widows, but until now she'd never figured they applied to her. She certainly wasn't ready to move into any kind of a relationship. Her loss was still too fresh. Sarah wondered when, if ever, that would change.

A glance through the tiny diamond of glass in the front door showed her that Kyle was standing there, his hand poised as though to knock again. She wasn't sure why he had come. She hoped his visit wasn't going to include an invitation to a relationship for which she wasn't ready. Sarah squared her shoulders, opened the door, and beckoned him inside.

"Sarah, how are you doing?" Kyle looked around. "I see the restoration people I recommended are at work," he said.

"Yes. Thanks for your help in that." She closed the door and pointed him toward the living room. "Detective Larson is here. I called him to say I'd remembered some other things that might be helpful to him, and he came by with some questions."

"What—"

"Connie reminded me of some events I'd either forgotten or repressed. I thought the police should know about them."

"But—"

"Kyle, I can handle this. But you're welcome to sit in if you like."

In the living room, Kyle exchanged greetings with Larson and took a seat in a chair at right angles to the sofa. Sarah eased down next to Larson, careful to keep some distance between them. She glanced at the two men and could tell the tension between them was almost palpable. Well, there was nothing she could do about that right now. She felt a bit of tension herself.

Larson had his notebook out now. "Tell me again about the events you mentioned," he said. "I need any details you can remember."

Sarah said, "They started about six months ago. My phone would ring well after midnight, sometimes as late as two or three a.m. The caller ID showed 'blocked number' or 'anonymous call,' I can't remember which. At first, I answered, but there was never anyone on the line. Pretty soon I just let it ring without answering."

"Did you try dialing star sixty-nine?"

"No, initially I figured it was either a wrong number or maybe some kids playing a prank. Then, when they continued, I tried to just ride it out."

"Did you think about changing your number?" Larson asked.

"I could have, I guess, but it would have been a hassle to do it. I'd have to notify lots of people—the hospital, other doctors—and I...Frankly, at that time I didn't want to invest the time and effort."

"How many times did this happen?" Larson asked.

"Probably four, maybe five, all about a week apart. Finally they stopped, and I thought things had run their course. But a few weeks later I saw a prowler outside my window. At least, I think I saw one."

"Tell me about that," Larson said.

Sarah suppressed the shudder she felt. "I went to close the blinds in the living room one evening, and I saw the bushes outside the window moving as though they'd just been disturbed. I looked past them into the yard and that's when I saw him."

"Who?"

"I saw what I thought was the outline of a man running away. I recoiled, sort of a reflex I guess, and when I looked again there was nothing there."

"Did you see a car?"

"No. I listened for a car starting, watched for headlights, something to show I wasn't imagining things, but the street was quiet."

Larson looked up from his notebook. "Was it a man or a woman? Tall or short? Did you see—"

"I have no idea. Frankly, I wasn't even sure I'd seen anyone outside. I decided it was my imagination."

"Did you go out to look?" Larson asked.

"No. I just closed the blinds, checked to make sure the doors and windows were locked, and went to bed."

"Did you call the police to report this?"

Sarah shook her head. "The more I thought about it, the more I wondered if I was imagining things. Maybe I should have reported the incident, but right then was a bad time for me. I was doing well to put one foot in front of the other."

"What about the next morning?" Larson asked. "Did you look outside in the daylight? Were there footprints in the flower bed?"

"Like I told you, I tried to ignore the incident. I wasn't sure I hadn't imagined it." Sarah said. "Besides, it rained that night. Wouldn't the rain have washed away any footprints?"

Larson ignored her comment and moved on. "Was this the only time you thought you saw a prowler?"

"I think so. But frankly, I kept the blinds closed day and night after that, so if someone was outside, I didn't see him anyway."

Larson looked up from his notebook. "Any other incidents?"

"No." Sarah said. "Do you think these are related to the fire?"

"They could be," Larson said. "At least this information gives me a time frame to start my investigation."

"All these happened after Harry died," Kyle said. "Right?"

Sarah nodded but said nothing.

Larson stood and pocketed his notebook. "I wish you'd let us know about these things when they happened, but I can understand how you must have felt about that time." He looked directly at Sarah. "I shouldn't have to say this, but I will. Keep your doors and windows locked. Arm your security system. Do you have a gun?"

"I...I don't have a security system," she said. "And I don't have a gun. Harry got rid of his when Jenny...when we knew we were going to have a baby in the house."

Kyle turned to Larson. "Do you think she needs one?" he asked.

"I can't give you an official position on that," Larson said. "But if you had a pistol, with a permit, and you knew how to use it, this would be the time to keep it handy. In the meantime, I'll arrange for a patrol car to drive by here periodically for the next few days. I'll be in touch, but call me if anything comes up before then." He handed her a card.

"I already have your card," Sarah said.

"This one has my cell number on the back," Larson said. "Use it...anytime, day or night."

After Larson was gone, Kyle said, "I came by hoping to buy you dinner."

"I can't eat, Kyle," Sarah said. "But thank you anyway."

Kyle stood and looked down at Sarah. She could tell he had something on his mind, but after a moment he simply nodded and said, "I'll give you a call in the morning."

Sarah was in the living room, staring numbly at the walls, when Tom Oliver found her to tell her they were leaving. He promised to be back tomorrow, Sunday.

"About what time?" she asked.

"I figured you might want to go to church, so I thought sometime after noon," he said. "It looks like we may be able to have almost everything done by sometime Monday. Maybe even late Sunday."

"Okay. I'll see you tomorrow."

Oliver stood there for a moment longer, apparently thinking. Then he turned away without saying anything more. In a moment, Sarah heard the front door closing.

After the house was quiet, she wandered around and found the crew had accomplished a lot. Bare floors in a couple of areas awaited new carpet that would be ordered Monday and put down when it arrived. No problem—she could stand uncovered floors for a few days. The smell of smoke was still there, but it was very faint. Soon that smell would be replaced by the odor of fresh paint. A few areas of soot staining around the door from her garage into the kitchen had been treated but needed more attention. That would undoubtedly be remedied tomorrow or Monday. She could look forward to having her house—her home—back soon.

Despite her approval of the work the restoration crew was doing, Sarah felt fear clawing at the back of her brain. She tried to fight it, but it wouldn't go away. Would her home ever feel normal? And, even more important, was this fire the last event she'd have to tolerate? Surely the police would find the person responsible and stop him...or her. At least, she hoped so.

Sarah tried to summon up enough courage to put aside her fears. Bill Larson was working on solving her problems. Kyle was available if she needed help. Right now, she'd concentrate on some of the routine things that usually occupied her on a Saturday.

When she finished remaking her bed with clean sheets, she noticed that the sun had set fully, leaving only pale gray twilight to illuminate the area outside her bedroom window. She had barely picked at her lunch. And what about dinner? Kyle had offered to take her somewhere, but she remembered telling him she wasn't hungry. No matter. Her stomach knotted when she thought of food.

Before she could move on to the next mindless task, Sarah's cell phone rang. She pulled it from the pocket of her slacks, saw who was calling, and remembered that she should have called Connie back long before this. Sarah dropped onto the edge of the bed and answered the call. "Connie, I'm so sorry for not getting back to you before this."

"I understand," her friend said. "What did the police say when you told them about the phone calls and the prowler?"

"Detective Larson felt I should have reported them, but I think he understood I had too much on my mind at the time."

"But did he think the person who set the fire was the same one who made the phone calls and was prowling around your house?"

"He didn't use those exact words, but I'm pretty sure he feels they were all part of the same thing," Sarah said.

"Have you been thinking about people who could be behind this?"

"I've tried, but I keep coming up with a blank. Harry and I didn't have any enemies."

The conversation went on for another fifteen minutes, and when it was over Sarah felt an overwhelming sense of fatigue. She lay back on the bed and closed her eyes. She wanted to do what she'd done as a child, huddling under her covers hoping that whatever monster she feared at the moment would disappear. If only she could go to sleep and awaken with this all behind her.

Apparently she did go to sleep, because when she awakened she looked outside her bedroom windows and saw it was now full night. Sarah swung her feet off the bed and padded over to close the blinds, but she stopped when she looked through them. There was a dark sedan parked at the curb across the street from her house.

She could just barely discern the shape of a man behind the wheel. When the headlights of a passing car illuminated the interior of the vehicle for a moment, she saw him turn and look in her direction. She couldn't discern his features at this distance. Nevertheless, Sarah wondered if she was finally seeing the person responsible for the trials she'd been experiencing. More than that, she wondered what would be next.

4

Bill Larson slouched in his easy chair, the TV tuned to a show where the police were able to solve whatever crime they were given this week in an hour, minus sixteen minutes for commercial breaks. He wasn't watching, having long ago discovered that there was very little relationship between television and real life when it came to police dramas. But he had also learned in the past few months that without the background noise and constantly changing images emanating from the set, his apartment was so cold and depressing it made the urge to drink almost too strong to resist.

He was in that special world halfway between dozing and wakefulness when the ring of his cell phone startled him into full consciousness. At first, he wasn't sure if the sound came from the television, but another ring followed the first, even after he'd muted the program. He was glad for the interruption, and even more when he saw who was calling.

"Larson."

"This is Sarah Gordon. I'm sorry to bother you this late, but…"

"No bother. Is something wrong?"

"The car…the man…someone outside my house." She paused. "I'm sorry. I shouldn't bother you with this. I guess this could have waited until morning."

The detective turned off the TV set. "If your original impulse was to call, it's probably something I should know. You said something about a car outside your house."

"I looked out the window a moment ago and saw this car. It's not unusual for a car to be parked at the curb there, but when the headlights of an approaching vehicle illuminated the interior I saw the man behind the wheel was looking toward me." She took a deep breath, and the sound in the phone receiver was like a sigh. "And I wondered if it was the same man I told you about earlier today—the man I thought was outside my bedroom window...watching me."

Larson scanned the area around his chair, wondering where he'd put his shoes. "Is he still there?"

"No, right after the headlights lit up the inside of his car, he drove away."

"Could you identify him if you saw him again?" Larson asked.

"No, I didn't really see his face that well. And before you ask, I didn't get his license plate number. All I know is the car was a dark sedan."

"Have you seen the police patrol cars I asked to drive by your house?"

"I haven't watched for them," she said. "Come to think of it, I wonder if it was the police car going by that lit up his vehicle. Do you think that's why he left?"

"Most likely," Larson said. He abandoned his search for shoes and leaned back in his chair. "He probably won't come back tonight, but if he does, call the number I'm about to give you. I'll alert whoever's on duty. Just tell the dispatcher the man's in front of your house. We can have a car with a couple of officers there inside of five minutes."

He read off the phone number, and Sarah dutifully repeated it back as she wrote it down. "Was it okay that I called you?" she asked.

"You did exactly the right thing," Larson said. "This could be a coincidence, but I'm willing to bet that man's the one who's behind these efforts at harassment. What we have to do now is find out his identity."

"Do you want me to do anything more tonight?"

"Just get some rest. And call if there's anything I can do." After the call was ended, he murmured once more, "Anything."

While she was talking with Detective Larson, Sarah heard the beep that told her another call was coming through on her cell phone. She glanced at the screen and saw it was Kyle on the line. What was he calling about this time? She ignored it, but when her conversation was over, she returned his call.

"Kyle," she said, making an effort to keep her tone civil. "Sorry I couldn't answer right then. I was on the phone with the police."

"Did something else happen?" he asked. "Do I need to come over? I can be there in fifteen minutes."

Kyle, give it a rest. You're pushing. "It's nothing that requires your coming over," she said. Sarah went on to explain about the car parked outside her house and her fear the driver was the same man who'd been harassing her.

"And you're sure you're okay?"

"I'm fine. Now, why did you call? Was there something you wanted to talk to me about?"

"I'm still worried about your security while the police sort this out," Kyle said. "I can arrange for you to stay at a hotel for a bit."

"No, Kyle. I'm not going to leave this house. And that's final."

"What about defending yourself, then?" Kyle said. "I can bring you a pistol. I'll bring it right now if you like."

"That's not necessary, but thank you." Sarah understood Kyle's anxiety over her—sort of. He'd been a friend of

Harry's, perhaps his best friend, and she could imagine that he felt he should look out for Harry's widow. But, friend or no friend, she'd had enough. "Look, can you stop worrying about me? My doors and windows are locked," she said. "Bill Larson has asked the dispatcher to send a patrol car by at intervals tonight. I'm fine."

"But what about tomorrow, and the next day, and the day after that?"

Sarah didn't want to tell Kyle that this was exactly the question that had crossed her mind earlier in the evening. She tried to sound confident when she replied. "I'm hoping the police will have the person behind all this in custody soon."

There was a moment of silence, and Sarah thought Kyle was about to hang up. Instead, his change of the conversational subject was so drastic it put her off-balance. "How long since you've been to church?" he asked.

"You mean sitting through a whole service without leaving because I couldn't stand it? I know the exact date." The last full church service she'd attended was the day she'd sat in the front row and stared at two coffins—one small, one larger. She couldn't recall any of the words said from the pulpit that day, although she was sure they were meant to bring comfort to her and those who joined her in mourning the loss of her husband and child. But throughout the service her thoughts were elsewhere, and they were not thoughts that brought her comfort. Instead, one question ran through her mind again and again: *God, why did You let this happen?*

Kyle's voice brought Sarah back to the present. "You mean you haven't been back to church since the day of the funeral," he said.

"I've tried to attend a couple of times since then, but my emotions got the best of me and I had to leave early. I kept flashing back to the service for Harry and Jenny. And probably my anger with God didn't help."

"I wonder if you'd like to go to church with me tomorrow," Kyle said. "I'll come by for you. I'll make sure you're safe, and I think it would be good for you."

Sarah declined at first, but Kyle somehow managed to be persistent without being pushy, and eventually she said, "Okay. You can pick me up about a quarter to nine. We'll need to come straight back here after the service ends, though. Tom Oliver said his crew was going to start back to work right after noon."

"Why don't I call Tom and ask him to hold off until about one thirty tomorrow? That way, I can take you to lunch."

Sarah was tired of resisting. "Whatever you say."

"Great," Kyle said. "In the meantime, call me if you think you're in danger."

"Right after I call the police," Sarah said. "But I'll be fine. Every door is locked."

"And you thought your garage door was locked," Kyle said. "If this guy, whoever he is, wants to get in, he will."

Sarah finally convinced Kyle that she'd be okay, but the uncertainty he'd planted wouldn't go away. As soon as she hung up, she went straight for the garage. Until this episode, she'd depended on engaging the "lock" button on her electric garage opener each evening. Now that she'd learned that the emergency lever could be tripped with nothing more technically advanced than a coat hanger, she wouldn't feel safe until she dealt with that.

She'd done an Internet search about ways to lock a garage door. Sarah wasn't certain her roll-up garage door even had a manual locking handle—she'd never looked for it before but seemed to recall Harry having pointed it out once, saying newer doors often didn't have these. Sure enough, in the spare keys hung on hooks in the washroom, she found a small key labeled "garage door." Now if she could just make it work.

She didn't want to go outside in the dark, but she also didn't want to rouse at every noise through the night, knowing there was a way for her stalker to get into her house. *You have to do this, Sarah.* She grabbed a hammer from the tools in the pegboard at the back of the garage, as much for protection as for use as a tool. She turned on the outside light that illuminated her driveway. She guessed the garage door should roll up and back smoothly enough for her to do it without the help of the opener motor. If the stalker did it, she figured she could as well. She pulled the emergency release, manually raised the garage door with no real problem, and stepped outside.

Her first priority was to see if what she wanted to do was feasible. Sarah pulled the door down and looked in the middle, about a third of the way from the bottom, where she found a T-handle with a key slot in it. She took a deep breath. *So far, so good.* She tried to turn the handle, but it seemed to be frozen solid. After a liberal dose of lubricant on the mechanism, followed by a few gentle taps with the hammer, the handle moved. As it did, she could hear the rods it controlled sliding into slots in the metal tracks on either side, locking the door. She unlocked the door, raised it, went inside, added more lubricant, and tried the handle from inside to make sure it worked freely. It did. Finally, she stepped out one more time and checked to make sure the key would lock and unlock the door. It would be awkward to use this, but it was better than worrying about someone entering through her garage.

With the garage closed and locked this way, no matter if someone had a remote to control the motor on the opener, the door would remain firmly in place. Even if the emergency lever were tripped, the door wouldn't move. True, it would be a pain to enter and exit the garage this way, but the peace of mind she gained was worth it. *Let's see you get past this, whoever you are.*

Nevertheless, that night she slept with most of the lights on in her house.

When Kyle pulled up to her house the next morning, he was surprised to see Sarah coming out the front door and hurrying to his car as he brought his car to a stop. Normally, he opened a car door for a lady, but she was inside and fastening her seat belt before he could get his own unfastened.

She was obviously nervous, and Kyle figured there was no need to ask her how she'd slept. If her current nervous state was any indication, sleep at Sarah Gordon's house had been somewhere between fitful and nonexistent last night. He decided on what he hoped was a neutral opening. "The weather isn't as hot as the first of June usually is here in Texas."

Sarah kept her eyes turned toward the side window. "I guess."

After that, Sarah continued her silence until the car pulled into the church parking lot. Kyle honored her obvious desire to avoid conversation, but after turning off the car's ignition, he turned to her and said, "Sarah, if you're uncomfortable being at church today, just say so, and I'll take you right back home."

Sarah didn't respond immediately. Instead, she seemed to concentrate her attention on people getting out of their cars and heading toward the church building. Finally, she turned back toward Kyle and forced a smile. "No, I guess I need to try it. And I don't think whoever's out to get me will do anything in the middle of a church service. After all, there are quite a few pairs of eyes watching."

Kyle decided not to say what he was thinking—that the most important eyes were those of God, who was watching over her as He had always been. Sarah probably didn't need to hear that right now, even from him. She'd made no secret of her anger at God because He didn't intervene when another driver robbed her of both her husband and daughter. Kyle tried to ignore his frustration at Sarah's failure to put her loss behind her. After all, that was what he'd forced himself to do following the death of his fiancée. Why couldn't she do the same? But maybe this wasn't the time to have that conversation. Maybe today he'd just let the service—the music, the prayers, the sermon—speak to Sarah. He'd bide his time.

"Thanks for taking me to church," Sarah said. "And for lunch."

"Glad church was good. As for lunch, you didn't eat enough to keep a bird alive," Kyle said.

"No, but it was good to talk with you. I guess I do need someone to listen to me ventilate." She opened the car door and turned in her seat to face Kyle, "Don't get out. I'll be safe now that I'm home." Sarah pointed to two vehicles, a red pickup and a white van, that were pulling in behind Kyle's Audi. "Besides, Tom's here."

"If you're sure you'll be okay," Kyle said.

"I'll be fine." Sarah paused with the car door open. "You've never told me how you know Tom Oliver," she said.

Kyle shrugged. "I did some legal work for him a couple of years back. I hope he's doing a good job for you."

"I think so," Sarah said. "What kind of work did you do? I mean, mostly you do criminal law. Has Tom been in trouble with the law? Should I be worried about letting him into my home?"

"The work I did for him didn't involve Tom, so I think you're fine," Kyle said. "Look, this involves client privilege. Why don't you ask him? If he wants you to know, he'll tell you."

"Well, thank you again for taking me to church and for lunch," Sarah said.

"Happy to do it." He paused, apparently trying to find the right words. "Look, I know a little of what you're going through. Remember, I've lost a loved one, too. Don't hesitate to call on me for help."

As Kyle pulled away, Sarah thought about the loss he'd suffered. She recalled the terrible incident when Kyle's fiancée, Nicole, went with a small group of church volunteers on a mission trip to Guatemala. They were constructing a church building when one of the heavy wooden crossbeams they were installing broke loose and fell, snapping her neck. She'd died instantly.

There was a time after the accident when Kyle's faith seemed to waver, but apparently he never lost it—at least, not that Sarah and Harry could tell. He mourned Nicole, but he didn't seem to blame God for the mishap. She guessed it said something about the strength of Kyle's faith, but it wasn't what happened with her. She couldn't bring herself to forgive God for the tragic accident that drastically changed her life. Maybe she should talk with Kyle about that sometime.

Tom Oliver climbed out of his pickup truck. "How you doing, doctor?"

"Doing okay, I guess," she said. "Tom, feel free to tell me if it's none of my business. Kyle mentioned in passing that he had done some legal work for you, but he wouldn't give me the specifics. He said those would have to come from you. Would you mind telling me what that's about?"

Oliver looked at his work boots, and for a minute Sarah thought he wasn't going to respond. Still looking down, he said, "It's sort of personal, and I'd appreciate it if you'd keep this in confidence."

"Of course."

"I have one son, Tommy. A couple of years ago he and another teenage friend were celebrating having just turned eighteen. They were in a car with Tommy's friend driving when it crashed into a vehicle driven by an elderly man. That man died. The boy driving the car Tommy was in had a blood alcohol over the legal limit. My son's BAC showed he'd had only one drink. Kyle defended my son and managed to get him off. The other boy went to jail for intoxication manslaughter."

"Oh," Sarah said. "That must have been a tough time for you."

"That's when I first met you," Oliver said. "You probably don't remember, but all three victims were brought to the emergency room where you're on staff. One of your colleagues worked on the old man but couldn't save him. You treated Tommy and the driver of his car. I think you were the one who drew blood alcohol tests on both boys."

"I see so many patients in the ER—"

"I'm sure you don't remember. That's okay."

After Sarah unlocked the front door, Oliver led his crew into the house, while she stood on the front porch trying to recall the incident. She had a vague recollection of examining the two teenagers. There had been some kind of argument at the trial that the blood samples had been switched. But, as she'd told Oliver, she saw so many patients...

She shook her head and walked slowly into her house. If only the boy hadn't been drinking. For that matter, if only the person who'd crashed into Harry and killed both him and their daughter had been more careful. Couldn't God have intervened? Why did good people have to die? Why had she been robbed of the joys of being a wife and mother? Why?

The more she thought about it, the more Sarah decided she'd seen too many tragedies at this point in her life. And not all of them had been in the emergency room.

Night was falling when Tom Oliver found Sarah and said, "That's it." He indicated the home with a sweeping gesture. "I think the painting's done. When it comes in, we'll be back to install carpet in a couple of areas, but other than that, we're through. If you see anything we need to correct or touch up, maybe some paint that needs another coat, just give me a call." He handed her a card. "Tomorrow's Monday. I'll talk with your insurance agent then about payment."

Sarah took the card and shoved it into the pocket of the jeans into which she'd changed right after church. "Thanks. And whatever's left after insurance pays, I'll give you a check."

She stood at the door with Oliver and watched his crew load the last of the ladders and drop cloths into their panel van. "None of my business," he said, "But have you considered a security system? You're here alone, which would probably be enough to make most women get one. Now I understand someone set this fire." He hesitated. "You know, my company doesn't just do restoration after fires. A lot of what we do is construction and repairs, but we also install home security systems."

Sarah shook her head. "I've thought about it, but I'm not ready to install one. I've heard too much from people who hate theirs—false alarms, maintenance, all sorts of problems."

"Suit yourself," Oliver said. "Some of my customers are happy to put in a system so they can get rid of the pistols they have for self-defense."

"I don't have one of those, either," Sarah said. "I know it's foolish, and maybe I'll change my mind on both counts, but for now, I guess I'll depend on locks and lights."

Oliver took a minute to think about this. Then he shrugged. "Call me if you change your mind." With that, he headed for his pickup.

After he was gone, Sarah went through the house in what she was sure would become a nightly ritual. She closed the blinds. She made certain all her doors and windows were locked. She double-checked that the garage door was locked as well, the bars firmly into the slots in the track.

Then she slumped into a chair in the living room, put her head in her hands, and wondered why she was fighting back the tears she felt damming up behind her eyes. There was no one to see them. But somehow she felt that Harry was watching—and she wanted to be brave for him.

Almost midnight, but the lights were still on throughout the house. He wondered if the doctor thought the illumination would scare him away. Was she in the house at this moment, cowering behind locked doors? Had she gone to bed, hiding under the covers like a frightened child?

He felt the comforting weight of the pistol in his pocket. His hand traced the outline of the 9mm Beretta semiautomatic. It had cost him over four hundred dollars, but it was worth it— lightweight, compact, deadly— the ideal gun for his purposes.

But he wouldn't be using it tonight. No, it was too soon. The doctor had to sweat, to go without sleep, to feel her heart beating in her chest like a trip hammer until she was certain it was about to explode.

She'd live every day not knowing when he'd strike next or what he'd do. And finally, when he thought he'd made her suffer as much as he could, he'd kill her.

5

Monday morning dawned bright and clear, the weather belying the cloud that seemed to hover over Sarah's head. She'd had very little sleep the night before, and what she'd managed had been far from restful. Her head had hit the pillow for the last time at about two a.m. and by six she was out of her bed and headed for the kitchen to turn on the coffee maker.

Her phone started ringing at seven a.m. The first call was from Dr. Chuck Crenshaw, the doctor who headed the group of physicians staffing the ER at Centennial Hospital. "Sarah, I was out of town this weekend, and I didn't hear about the fire at your place until last night. Are you okay?"

"Yes, thanks, Chuck." She went on to explain about the minimal damage, deciding not to get into the emotional upheaval the event had caused. "I'm planning to work my shift as scheduled this evening."

"Well, let me know if you need someone to cover for you. And if there's anything any of us can do..." He let the sentence hang unfinished, but Sarah knew what the thought behind it was.

"Thanks," Sarah said, and ended the call.

If there was anything that could be done for Harry's widow... If anyone could help out in this stressful time... If she needed... The sentiments were the same ones she'd heard eight months ago when her husband and daughter were snatched from her by the auto accident. She'd appreciated the gestures then. She appreciated them now, but they also served as a reminder of her loss. More than that, they marked a change in her, a change that doubtless others saw as well. *What's happened to me? A woman doctor's supposed to be strong. An ER doctor has to be independent. I still function adequately in my professional role, but I've lost the edge I once had.*

After she married Harry, Sarah had developed the habit of shedding her independence when she left the hospital. At work, she had to be decisive, in charge, always ready to take over. But when she got home, she relaxed. Here Sarah could be a wife and mother, part of a team, sharing responsibilities with her husband. Harry was a great husband and father, always there to help. After Jenny was born, Sarah didn't have to be a supermom. In a manner of speaking, she'd learned to drop her cape at the door.

Now Sarah was finding it hard to dig out of the pit of despair the loss of her husband and daughter had put her in. She still managed to do her job in the ER. There she made tough decisions and acted on them, although perhaps not as effectively as before Harry's death. But at home, in the midst of constant worry and uncertainty, she sometimes found the smallest decision too much for her. Her personal life was in tatters. Why couldn't things be like they used to?

Why had God let this happen? When Harry and Jenny had been killed, Sarah's first thought was that God had made a mistake. Why would He let the fatal crash take place? Why didn't He intervene? Then, when the reality of her loss finally soaked in, Sarah tried to lean on her religion to help her through the troubled times. She'd heard and read all the sentiments when they came from others in times of distress. Lean on God, and He'll uphold you. But that strength didn't come. Instead, she found herself constantly asking God, "Why?"

Of course, God wasn't the only target for her anger. She'd never told anyone about this, but there were times—many times—when she was angry with Harry. Oh, she knew he didn't want to have that accident. He didn't plan to die. Harry didn't plan to take their daughter with him, leaving Sarah alone. But she couldn't help being angry with him. Sometimes, in the dead of night, alone in her room, she'd find herself saying again and again, "Harry, why have you left me? Harry, why did you do this? Why?"

Her attendance at church yesterday marked the first time she'd sat through an entire service since she'd exited the building behind two coffins eight months ago. Was she ready to turn to God once more? Despite what everyone said about seeking Him in time of trouble, Sarah couldn't bring herself to make that leap. Not yet.

When her phone rang again, it startled Sarah. She looked at the caller ID and sighed. It was Kyle. Good old Kyle. He'd been the first person she thought of when she needed help, and she was glad to have him around for support. But recently she'd come to suspect that his closeness had more behind it than willingness to help his friend's widow.

"How are you doing, Sarah?" Kyle asked.

"I'm making it okay." It occurred to Sarah that Kyle was acting just like Harry always had. He was trying to protect her. *Kyle, you might have been my husband's best friend, but stop trying to replace him... in any way.*

Sarah took a quick sip of coffee and tried to steer the conversation in a different direction. "Thanks for recommending Tom Oliver. He and his crew did a nice job of restoration. The house is back to pretty much normal." *Except that I know someone's been in it. Did he touch anything? Did he sneak up the stairs to Jenny's room? Who was it? Why did he do it? And... will he come back?*

Kyle's voice brought her out of her musing. "Are you going to—"

"If you're wondering if I'm going to work today, the answer is yes." She took another swallow of coffee, half emptying the cup this time. "Look, Kyle. I appreciate your concern, but at this point I have to gather up the pieces of my life and move on. I imagine I'll hear from Bill Larson before I head to work this afternoon. If I think I need a lawyer, I'll give you a call."

"I'm available anytime, Sarah."

The third call didn't come until mid-morning. "This is Bill Larson. How are you today?"

If one more person asks how I'm doing... "I'm surviving. And I'm glad you called. Yesterday I was talking with a man who reminded me that I was responsible for drawing the blood alcohol tests on his son and another teenager after they'd been involved in an accident. Apparently, one of the defense attorneys made the argument that I got the samples mixed up. I'm sure I didn't, but I guess you were right. There are people who've come in contact with me through my emergency room duties who might have ill will toward me, if I can use an old-fashioned phrase."

"One of the things I planned to do was go through ER records looking for the names of people like that," Larson said. "Because of the privacy laws, I'd have to get a court order to do it. If you'd be willing to go through the records and give me that list, it would be a lot easier. Would you?"

Sarah didn't waste a lot of time thinking about it. "If you think it might help, I'm ready. When do you want to start?"

Bill Larson had a pounding headache. It wasn't that his eyes were tired from personally scanning hundreds of emergency room records. Sarah had done that, giving him names when she decided the person involved might have a grudge against her. But the repetitive task of writing down those names and contact information, consulting with her for details of her encounter with them, sitting in a stuffy medical records room under unforgiving fluorescent lights, squirming as he tried to find a comfortable position in an uncomfortable straight chair—that was enough to give anyone a headache.

"Are you sure you want to do this?" Larson asked Sarah. He almost hoped she'd tell him she was ready to quit.

"There are a lot of things I'd rather be doing, but if this is what it takes to give you some leads, I'm willing."

So he'd continued, jotting down names that might turn out to be Sarah's "stalker." Despite what appeared at first to be a hopeless task, Larson figured that good detective work—asking questions, looking for relationships, examining evidence, sifting through interviews—would eventually unmask the man.

Sarah looked up at the clock on the wall of the hospital record room. "I have to go to work pretty soon. Do you need some more names? If so, I can meet you here again tomorrow morning."

Larson looked at the list of names he'd accumulated. "How far back in the records have we gone so far?"

"About a year. Think that's enough?"

"Possibly. Let me make a note of the last date in the pile. Then I'll start working on what we have. If I need your help again, I'll give you a call." He paused and looked directly at her. "And you know we're also going to have to look into your personal life. I hope you—"

"Whatever it takes. No apologies necessary." She picked up her backpack, evidently what she used as a purse when going to work in the ER. "Truthfully, do you think what we did today might help you?"

Larson rose and stretched, hearing his neck pop and feeling the muscles in his shoulders rebel at the movement. "We never know. I'll just keep checking on all the leads. Meanwhile, what are you doing about security?"

The two of them moved toward the door of the records room. When she reached it, Sarah stopped with her hand on the doorknob. "I've been locking my garage door manually since you showed me how the emergency release lever could be tripped with a coat hanger. I'll get a security guard to walk me to my car when I leave the hospital tonight. I make sure all my doors and windows are locked. I think that's about all I can do."

"Anything else?"

"I've been thinking about an alarm system for the house," she said.

"Probably a good idea," Larson said. "And don't forget, you have all my numbers. Call anytime you want, even if you think it's something trivial. I promise you won't be a pest."

She thanked him and went out the door. He followed, then stood watching her walk down the hallway. *Sarah, you could never be a pest. Why couldn't I have married someone like you?*

When Sarah entered the ER, she walked into what might seem to the uninitiated to be chaos set against a background of shouts, moans, beeps, and various other noises. To her, it was home.

"Glad to see you," Dr. Craig Perkins said as he passed her. "You sure you're okay working today?"

"I'm fine. What's going on, and where shall I start?"

After getting a quick update on the patients in the ER, Sarah said, "I'm on it. You take off."

As Sarah approached the first enclosure, she heard a child crying inside. She pulled aside the curtain to see a neat but plain-looking woman, probably in her early twenties, holding a young girl in her arms. The child looked to be about two...the same age as Jenny. Sarah blinked hard and swallowed to loosen the lump in her throat. She'd been warned there would be emotional triggers at random times, but so far she hadn't encountered one during an ER tour. Now she had. Sarah fought back the impulse to cry.

Sarah took a few calming breaths. "How can I help you?"

"My daughter…my daughter fell this afternoon. I didn't think much about it. I mean children are always falling. But she's still crying, and I'm afraid her arm is broken."

Gently, Sarah touched the arm. The little girl jerked it away, but not before the doctor noted it was slightly swollen just above the wrist. She hadn't been able to feel any crepitus, the grating sensation caused by ends of bone rubbing together, but that might not be present if the fracture were non-displaced. In any case, an X-ray was going to be necessary. If the arm were fractured, the mother would have to care for a little girl with a cast on her arm for four to six weeks. *But at least her daughter's alive.*

Sarah stuck her head out of the cubicle and called to Connie, who was working that shift. The nurse hurried over.

"You want an X-ray?" she asked.

"It's a possible Colles' fracture," Sarah said. "I'll put a short arm splint on it until we can get the X-rays. Maybe that will stop some of the pain and prevent any neurovascular injury."

Later, after Connie left to escort the mother and daughter to get the X-ray, Sarah leaned on the wall in the vacant cubicle and fought to calm the storm she felt inside. *They warned me about triggers, but this one caught me off guard. How long will I have to be alert for them?* Thus far, she'd had no such reaction when called upon to treat an adult trauma victim. But this child, who was about Jenny's age, had made her heart feel like it was breaking. *Jenny. I miss Jenny. I miss her so much.*

As it turned out, the little girl's arm wasn't broken, and a relieved mother left the ER with her daughter's wrist supported by an elastic bandage. Sarah didn't see them go, because she was already involved with the next patient. And she knew that would be the way things went for the balance of her tour.

It was almost midnight when Sarah, feeling rather foolish, walked beside the security guard to her car in the physicians' parking lot. "You know, I appreciate this."

He touched the holstered pistol on his hip. "Doctor, it's part of my job. Not many people want to tangle with an armed man, and I'd always rather prevent a problem than deal with the consequences after it's too late."

Sarah kept her car doors locked as she drove through the deserted streets. At her house, she stopped her car in front of the locked garage door. She automatically reached for the opener clipped to her sun visor, then pulled her hand back. It wouldn't work, because the door was locked. Sarah ran her choices through her head and decided a quick run to the front door was safer than getting out, unlocking the garage door, then pulling in. And it would be daylight when she left the next day, so getting into her car in the driveway shouldn't put her at risk then.

She started to breathe a silent prayer for safety but stopped, remembering the apparently ineffective prayers she'd offered when she got the news of the wreck that claimed the life of her husband and child. Maybe speed and determination would substitute for divine protection. Sarah shook her head, opened the car door, and dashed for her house, reaching over her shoulder to beep her car locked as she went.

The man was grateful that the color of his vehicle allowed the car to blend into the darkness. He'd found a parking place between two other cars, almost directly across the street from Dr. Gordon's house. He was in a spot equidistant from the streetlamps at either end of the street. Black clothes let him merge with the shadows inside his vehicle.

The houses on the block were all dark by now. The exceptions were what seemed to be nightlights. No bluish illumination from TV sets flickered through partially covered windows. Aside from the occasional bark of a dog, the neighborhood was quiet.

Each time a pair of headlights came down the street, the man slid down behind the wheel until he wasn't visible through the windshield. Twice he'd done it, only to see the headlights pass and be replaced in his rearview mirror with the twin red dots of taillights receding in the distance.

This time, the vehicle bearing the headlights slowed as it approached the doctor's house. After it turned into the driveway, he eased up from his hiding place behind the steering wheel and watched the car stop with its nose just feet from the locked garage door.

He knew it was locked, because less than an hour ago he'd parked farther down the street, walked innocently past Gordon's house, then ducked back to try his coat hanger trick on the door. He could trip the emergency release lever but was unable to budge the door. So she's discovered how to lock it. That may make her safer in the short term, but it's inconvenient for her, and all it means for me is that it's time to step up the action.

Dr. Gordon sat for a moment in her car, apparently deciding how to proceed. Either way, the man was prepared. He pulled his pistol from his waistband, lowered the driver-side window of his vehicle, and, resting the pistol barrel on the window ledge to steady it, aimed the Beretta toward Gordon's front door.

When the car door opened and she started her dash toward the house, the man smiled. He took in a deep breath, let it partway out, and gently took up the tension on the trigger. The noise of the gunshot was no more than a flat clap that quickly died away. A dog a few houses down the way let loose a series of sharp barks. Then everything was quiet once more.

The man rolled up the car window, carefully stowed the pistol, and drove away, not turning on his lights until he reached the end of the block.

6

Sarah stood in her living room and tried to ignore the noises coming from the darkness outside the closed front door of her home. Instead, she concentrated her attention on Bill Larson, who was saying, "Tell me one more time what happened."

She'd been over it so many times Sarah almost had the words memorized. She described again the events of less than an hour ago. "When I heard the shot, I dropped to the ground. I reached up, unlocked the front door, rolled inside, and locked it behind me. Then I pulled out my cell phone and called 9-1-1."

"You're certain you only heard one shot?" Bill Larson said.

Sarah Gordon forced herself to relive that terrifying moment. "Yes. One shot."

"And what happened before that?"

"I sat in my car, trying to decide if it would be safer to get out, unlock the garage door, and pull in, or simply make a dash for the front door." She took a deep breath. "I chose to run for it. I had almost reached the front door when I heard the shot. At about the same time something hit the door frame above my head."

The front door opened and a patrolman stepped into the room. "Here's the slug," he said. He held out a small plastic envelope containing a misshapen piece of gray metal. "We dug it out of the wood just above the door. Looks like it could be a 9mm, but I imagine it's too deformed for ballistics to tell us much."

"I guess I'm lucky it didn't hit me," Sarah said.

"Either that, or he wasn't trying to hit you," Larson replied. "If we assume the same person is behind all these episodes, then consider the progression of events. First, some phone calls after midnight. I understand why you'd ignore them. It was easy enough to write them off as the work of a practical joker, maybe some kids getting their kicks. And you were still trying to recover from the death of your husband and child."

Sarah nodded, trying without success to relax the tight knot growing in her stomach.

"Then you saw a man standing outside your window, something you should have reported to the police, but didn't."

"I wasn't sure I saw him. Maybe I should have called them, but I was—"

"I understand," Larson said. "Let's focus on what happened afterward. You had a fire that was set in such a way that it probably wouldn't burn down the house. Then you saw a suspicious person sitting in a dark sedan parked outside your house. And now someone puts a bullet into the door just above your head."

"So…"

"So, I think someone is trying to frighten you. There's been a definite progression to the attempts, but so far it seems he may only want to scare you. But what he's doing is a little more serious each time. That's not to say he isn't going to make an attempt on your life at some point, but first it seems he's getting his jollies making you sweat."

"Well, he's succeeding," Sarah said. "And you're right about the escalation. Now I find myself constantly worrying what will be next… and whether it will be fatal." She reached behind her, felt the couch, and collapsed onto it.

"Are you still adamant about staying in the house?" Larson asked.

"Yes. I'm not going to let him drive me out of my home. It's the one Harry and I bought. It's the one I brought Jenny home to from the hospital. It's..." She shook her head. No need to say it yet again.

"Then you'd probably better get that security system we've talked about," Larson said. "I also recall mentioning a pistol for you. Unofficially, that's not a bad idea."

"Security system, maybe. Gun, never," Sarah said. "Are you any closer to finding the person behind this?"

Larson shook his head. "It's too soon, I'm afraid. I have that list of people you've seen in the emergency room, and I'll start interviewing them tomorrow." He looked at his watch. "Or actually, later on this morning. While I'm doing that, I'll probably ask the other detective with whom I work to look into some other areas."

"And if nothing comes of what you're doing?"

"Then we'll keep at it," Larson said. "Don't worry. I'll catch the person behind this."

"But meanwhile, I have to go about each day with a target on my back, wondering when and where the next event will take place. And, of course, not knowing when he'll get tired of playing the game and decide to end it... and my life."

Tom Oliver's voice carried traces of sleep when he answered his phone at half past seven the next morning. "Dr. Gordon, the caller ID showed it was you. If it were anyone else calling at this hour, I'd have let it ring, but I figured you wouldn't call this early if it weren't important."

"You're right, Tom, and thank you for answering. I've thought about what you said, about a security system. How soon can you or someone from your crew get to my place and put one in?"

There was a pause. She guessed the man was thinking about his schedule.

"Since it's for you, I guess I could shake loose and install it myself. I'll do it today. There are several choices, though. What did you have in mind?"

They spent the next fifteen minutes discussing options. Sarah's decision was to arm every door and window so that a breach would not only set off an alarm in the home, but also notify the security company. Sarah had a number of questions, and Tom seemed prepared to answer all of them.

"How do I use my garage door opener and not call out the police or National Guard or whoever?" she asked.

"You'll be able to arm and disarm the system a number of ways, including a key fob you can put on the same ring as your car keys," Tom said. "When you leave, you'll arm the system after you watch the garage door close. When you return, you disarm it, open the garage door, close it behind you, and rearm it."

"So I can go back to using my garage opener?"

"Right. Any other questions?" he asked.

"Can you have it done today before I leave for work this afternoon?"

Another pause. "I guess I could do that. I'll pick up the material and be at your house by nine. I should have you ready to go by noon."

"Thanks," Sarah said. "Oh, and while you're here, I'm going to need you to patch a bullet hole above my front door."

Sarah hung up. Then two thoughts crossed her mind. The first was that her final words of the conversation should give Tom something to think about as he gathered the material for the job. The second was more troubling. Was it really a good idea to have Tom, whom she'd known for just a few days, install the security system on which she'd depend for her safety? Or had she made a mistake—a big one?

Suppose Tom was in some way involved in this game of cat and mouse. Maybe he or his son... No, that made no sense. *You're getting paranoid, Sarah.* Well, sometimes paranoia wasn't such a bad thing. In this case, she could only hope it would keep her alive.

The hairs on the back of Sarah's neck prickled as she walked into the emergency room of Centennial Hospital that afternoon. The trip from her home, where Tom Oliver had just completed the installation of her alarm system, was a terrifying one for her. She wasn't sure why her fears seemed to have heightened. Maybe the installation of the security system had made it all more real to her. But whatever the cause, Sarah was more nervous than usual today.

She'd kept her eyes moving, scanning in all directions for someone who might ram her car or shoot at her. Once in the hospital parking lot, she debated phoning for a security officer to escort her, a tactic she decided with some regret to forego. *Get real. It's broad daylight and shift change time. People are coming and going all around you. You're safe, Sarah.*

Sarah shoved her backpack into her locker, closed the door, and spun the dial of the combination lock. As she was turning away, Connie Douglas hurried into the break room of the ER. "Are you coming on duty?" Connie asked.

"I thought I'd check first with Dr. Perkins to see if there's anything special I need to know," she said, "but, yes, I've got this shift."

"Well, don't bother talking with Dr. Perkins. I need you now," Connie said.

She hurried away without another word, leaving Sarah to follow. Connie had worked in this ER or others like it for a couple of decades. She was no rookie, and when Connie said to hurry, it was best to do just that.

As she exited the break room, Sarah noted a flurry of activity in one corner of the emergency room. The curtains weren't completely drawn around one of the spaces, and she could see Dr. Craig Perkins bending over an elderly man, doing cardiac compressions. She recognized an anesthesiologist at the patient's head, evidently trying to place an endotracheal tube, a polyethylene tube inserted into a patient's airway to administer anesthetic gases, or in this case oxygen. Other people were there as well, although Sarah could catch just a glimpse of them as they worked.

This explained why Connie needed Sarah in a hurry. Apparently, she was aware of a patient needing immediate medical attention, and it would take a few moments to get another doctor down here. Sarah quickened her pace.

Sarah wasn't sure what she expected to see when she followed Connie through the curtains into a cubicle opposite the one where Craig was working. On the gurney parked in the center of the space was a young woman, no more than a teenager was Sarah's guess. Beside her was an older female who bore a slight resemblance to the patient—perhaps a mother or other relative, Sarah thought.

An IV was running into the patient's hand. The two prongs of an oxygen catheter led into her nostrils. A monitor beside the gurney displayed her heartbeat and blood pressure, and the leads from another monitor led under the sheet onto her distended belly. She was obviously pregnant, and although it appeared she was in labor, she remained silent.

"Miss Young has been having contractions for a couple of hours," Connie said, slightly emphasizing the *Miss* in case Sarah missed that information on the clipboard she was handed. "She has no obstetrician. I phoned the OB on call when she arrived, but in the meantime the fetal heart tones have dropped."

Connie's voice never displayed the concern Sarah knew she was experiencing. Sarah felt it as well. As soon as the situation became clear, Sarah felt tentacles of fear grip her heart. This was one of the true emergencies in obstetrics—fetal distress.

"How far along in your pregnancy are you?" Sarah asked as she moved to the patient's side. "Do you know when the baby's due?"

"I...I think I'm about nine months along."

"First child?" Sarah figured that, given the age of the patient, the answer was probably "yes," but she'd learned never to assume anything.

"I...I had an abortion about a year and a half ago. My boyfriend wanted me to do the same thing with this pregnancy, but I...I refused. I want this baby, even if he doesn't."

Sarah placed her hand on the young girl's abdomen. There was no fetal movement, and although that wasn't a definitive sign, it was enough to concern her. What she could feel, though, were frequent and somewhat irregular contractions of the uterus. "What FHT rate did you get?" she asked Connie.

"Here. Take a look at the electronic fetal monitor tracing." Connie handed Sarah a broad paper strip with two irregular lines, one below the other.

Sarah's own pulse quickened as she noted that the baby's heart rate wasn't the normal 120 to 160 beats per minute. The FHT, the fetal heart tones, demonstrated wide swings in rate, dropping and peaking in a pattern that told her there was definite fetal distress. And the monitor confirmed that the uterus was contracting frequently.

"Let's have a quick look," Sarah said, reaching for exam gloves. What she feared was evident the minute she looked beneath the sheet. The young girl was bleeding. She undoubtedly had some degree of placental abruption, a turning loose of the placenta that left the fetus starved for oxygen. Whether the contractions had caused this or vice-versa was a chicken-and-egg question, one she didn't need to address. The important thing wasn't the cause—it was the solution. The situation called for an immediate Caesarian section to save the baby.

"Who's the OB on call?" she asked Connie.

"Dr. McClelland. I called him already," Connie said. "His service was going to give him the message."

"Call again. Do whatever's necessary to get through to him. I'm going to call upstairs and alert OB to prepare for a C-section."

The patient looked up at Sarah, fear obvious on her face. "What's happening?"

"The placenta—the thing that gets blood to the baby—part of it is coming loose from the wall of the uterus. We'll need to take the baby surgically—what we call a Caesarian section—as quickly as possible."

"I...I don't have a doctor," the young girl said.

The woman at her side spoke for the first time. "I'm her sister. We don't have insurance. But I'll make sure the doctor and the hospital are eventually paid every penny. Just do whatever you have to. This baby is important...to all of us."

Sarah looked to make certain the IV was running. The girl's vital signs were abnormal, but Sarah's real worry lay in the tracings from the fetal monitor, still showing significant swings in the heart rate of the baby. She pulled out her cell phone and started to dial the labor and delivery section of the hospital. "It's important to me, too. And I promise you we'll do whatever's necessary to make sure this baby gets here safely."

Connie sat just off the ER in the room that served the staff as both lounge and locker room. She held a cup of coffee, occasionally blowing across the surface of it before sipping, as she took advantage of her supper break. Connie often chose to combine eating her meal with reading a few pages in her Bible, and that's what she was doing today.

She didn't flaunt her religion, but neither did Connie try to hide it. She'd discovered that some of the patients she dealt with in the emergency room appreciated a nurse with a spiritual connection. As for the others—well, she simply tried to witness to them in whatever way she could. Matter of fact, that's what she'd been doing to her friend Sarah for several months. She looked up to see the doctor coming into the room.

"Hiding out, are you?" Sarah asked.

"No, just taking my supper break," Connie said. She motioned to Sarah to sit down. "Have a seat. What's the latest on the Young baby?"

Sarah eased down onto the sofa beside her friend. "I took the patient up to the delivery room, hoping Dr. McClelland would arrive on time. As it turned out, he was already up there, waiting for a patient to deliver. He agreed with us about the placental abruption and took Ms. Young right in for a C-section."

Connie watched as Sarah touched the corner of her eyes with a tissue, blotting away tears. "Did everything go okay?"

"I had to hurry back to the ER, but I just called labor and delivery, and mother and baby are doing fine."

"So why are you crying?"

"The mother had already picked out a name for the baby. It's a little girl." She took a moment to gather herself. "She named her Jennifer."

Connie reached for the hand of her friend. "Then let's take a moment and pray for Miss Young and Jenny." *And for you, Sarah. Definitely for you.*

7

It had been an emotionally draining shift, as well as a physically tiring one, in the ER. Sarah made certain the doctor relieving her was clued in on the patients she'd sent to X-ray, the ones awaiting lab work, and the few other bits of information he'd need to make the transition seamless. At last, she trudged to the break room and pulled her backpack from her locker. Although her inclination was to put an audible full stop to the day by slamming the locker door, she gently closed it.

"Want me to walk to your car with you?" Connie said from a corner of the room.

"Oh! I didn't see you there," Sarah said. She slumped onto the sofa. "No, I'll be fine. I'm going to sit here for a minute while my thoughts sort themselves out. Then I'll probably get one of the security guards to walk me to my car."

"Is that what you're going to do every night until the police catch the creep who's behind these attacks?"

"I honestly don't know," Sarah said. "I'm just taking it one day at a time, hoping that Detective Larson will find him soon."

"Have you—"

"I'll bet I know what you're going to say. Yes, I've had a security system installed at my house. They put it in today, matter of fact. But I refuse to get a gun."

"Good on both counts," Connie said. "A security system for a woman alone is an appropriate precaution. But I don't like the idea of having a pistol in the house."

"Harry had one, but I made him get rid of it when...when Jenny..." She stopped and fought the tears that, despite her efforts, started rolling down her cheeks.

Connie sat on the couch and put her arm around Sarah's shoulder. "That's okay. Your emotions are going to be pretty unstable for quite a while, going up and down at the slightest provocation. Take it from me. The best thing you can do is let the tears out when you feel them coming. Holding them in just makes the next time this happens even worse."

"How would you know?" Sarah muttered softly.

"Because I've been where you are," Connie answered. "I lost a child many years ago. She was four when she got sick. The pediatrician made the diagnosis quickly—meningitis. He got her transferred to Children's Medical Center in Dallas, but despite everything they could do, she passed away. So I know about loss...and triggers...and...I won't say healing, because I'm not sure you're ever the same. However, I do know that you'll reach a point where the good memories overcome the bad ones."

Sarah looked up at her friend and marveled that they'd worked together for years, yet she'd never heard about this part of Connie's life. "So what I'm going through is normal?"

"It's different for everybody. For you, your loss is twice what most people experience because two of the most important people in your life are dead now. And piled on top of that, you have this unknown person attacking you. Sure, it's normal for you to be on an emotional roller coaster."

"I just feel...I feel like I'm different. I don't know if I can get back to the person I once was."

"You're thinking of the doctor who could look at things unemotionally and make decisions. No, you may not ever be that person again. But that's not all bad. Most people who've experienced the loss of a loved one find themselves more tender." Connie handed Sarah a tissue from a box on the table in front of them.

"There's... there's another thing," Sarah said. "Something I don't talk about."

"You mean being angry with Harry for leaving you alone?"

"How did you know?" Sarah asked.

"It happens to most people. They may not admit it. And logic tells them the person who died didn't do it on purpose. But they still feel like they've been betrayed."

"How can I get past this? Do you have any suggestions?" Sarah asked.

"This might be a good time for you to reacquaint yourself with God."

"I'm—"

"I know," Connie said. "You're mad at God. Your first reaction is to ask why God would let something like all this happen. I did. And I've discovered that the answer is, 'I don't know.' We can't see what God can, so we have to trust Him."

"How can I trust Him when my world has fallen apart? Why did He do this to me?"

"We live in an imperfect world. Bad things that happen are part of that. They're not punishment. But God doesn't make bad things happen. And no matter what we experience, God's still in control."

"It doesn't seem like it," Sarah said.

"You may not see it now, but you will. I don't know how God will handle your situation," Connie said. "What I can tell you from my own experience is that things will get better. You will survive. You may even come out of this stronger... or you may not. But either way, you can trust God."

"That's hard for me to believe," Sarah said.

"Believe it. Right now, you're angry with God," Connie said. "That's not unusual. Look in the book of Psalms and think about David, who wrote that book. There were times he believed God had deserted him. But he never stopped trying to talk with God."

"And..."

"And you might consider doing the same thing."

Sarah drove home with the same care and caution she'd used to navigate her way from her house to the hospital. She was careful to scan both sides of the street near her home for suspicious vehicles, but all she saw were the SUVs and sedans her neighbors parked there on a regular basis.

She pulled into her driveway and thought her way through the process ahead of her. Confident that she knew what came next, she thumbed the button on her key chain that disarmed her security system. Then she reached to the remote clipped to the sun visor of her car and punched the button to raise her garage door. When she was safely inside the garage, she reversed the process. Thank goodness she no longer had to manually lock and unlock that door.

Was this what she was going to do at least twice a day for who knew how long? Well, if it would keep her safe—no, if it would keep her alive—she was willing to put up with any amount of nuisance. Besides, as her friend Connie had said, a security system was a good idea for a woman living alone. Still, she wondered what progress, if any, Bill Larson was making with his investigation.

As she sometimes did when coming home from a particularly stressful shift at the hospital, Sarah made a cup of hot tea, put a few cookies on a plate, and sat down in the living room to watch a recorded sitcom. She'd seen this particular program so many times she found herself mouthing the lines along with the actors, but it didn't matter. For Sarah, the ritual was more important than the elements of the experience.

When Harry was alive, she'd worked the day shift and a nanny had taken care of Jenny. In those days, after their evening meal, after Jenny was fed and bathed and asleep in her bed, Sarah and Harry would go through this same routine, sharing the events of their day, sipping hot tea, while ignoring the program that played out before them.

Without Harry to share the experience, Sarah didn't find the same comfort she had in those days. Nevertheless, tonight she felt a need to draw a dividing line between the stress and excitement of her work and the shelter of her home. It was the equivalent of what castle owners must have felt when they raised the drawbridge and flooded the moat.

When the program was over, she turned off the set. The dishes could wait until morning. Sarah yawned, but she knew she was fooling herself. She wasn't sleepy. Despite locked doors and windows, despite a security system that would sound an alarm and send a message for help at the first breach of the fortress her home had become, she wondered if he was out there. He—the man whose face she couldn't see but whose outline was there each time she closed her eyes. He—the man who had broken into her home, set a fire in her garage, sent a bullet into the door frame above her head.

A warm shower and climbing between clean, crisp sheets did nothing to make Sarah think she'd get some sleep tonight. Then she thought about the time she'd spent with Connie earlier in the evening. Her friend's words came back to her—"God doesn't make bad things happen." If that was true, Sarah had wasted lots of hours being angry with God. Now was she supposed to just reverse her course? Was God really interested in her, even when she'd turned her back on Him after the loss of her family?

Sarah lay in the dark, tossing in the loneliness of the king-sized bed. Finally, she gazed into the blackness that surrounded her, and without editing them, not caring how they sounded, she spoke aloud the words that were in her head. "God...please help me." She took a breath that was almost a hiccup. "I miss Harry and Jenny. I'm scared of the things happening to me right now. I don't know where to turn." A tear rolled down her cheek and she brushed it away. "God, I need help. Please."

On Wednesday morning, Sarah had just rinsed the plate that had held her English muffin and was about to pour her second cup of coffee when her cell phone rang.

"Dr. Gordon, this is Tom Oliver. Am I calling too early?"

"No, I've been up for a while." She trapped the phone against her shoulder and lifted the coffee pot off the warming plate, grabbing her cup with the other hand.

"I wanted to follow up on that security system I installed. Any problems?"

"So far, so good. But I appreciate you checking." She poured coffee into the cup, then added sweetener as she continued to talk.

"And the restoration? The carpet we ordered should be in soon. Shall I call you to set up a time to install that? Shouldn't take long."

"Fine. Let me know when it comes in," Sarah said. She rolled her head left to right and back again, but the tension in her neck and shoulders didn't abate. Perhaps it wouldn't until all this was over.

After a few more minutes, Tom ended the call. Sarah sat down at the kitchen table and sipped her coffee. She appreciated Tom's following up, but his last words to her yesterday had been, "Just call if there are problems with the system." Since she'd had none, she hadn't really expected a follow-up this morning. In addition, she thought they'd already arranged that he'd set up a time for installation of the carpet when it came in. Although the reasons he cited were probably valid, it seemed to Sarah that Tom's call was really unnecessary—unless there was some other motive behind it.

Was he checking up on her? Did he want to know if she was home? After all, he could probably circumvent the alarm system that he'd installed, which meant he could get into the house easily enough. Had he seen her program in the alarm code? She'd been in such a hurry to get to work that

Sarah paid little attention to shielding Tom from the keypad when she entered the numbers. Could he have programmed in a "back door" code that would allow him to disarm the system?

Sarah started to head for her computer to check this notion on the Internet before she forced herself to stop. *That's paranoid thinking. Tom has been nothing but helpful. Stop being suspicious of everyone around you.* Sarah wondered what it would take to stop this mindset of hers, the tendency to suspect everyone, trust no one. Would it end when her stalker was found and brought to justice? Or when he finally decided to stop toying with her and snuff out her life? No, she would take normal precautions to avoid making herself vulnerable, but this business of seeing attackers behind every bush and ulterior motives in the attentiveness of others had to stop.

Sarah remembered that she had errands to run, and it would probably be best to do them in broad daylight. She opened cabinets, checked her refrigerator, and came up with a list of groceries that should get her through the next several days. Most of her clothes were washable, but she had a couple of dresses that should go to the dry cleaners, so she gathered these and put them by the kitchen door that led to her garage. Sarah started washing a load of clothes, and made sure the dishwasher was going. By the time she headed out the door she felt almost as though things were back to normal.

It seemed to Sarah that she'd slept reasonably well last night. Perhaps the change had something to do with her conversation with Connie, followed by her attempt at prayer before she dropped off to sleep. But, whatever the cause, it seemed the day was starting out on a better note.

Sarah backed out of her driveway, went through the routine of lowering the garage door, then arming the alarm system, and started driving down the street. She'd only gone a block before she realized she hadn't picked up the clothes she'd wanted to drop off at the cleaners. Since she'd worn one of the dresses to church a few days ago and she'd likely choose the other if she went back this Sunday, she needed to get this done today. Sarah made a couple of left turns and headed back toward her house.

As she drew near, Sarah saw an unfamiliar black sedan at the curb directly across from her house. She knew most of the cars that were usually parked on that street, and this wasn't one of them. As best she could tell, the car was empty. Was someone at that moment trying to get into her home, preparing to lie in wait for her return? The security system should stop an intruder, but what if this was Tom Oliver, circumventing the alarm system to gain entry? Or maybe he'd given the code to someone else, perhaps sold it? Even if the alarm system were working, could someone be at the side or back of the house, waiting for her to disarm the system so he could open a window or jimmy a door lock and get in?

Sarah stopped short of her house and edged her car to the curb, making sure she had a good view of the black sedan. She got out her phone, entered 9-1-1, and sat poised with her fingers over the keyboard to hit "send." Then she saw someone open the door of the house across the street from hers. A middle-aged woman with dark hair, carrying a large purse, emerged and started down the walk. Sarah pressed the button to roll down the passenger-side window of her Subaru just in time to hear the woman call back toward the house she'd just left, "Your Avon order will be here in about a week. I'll give you a call when it comes in."

"Just let me know," replied a woman's voice.

"And when I deliver it I'll expect some more of those delicious cookies," the woman said. She opened the door of the black sedan, tossed her purse onto the passenger seat, and climbed behind the wheel.

As the car pulled away, Sarah cleared the numbers from her phone, then leaned back and drew her arm over her forehead, wiping away perspiration that wasn't due to today's Texas heat. Well, better to make a mistake like this than to walk into a trap. Sarah took some deep breaths in an attempt to slow her racing pulse. It didn't work. Even after she heard the garage door close behind her, she still felt the effects of her adrenaline rush.

Bill Larson reached for the coffee cup at his elbow and found it empty. He shoved it aside, deciding he'd had enough for now. His desk was awash in papers, but this was nothing unusual. He knew where to find each sheet and what it represented. The papers in this particular pile were notes he'd taken when—sometimes by phone, sometimes in person—he'd interviewed the list of potential suspects gleaned from the ER records of patients Sarah Gordon had seen. He'd put in the time and effort, but so far he hadn't come up with a viable suspect.

"Hey, partner. Any progress on your case?" Cal Johnson leaned on the edge of Bill's desk. His Styrofoam cup was almost hidden in hands large enough to palm a basketball. Today, in contrast with his weekend attire, Cal was dressed in a suit, dress shirt, and tie.

"Not really." Larson looked up at the detective. "Got a court appearance today?"

"Yep. And I'll bet that after I sit in the hallway outside the courtroom for half a day, the defense lawyer and the DA will get their heads together and work out a plea deal."

"That happens sometimes," Larson said. "Just be glad if they agree on an outcome that will get another criminal off the street, even if it's not for as long as we might wish."

"Yeah," Cal said. "We just catch them. It's up to the legal system to decide what to do next."

Larson leaned back and tugged at the tie hanging below his open collar. "I just wish I had a lead on the Gordon case."

"No luck on the ER patients?"

"There are a few who seem to have a motive to carry out the fire or shooting, but excluding those who've moved or died, the others were sound asleep next to a spouse who was willing to testify they never left the house."

"What's your next move? Wait until our perp does something during daylight hours, when it will be harder for him to establish an alibi?" Cal said.

"Actually, when you're through in court I'd like you to begin looking into the doctor's personal life. Maybe that will point us toward whoever's doing this."

"Think there's anything there?" Cal asked.

"Not really, but you know as well as I do, it's part of the process."

"And then again, maybe we'll catch whoever it is in the act," Cal said.

"That would be nice, so long as it's not an act that's fatal for Dr. Gordon."

Kyle Andrews leaned back in his office chair and put one foot on an open desk drawer. His tie was at half-mast, the sleeves of his dress shirt were turned back two folds, and his coat was on a hanger dangling from a hook on the back of his closed office door. He picked up his phone, dialed a number he knew by memory, and when the call was answered, said, "How are you holding up?"

"About like you'd expect, I suppose." Sarah's voice was hesitant, as though she were trying to avoid awakening someone in the room with her.

"Are you okay? You don't quite sound yourself."

"I'm not myself, Kyle," she said. "I haven't been myself for quite a few months. And just about the time I feel like it's coming together for me, someone sets my house on fire. Then, just to keep me on my toes, they shoot at me as I'm hurrying into my house."

"I'm sorry—"

"I'm not finished," Sarah said. "I've had a security system installed and felt a little more secure. But then I started out to run some errands, had to turn back to my house to get something I'd forgotten, and almost had a heart attack when I saw an unfamiliar black sedan parked in front of my home—a car belonging to an Avon lady."

Kyle started to grin at the image, but stopped when he realized the emotions Sarah must be feeling right now. "I'm glad you have a security system now," he said.

"And that's fine, except part of me wonders if I can trust the man who installed it. Maybe he sneaked a peak at the code I chose and now can get into my house anytime he wants."

"Sarah, Tom Oliver is a straight arrow. He'd never do anything like that."

"But you had to defend his son," Sarah said.

"Don't hold Tommy's mistake against his father," Kyle said. "Besides, you have to trust someone. I hope you trust me, and I'll vouch for Tom Oliver."

The silence on the other end of the phone lasted too long for Kyle's comfort. Finally, he said, "Did I catch you at a bad time? I just wanted to check on you."

"There may never be a good time," Sarah said. "I appreciate your concern, but I'm afraid that my trust level for just about anybody is pretty close to zero. Now I really have to go."

After the call was over, Kyle leaned back, put his hands behind his head, and thought about what Sarah had said. It was pretty evident that she included him when she referred to her zero trust level for everyone. Was this just hyperbole, or had she truly reached that point? And, if that were the case, how could he change her mind?

Sarah looked at her watch. She'd gotten bogged down running errands and straightening around her house, and now it was time to head for work. Had she eaten lunch? No matter. She wasn't terribly hungry. She decided she'd pick up something at the hospital food court on her break this evening.

She went through the routine of disabling the security system, pushing a button to raise her garage door, backing her car into the driveway, lowering the door, and arming the system again. To do that for a day or two was a nuisance. To do it for a couple of weeks would be an inconvenience. But to continue this way for the foreseeable future—that was something she didn't want to consider.

Then again, was it really the routine she disliked? No, she could adjust to it, inconvenient as it might be. It wasn't the routine, it was the constant fear of what she might find when she came back, of what would happen to her next. She'd learned in medical school that one definition of anxiety was fear of the unknown. Well, that was what she faced every day now.

Surely it wouldn't be long before Bill Larson learned the identity of the person behind these attacks and brought him to justice. She had to believe that, because Sarah was certain she couldn't go on this way.

He was parked in a different spot today, not directly across the street from Dr. Gordon's house this time. His car was a bit farther down the street, tucked into a space between two others—too far away for a shot from his pistol to hit her, but close enough that he could see her when she left. Was it his imagination, or did she seem a bit harried when she backed her car out of the driveway and pushed the button on her remote to lower the garage door?

After she was satisfied the door was fully down, the doctor reached toward where her ignition keys would be. That probably meant she was finding the fob on her keychain to arm her security system. Before she left the driveway, she picked up her phone and punched several buttons. She waited a few moments, silently shook her head, put down the phone, and drove away. Whoever she was calling didn't answer, and it seemed to frustrate her. Frustration was good.

So far, it looked as though she was using the alarm system regularly. He figured it wouldn't be long before someone or something set it off. Enough false alarms and perhaps she'd stop using it. Or maybe she'd forget to set the alarm as she left. That happened quite often with these systems. In either case, when that happened he'd pay her another visit. Would it be the final one? Too soon to tell. For now, he'd just let her stew.

8

"I APPRECIATE YOU TAKING THE TIME TO SEE ME," BILL Larson said. He sat at a corner table in the hospital's food court, a cup of coffee cooling before him. Although people were coming and going all around, the tables nearby were empty and the low buzz of conversation was like white noise, masking their conversation from the ears of others. This setting was probably as good as any for this meeting.

Sarah took a bite of her tuna sandwich, chewed, and swallowed. "So what's going on?"

"You gave me a list of adult patients and parents of children you saw in the ER who might have a reason to hurt you. Detective Johnson or I have checked out every one of them. So far none of them seems likely to be the person we want. I'm going to need you to sit down with me again and help me get more names from the emergency room records."

Gordon picked up the remaining half of her sandwich but held it without eating. "Why?"

"Because my gut tells me the person who's doing this to you is somehow related to a decision you've made in the ER."

Dr. Gordon chewed another bite of tuna sandwich, following it with a swallow of milk before saying, "I'm an ER doctor. The patients I see think they have an emergent medical condition, whether they do or not. Many of them I can treat myself, for some of them I have to call in a specialist, and a few I send home with medications and as much reassurance as I have to give them."

"I get that," Larson said.

"It may surprise you to hear this, but doctors aren't perfect," Sarah said. "We make mistakes. But I…actually, all the doctors working in that ER, exercise our best medical judgment every day. But are there patients who get so upset when we make a mistake that they want revenge? So far, I haven't encountered any."

"Tell you what. Will you give me another hour tomorrow, going over ER records? If we don't turn up anything promising, I'll let that end of it drop while we pursue some other areas."

"Such as—"

"Right now, Detective Johnson is taking a deeper look into your personal affairs. He'll be checking relationships, tradesmen with whom you've done business, anyone we can think of who might be carrying a grudge."

"No problem," Sarah said. "I'll meet you in the records room about one p.m. tomorrow. And as for digging into my private life, have at it. I don't think there's a chance in the world you'll find anyone there who's out to get me—certainly not anyone who'd set my house on fire or take a shot at me."

"Let's hope not," Larson said. "But we have to look."

Kyle Andrews sneaked a peek at his watch. He'd wanted to talk with his pastor, but when he made the call he hadn't realized that Dr. Farber met with the Board of Elders of the First Community Church on the first Wednesday evening of each month. And that was today. Kyle offered to let his visit slide until another day, but the pastor insisted they meet at his house after his meeting was over.

"Tell you what," Farber had said. "I'll call you when I leave the church. By the time you get to my house, I'll have some fresh coffee started, and we can finish off the pound cake one of the ladies of the church dropped by a few days ago."

Now it was nine thirty—not yet too late for a chat between friends, but if the pastor didn't call soon... Then Kyle's cell phone rang. He checked the caller ID. "Dr. Farber?"

"Kyle, how many times have I told you calling me 'doctor' or 'pastor' isn't necessary when we're in a social setting? Just call me Steve. Anyway, I'm leaving the church right now. I should be home before you get there, but if not, I won't be far behind you."

It took Kyle fifteen minutes to reach Dr. Farber's... er, Steve's home. Sure enough, the pastor's garage door was just going down as Kyle parked his car at the curb. By the time he reached the front door, the pastor had it open, beckoning him inside.

"Come in, come in," he said. "I just got here myself. I'll start the coffee, then get rid of this tie and change into some comfortable shoes. Make yourself at home in there," he said, pointing to a room down the hall to Kyle's right.

The room was probably where Farber studied, prepared his sermons, and counseled visitors. The walls were lined with bookshelves. A desk in the corner had open books and sheets of notes scattered over its top. But the room also appeared to be where he relaxed and read. There was a comfortable wing chair in one corner with a lamp behind it to the right. A small table to the left of the chair held a few magazines and a couple of novels. Sections of today's newspaper were scattered on the floor beside the chair.

Kyle eased into a leather-covered club chair facing the wing chair and crossed his legs. In a few moments, Steve came through the door. The pastor was tall but by no means thin. His silver-gray hair was combed straight back, his moustache neatly trimmed. Blue eyes behind metal-rimmed glasses managed to seem both guileless and inquiring at the same time.

The pastor had exchanged his dress shirt and tie for a golf shirt and replaced the shoes he'd worn earlier with slippers worn over bare feet. "The coffee should be ready in a moment," he said, before taking a seat facing Kyle. "While we wait, why don't you tell me what's on your mind?"

"You know about Sarah Gordon's situation."

"Of course," Farber said. "She lost her husband and two-year-old daughter about eight or nine months ago. Then she had a fire at her house recently. She's certainly had her share of problems."

"More than you know," Kyle said. "There've been other incidents beside the fire. It appears that someone is making an effort to frighten her...perhaps to kill her."

The pastor whistled silently. "I didn't know. I saw Sarah in the service with you on Sunday. I was glad she came. I hope that was your doing. I've tried a few times to call her but got no answer. I wondered if she saw my name on caller ID and didn't pick up. I mean, that would be the reaction of a lot of people, getting a call from their pastor after a loved one dies."

"What do you mean by that?"

"They're too busy with their feud with God to talk with me. 'Why did God let this happen? Why didn't God intervene?' Surely you had thoughts like these when your fiancée died. I certainly did when I lost Mary." He held up his hand. "Let me bring in the coffee. I think this may be a long conversation."

"You're working late," Cal Johnson said as he spied Bill Larson hunched over his desk, squinting at the screen of his computer.

Larson eased back in his chair and stretched. "I lost track of time, I guess. Then again, I don't have anyone waiting for me at home. You, on the other hand, should be there with Ruth."

"She had a meeting at the church tonight. I was home for supper, but I got tired of watching TV so I thought I'd check back and see if you've made any progress." Cal eased one hip onto Larson's desk and peered at the computer screen. "But if you're still here..."

"I've used the various databases available to us, looking for some reason our mystery man is trying to scare Dr. Gordon, but nothing so far. Then I decided to do a plain Internet search." He pointed to the computer. "On Google there were thirty-five million hits for the name Sarah Gordon alone, but that will drop as I add the various filters. And I haven't even begun looking for things that have to do with her late husband." Larson stretched. "I'm probably going to ask you to do some of this. But not tonight."

Cal looked at his watch. "Well, if you don't need me, I've got to head home so I'm there to meet Ruth when her meeting's over. So far, I'm doing pretty well at making this marriage work." He eased off the desk. "I'd ask if you wanted to have a drink with me before I head home, but I guess you're still on the wagon."

"Day at a time," Larson said. "Let me give you some advice, Cal. Sometimes it's a temptation to reach for booze to help you forget a bad day. Cops do it all the time. It's an easy way to distance ourselves from some of the things we encounter. But don't do it. Instead, talk with your wife." He shook his head. "I wish I had."

Cal nodded. "I'll try." He turned to walk away, then said over his shoulder, "See you tomorrow."

Steve Farber looked regretfully at the plate of cake crumbs sitting on the low coffee table in front of him. He reached out to pour a bit more for himself from the pot that rested on a tray beside the remains of the cake. "Help yourself to more coffee," he said to Kyle. "I'm sorry there isn't more cake."

Kyle Andrews filled his cup, added sweetener, and stirred. "No problem. I normally don't have dessert with my evening meal."

Farber patted his stomach. "Unfortunately, I attend enough meetings that include coffee and sweets that I've had to make a conscious effort to leave off desserts if I'm going to keep my weight from ballooning." He smiled. "But sometimes I make an exception." He brushed a few crumbs from his moustache, took a sip of coffee, and looked at Kyle. "Now let's get back to the subject of our conversation. You seemed surprised when I talked about being angry with God for letting a loss or a death happen. Were you shocked that a pastor would go through that himself?"

Kyle didn't respond immediately. He put down his cup, pursed and relaxed his lips, and thought about the question. Finally, he said, "I guess I was."

"Didn't those thoughts cross your mind when your fiancée died? After all, a crossbeam fell on her while she was on a mission trip helping build a church. There she was, doing the Lord's work, and she was killed by a freak accident. Didn't you want to lash out at God?"

Kyle bowed his head. "Yes. But I figured that would be somewhere between disrespectful and sacrilegious. So I kept things bottled up, said all the right things, and eventually I came to accept my loss." He looked up at Farber. "You didn't do that?"

"Nope. You may think that's the Christian thing to do, but I can tell you it's certainly not the way most people react."

"I guess I didn't know about your loss. What happened?"

"Mary, my wife of twenty-five years, went to our family doctor for a physical. The doctor apparently missed a lump in Mary's breast. When it was big enough for her to find it herself, she called him, and he sent her to a surgeon. She had surgery, chemotherapy, radiation—the works—but she died.

After that, I asked for a three-month leave of absence from the pastorate, because I figured it would take that long for me to get over the loss. Frankly, I wondered if I could ever be a pastor again. The church was generous—they gave me the leave of absence."

"I agree. Most churches wouldn't be so generous," Kyle said.

"Especially after the other problem the elders knew I had when they called me."

"What was that?"

"Not important right now." Farber shook his head. "Let's just focus on the way I handled Mary's death. I spent the first six weeks of my leave railing at God. I really thought I had no business being a pastor."

"What changed your mind?"

"I decided my constant complaining to God wasn't getting me anywhere. I needed to give Him a chance to respond. So I opened a dialogue with Him."

"How did you go about that?" Kyle asked, seeming genuinely interested.

"I began by studying the Scriptures," Farber said. "Not just cherry-picking the ones I wanted, but reading whole sections, whole books of the Bible: first Psalms, then Job, then the Gospels. Finally, I started praying again. And, although I never heard a disembodied voice or saw handwriting on the wall, I was aware God was speaking to me. So I stopped talking to Him long enough to listen. And that's when it dawned on me."

"What?"

"What I'd been preaching all these years was true. I just hadn't believed it enough to apply it to my own life. What happened to me wasn't His judgment. He didn't cause it, but He was there to help me through it. And when I turned back to Him, He was still right where He was before I lost Mary."

Kyle shook his head. "You know, I came here hoping you'd tell me the secret of helping Sarah get over her loss and the stress she's under now. Instead, I found that what she's been feeling, what she's doing, isn't unusual. I guess the time frame varies for different people to get past their loss, and it's not abnormal for her to react the way she has."

"So what are you going to do?" the pastor asked.

"I guess that instead of worrying that Sarah isn't recovering the way I think she should, I'll work on being her friend, however long it takes," Kyle said. "And maybe I'd better let out some of the feelings about my own loss that I've buried."

Sarah had heard it all her professional life: Working in an emergency room was predictable only in its unpredictability. It had been a relatively quiet Wednesday evening, but that changed about the time she was scheduled to go off duty. Sarah had given her report to Chuck Crenshaw, the doctor relieving her, and was headed for her locker when the double doors into the ER crashed open.

A female paramedic, one Sarah recognized as being relatively new on the job, pushed and guided a stretcher while a more senior EMT hurried alongside doing chest compressions on an elderly man. An IV was in place and an oxygen mask covered the patient's bloody face.

Right behind them came another team. The patient on this stretcher was a girl, probably a pre-teen. She was bleeding from cuts on the face and scalp. Her blonde hair was matted with dried blood. Her eyes were closed. Sarah wasn't sure if she was unconscious or lying still in a vain attempt to shut out the horror of the situation.

"MVA," the female paramedic pushing the first gurney said in a loud voice, heading toward an open cubicle. "He was driving. Didn't have his seat belt on. Air bag didn't deploy. Blunt trauma to the chest from the steering wheel, cuts where he hit the windshield. He went into cardiac arrest while we were getting him onto our stretcher."

"I'll take this one," Chuck said.

That left the young girl for Sarah. "Same motor vehicle accident?" she asked.

The EMT guiding the stretcher nodded. "Mainly cuts from flying glass, but she hit her head on the vehicle's dash. She's been in and out of consciousness since we picked her up."

In a cubicle, Sarah did a quick assessment. The bleeding had slowed, but at least one scalp laceration would require stitches, and a couple of the facial cuts might, as well. The girl kept her eyes closed, but opened them on command, only to shut them tightly again afterward. A preliminary neurologic exam showed no localizing signs. She knew who she was. She knew today's date. But when asked repeatedly what had happened, she didn't respond. Sarah couldn't decide if she was blocking out the accident or if this was a consequence of her head trauma. She asked for a CT scan of the girl's head and neck.

Sarah cleaned up the largest of the lacerations herself, then covered them with sterile gauze. Meanwhile, the nurse assisting Sarah arranged for a stat head and neck CT. As the nurse and the X-ray tech rolled the girl's stretcher away, Dr. Crenshaw came over. "Want me to take over here?"

"I can stay until we're sure she's stable," Sarah said. "Was the man brought in by the other ambulance her father?"

"Grandfather."

"And..."

"He didn't make it," Chuck said. "This was a one-vehicle crash. He wrapped his car around a light pole. My guess is that he had a heart attack while driving. How about the girl?"

Sarah briefed him on her findings. "I've ordered a head and neck CT. If they're negative, just suturing her lacerations will probably take care of her, although she may need to be admitted for observation." She looked around. "You say he was the grandfather. Are the girl's parents coming?"

"Not immediately. I talked with the police right after I pronounced the driver DOA. It seems the grandparents are taking care of the girl while her parents are out of town."

Sarah's heart sank. She knew firsthand the pain the family would experience as a result of the accident. Sometimes, she felt as though her own hurt were still fresh.

It was after one in the morning before Sarah left the hospital. Her mind was still working on the most recent events when she turned into her driveway. She went through her routine, determined that she wasn't going to be distracted and let her assailant get to her. She sat in her car, the doors still locked, the light from her headlights illuminating the garage door and surrounding area. She pushed the button on her key fob to disarm the alarm system. She had her hand on the button to raise the garage door when in the light spill from her car she thought she saw a small bundle on her front stoop. Her initial instinct was to check it out, but instead she pulled into the garage and lowered the door before unlocking her car and climbing out.

Inside the house, she dropped her backpack in the living room and turned on the porch light. She looked through the viewing window of the front door and saw no one around. Only then did she unlock the door, step onto the small porch, and pick up the bundle wrapped in what appeared to be a baby blanket. She lifted one corner of the blanket and tears came to her eyes. The bundle held a doll, one like the doll lying on Jenny's bed upstairs—her dead daughter's favorite.

She looked more closely at the figure in the blanket. It seemed to be an exact duplicate of the doll Jenny had carried around from morning until night for months before her death.

Then Sarah had a thought that made her blood run cold. Was this Jenny's doll?

9

STILL HOLDING THE DOLL, SARAH BACKED INTO THE HOUSE, slammed and locked the front door, and leaned against it. If whoever was behind this was trying to get to her, he'd succeeded. Acting by muscle memory, not volition, she reached for the keypad on the wall next to the front door and rearmed her security system.

The thought continued to eat at her—how did her stalker know what doll to buy? How could he know the doll left on her front steps would be a duplicate of the one her dead daughter loved? Or, could this be Jenny's doll?

Now she wished she had a gun. What if her stalker, the man who'd left the doll, hadn't left? What if he was still upstairs? She looked around for a weapon, something heavy. She finally settled on a brass lamp sitting on the end table in the living room. She unplugged it, wound the cord around the base, and removed the shade. Sarah unscrewed the bulb and laid it aside. Holding it by the empty light socket, she hefted the lamp. Not a substitute for a gun, but at least she had a weapon.

Holding the lamp in one hand, the doll tucked under her other arm, she slowly climbed the stairs and headed for Jenny's bedroom. She paused at the door, wanting to know yet afraid of what she'd find. Finally, Sarah summoned up the courage to ease open the door. The room was dark. She listened hard but heard nothing. Finally, she flipped on the light and looked around the room. There was no one there. Jenny's doll was still on her bed, right where Sarah put it when the police returned it to her.

But if the doll in the bundle from her porch wasn't Jenny's, that raised another question. How did her stalker know which type of doll to leave on the porch? The only answer Sarah could think of was that he'd been in the house at some time, had probably been in this room, touched Jenny's things, more than likely handled her daughter's doll. A sense of violation made Sarah shudder. She swallowed hard, working to choke back the bile she could taste in the back of her throat. It took a moment for the sensation to pass.

Finally, she turned off the light, closed the door, and eased down the stairs. *I don't know how much more of this I can stand.* Sarah restored the lamp to its position on the end table. She'd plug it in and put the shade in position later. Not now.

Sarah collapsed onto the sofa. She dropped the doll beside her, clutched her arms around herself, and hugged—not because she was cold, but because she was afraid. Her breathing was still ragged. She heard her pulse pound in her ears.

She didn't know how long she sat, reliving the incident in her mind. Finally, as though waking from a dream, Sarah pulled out her phone to call Bill Larson. She had the number partially dialed before she broke the connection and dropped the phone. She didn't feel like talking, even with the police, even with someone like Bill Larson. Not tonight.

She'd call in the morning and tell him of this latest development. Whoever left the bundle was probably long gone. Larson might criticize her for waiting, but when she thought about it, what could the detective do right now? Tomorrow he could pick up the doll, have his lab check it for fingerprints, canvass stores that sold them. But Sarah didn't have high hopes for his learning the identity of her stalker. Whoever was doing this was too smart, and she had a sinking feeling that Larson would come up empty.

After she talked with Larson, Sarah decided it was time to phone Kyle and ask him about the pistol he'd offered. But she'd do all that tomorrow. Tonight, she wasn't up to it.

Her emotions, which she'd finally brought under control, boiled to the surface once more as Sarah headed for the bedroom. She felt the tears she'd been holding back coming again. This time she fell onto the bed, buried her face in her pillow, and let them flow freely. *When is this going to stop?*

Her body shook with sobs as she thought about what she'd lost—a precious child, a loving husband—both gone in an instant. The accident that took them was very much like the one that had sent two patients to her in the ER tonight. Sarah recalled Connie's words about emotional triggers. Well, this was a big one. She wondered how long it would be before they stopped lurking around the corner waiting to surprise her.

The tears slowed, the sobbing subsided, and Sarah heard the words just as certainly as though Harry were standing beside her. *Stop thinking about the past. It's over. Pay attention to the danger facing you right now.* There was someone out there, someone who seemed determined to torture and perhaps kill her. That's where she should focus her attention.

Maybe Connie was right. Maybe Sarah needed to look toward a source she'd turned her back on months ago for the help she needed now. She bowed her head and pondered how to begin. As before, she ended up simply voicing the emotion in her heart. "God, I'm reaching out to You. Will You help?"

"Are you sure you want to do this?" Kyle held out the revolver, barrel first.

"I'm sure," Sarah said. She took the pistol from him, holding it by the grip but keeping her finger outside the trigger guard. "It looks sort of small."

"It's large enough. That's a Smith & Wesson .38 caliber revolver. Holds five shots, weighs less than a pound, and is accurate at close range," Kyle said. "It's unloaded. The first thing to do is make sure you know how to use it. I'll also get you started on the application process for a concealed-carry permit."

"Do you have a permit?" she asked.

"Yes. I'm an attorney practicing criminal law, and when I hung out my shingle I was told by some experienced lawyers that I should arm myself." Kyle pulled up the cuff of his trousers to reveal a small pistol, the twin of the one she held, in a holster strapped to his ankle. "Fortunately, I've never had to fire this in anger, but I'm licensed to carry it."

"If you still have yours—"

"That pistol is for you. I bought it right after someone tried to set fire to your house. I feel better about your safety now that you've finally decided to accept it." He let the trouser cuff drop. "You can have it with you in your home or keep it out of sight in your private vehicle."

"So what's next?" she asked.

"I fire my pistol once a month to keep up my proficiency, so I'm a member of a gun club. We'll go there in a few minutes and get you started." He looked at the pistol in Sarah's hand. "Even with the proper permit, you shouldn't have a gun unless two criteria are met—you know and practice firearms safety, and you're prepared to shoot if necessary."

"No problem there," Sarah said. "Harry taught me how to handle a pistol, so I'll just need to brush up on a few things. And, given the recent events in my life, if it will put an end to this nightmare, I'm ready to shoot."

Bill Larson held his cell phone to his ear and looked around at a squad room that was quiet this early in the morning. The doll on the doorstep was another link in the chain. At least it wasn't an action that would hurt Sarah physically, although the emotional damage was still evident in her voice, even on the phone.

"He must have been in the house and gone to Jenny's playroom," she said. "How else would whoever left it know that doll was the same as Jenny's favorite?"

"Maybe you posted a picture or two on Facebook of Jenny holding her favorite doll. It wouldn't be difficult for someone to enlarge the image and identify the doll."

"I guess so," Sarah said. "Ordinarily we tried to keep Jenny's picture off social media, but she got that doll last Christmas, and, come to think of it, it may have been in a few of the pictures we shared afterward."

"I'll have someone pick up the doll this morning. We'll run some tests, maybe see if we can find where he bought it." Larson didn't tell her that the odds were that all this would have a negative return. Maybe she'd already reached that conclusion as well.

Larson ended the call and scribbled a note to have someone pick up the doll. But there'd been a second bit of information in that call. *So Sarah is going to get a pistol.* He didn't disagree that she needed a gun for self-protection, even though he couldn't officially recommend she get one. And she'd already started the process of getting a permit for it. So why was he bothered by the fact that now she was armed? Was it because it underscored his inability to identify the person who was after her and close the case? Or could his unease be because she got the pistol from Kyle Andrews, rather than from him?

He looked up and saw Cal Johnson approaching. Today Cal wore an open-necked sport shirt beneath a lightweight sport coat. The coat flapped open as he walked, revealing the butt of the service revolver that rode on his right hip.

Normally, Cal was easygoing, with a ready smile for his fellow detective, but not this morning.

Larson ventured a guess at the cause. "Trouble with Ruth?" he asked.

"Sort of," Cal replied. "I was home when she came in from the meeting last night. We had some together time, and things were going well. Then our phone rang. It was Betty."

"Your first wife was calling? Why?"

"She was drunk. She wanted me to send her some money."

"Did Ruth know who it was?"

"As soon as I mouthed 'Betty,' Ruth pointed to the speaker button, so she heard the whole conversation."

"I didn't think your divorce included any alimony," Larson said.

"It didn't. We had a clean break. She was already seeing this other guy by the time our marriage was over. The two of them moved out of state, and I thought that was the end of it."

"But—"

"But he lost his job, so his drinking increased. And if he was drinking, she was drinking. And last night she drunk-dialed me to ask for money."

"What did you do?" Larson asked.

"I managed to calm her down. I suggested some places she could turn to for help. And I finally got her off the phone." Cal shook his head. "I could tell Ruth was sort of ambivalent about the episode. After all, she'd just come from church, where the women talked about loving their neighbor, so she felt like we ought to help Betty. On the other hand, Ruth obviously didn't want to worry for the rest of our married life that my first wife would be calling every time she got into trouble...or had too much to drink."

"Where does it stand now?"

"I think Ruth realizes she's married to a man who has some baggage. I mean, I've tried hard not to let my police

Medical Judgment

work interfere with my home life, and I appreciate what you've done to help there. But I've made some mistakes in my life, and last night, one of them popped up again." He spread his hands. "I don't know what to do."

"Cal, we all have baggage. You have a failed marriage. I have alcoholism. I suspect that if she looks hard enough, Ruth will find she's carrying some as well. None of us is perfect. But we have something going for us: God is always there to help us when that baggage tries to drag us down."

"So what do you think?"

"I think you should call Betty back. First, talk with Ruth, though. She needs to be involved in the decision. Be sure she knows that your first wife is no longer a part of your life. Assure her that this call to Betty will be a one-time thing, an attempt to talk with her while she's sober, to see if you can help."

"I don't know..."

"You can suggest Betty try AA, if she's willing. She might want to try to get some help from a pastor or someone at a church. And Ruth may have some ideas, too."

Her new pistol was like a loose tooth she couldn't leave alone. Sarah picked up the revolver, opened the cylinder, unloaded it, put the same four .38 caliber bullets back in, closed the cylinder with an empty chamber beneath the hammer. There was no safety—most revolvers didn't have them—but Kyle had assured her the revolver was safe from accidental discharge so long as she observed a few common sense rules.

Her first thought when Kyle began his instruction at the gun range was that she didn't have enough ammunition in the revolver to defend herself. "Five bullets won't be enough."

"No, you'll have four," he said. "Remember, you should always keep an empty chamber under the hammer. But you'll only be firing as a last resort and in self-defense. You'll be shooting at almost a point-blank distance, and if four bullets aren't enough, a dozen probably won't do it, either."

It hadn't taken her long to get used to the pistol. Harry's gun had been larger, heavier, held more bullets. But Kyle was right. This revolver had enough stopping power. All she had to do was point it and pull the trigger.

It was time to leave for work. Sarah picked up her backpack and checked its contents. She reached for the pistol, drew her hand back, reached again, and picked it up. This was a new experience for her. Despite the assurances she'd given Kyle, she wondered if she'd really shoot the person responsible for everything that had happened to her. Then she thought of the doll, now in the hands of the police who'd go over it for fingerprints and anything that would help identify the person who left it. She considered for a moment more, then resolutely picked up the pistol, hefted her backpack, and headed out the kitchen door into the garage.

She carefully placed the pistol out of sight in the glove compartment of her car. Kyle had warned her that, until she received her permit, she shouldn't be carrying the pistol. But, considering the circumstances, he was relatively certain the police would understand if the matter ever came up. Better to have an unlicensed firearm than continue to be a helpless target.

Her routine for leaving the house was easier to follow now. Lock the car doors from the inside, disarm the security system, punch the button to raise the garage door, back out, close the garage door. She was about to rearm the security system when her cell phone rang.

It was Kyle calling to see if she had any questions about the pistol.

"No, but I appreciate your checking. And I'd be glad to reimburse you for the cost of the gun. I thought it was an extra you had. I didn't know you'd bought it just for me."

Kyle would have none of that. "It makes me feel good to know you're more secure. I'll let you get to work, but call me anytime."

Sarah finished backing out of the driveway and headed to work. After half a block, she wondered if she'd re-armed the security system. Should she go back and make sure? No, she didn't have time. Besides, the routine had become automatic. She was probably worrying needlessly.

He'd thought he might have to wait longer, but the doctor had already made a mistake. As best he could tell from his observation point, the phone call had interrupted her routine enough that she left her house without setting the security system alarm. Undoubtedly, the doors and windows would be locked, as usual. Since the police had discovered his trick for getting into the garage by tripping the emergency release, he'd acquired a little electronic gadget that would activate any garage door motor, no matter how sophisticated the code. If the security system wasn't armed, he could always get in through the garage. And when he did... Well, he'd decide what to do after that.

He looked at his watch. She was going to be gone for at least eight hours, and more likely nine or ten. He should wait until it was dark to make his move. Then he'd enter the unalarmed house and wait to greet the doctor when she returned. He wasn't certain just yet what would follow, but whatever it was would certainly be a surprise, one that would help make up for the suffering her husband had caused.

10

Bill Larson put down his menu and looked across the table at his pastor. "Dr. Farber, I'm glad you were free for dinner this evening."

"Forget the 'doctor.' It's Steve this evening. And I'm glad you called," he said. "I think most of my congregation feel a bit uncomfortable when they're around their preacher. You probably get that as well, I guess. They're ill at ease in the presence of a detective, even when they have nothing to hide."

"I think everyone has something to hide," Larson said. "For instance, I'm an alcoholic. I tried for years to conceal it before I eventually admitted it to myself and began taking steps to fight it."

The waiter arrived at their table and asked for drink orders. Both men settled on iced tea. "I hope you didn't do that on my account," Larson said, when the waiter left. "You could have had some wine with dinner if you wished."

"No I couldn't," Farber said.

He left it at that, but Larson nodded and filed away the information. He'd had suspicions, and Steve just confirmed them. The pastor was fighting the same battle as the detective.

The conversation was casual until they finished their dinner. Both of them passed on dessert but asked for coffee.

After it was served, Larson said, "I wonder if I could ask you a few questions."

Farber smiled. "I was curious about when you'd get around to it." He held up his hand like a traffic cop. "That's okay. I've enjoyed dinner with you. As I've said, most people feel uncomfortable around their pastor. The opportunities I've had for dinner out since Mary died were mainly church affairs, and those are sort of have-to invitations."

"And I don't go out much either," Larson said. "So it's been a nice change for me." He pulled a notebook and pen from the inside pocket of his sport coat. "But now it's time to ask you some questions about Sarah Gordon."

"Has something new come up?"

"No, we're just pursuing all the leads we can find. My question, I suppose, is whether you know of anything that might lead someone to do all this. I mean, the phone calls and even the stalking are one thing, but the fire and the gunshot tell me this is escalating out of control."

Farber frowned for a moment, obviously thinking about the question. Then he shook his head. "Sarah Gordon, before Harry and their daughter were killed in that crash, was regular in her attendance at church. Everyone loved the whole family. You've heard the expression, 'Didn't have an enemy in the world.' I believe that could have been applied to the Gordon family."

The detective asked a few more questions. Sometimes getting at the information needed from a different direction worked. In this case, it produced the same results. Everyone loved the Gordons. No one had any reason to do this to Sarah.

Larson drank the last of his coffee, caught the eye of their waiter, and motioned to his cup. After the waiter had served both of them, the detective said, "You know, even if you haven't shed any light on the case, it's been nice to sit down to a meal instead of snatching some fast food or nuking a Lean Cuisine."

"Well, if I think of something, I'll give you a call," the pastor said. "And you'll have to let me treat you to dinner some evening. I think we have a lot in common. And I don't have many real friends with whom to share."

"Same goes for a detective," Larson said. "But I think tonight we've both felt comfortable."

"Perhaps that's because neither of us has tried to hide any secrets," Steve said.

No, and now I know you and I share one. Since neither of us has chosen to lean on AA, maybe we can help each other when it's needed.

Sarah was in the ER, working hard to do what doctors often must: compartmentalize their lives and focus their attention on the situation at hand. When she found her tormenter's actions creeping into her thoughts, she shored up the wall that kept them from impinging on the attention she gave each patient she saw in the emergency room. The clock on the wall told her she had only another hour until this shift was over. Tomorrow was a day off, but she couldn't afford to let her focus drift.

She was just about to say something to Connie, her nurse friend, when the double doors into the ER opened to admit two EMTs pushing a stretcher on which a middle-aged man was actively convulsing. He was restrained to the gurney with straps. A woman walked beside him, holding a padded tongue depressor between his teeth, a worried expression on her face.

Connie met them a few steps inside the door and steered them to an open cubicle, with Sarah a few steps behind. "What do you have?" she asked the lead EMT, a middle-aged man whom she knew by sight but not by name.

"According to the patient's wife, he began seizing right before she called 9-1-1. No known head trauma, non-drinker, no history of recreational drugs. Good general health except hypertension, controlled with meds."

She noticed there was no IV running, but before she could comment, the EMT said, "We couldn't get a vein. I gave him ten milligrams of diazepam IM about..." He looked at his watch. "I gave it ten minutes ago. It didn't seem to slow his seizures, though, so you may want to repeat it."

Sarah moved in, signaling for Connie to hold the tongue depressor. She started her exam with the man's head. Her fingers found it quickly—an abrasion and area of swelling toward the rear of the skull on the left. She turned to the woman who'd accompanied the patient and said, "Ma'am, are you his wife?"

"Yes," the woman said, hovering just behind Sarah as though by her very presence she could help.

"When did he hit his head?"

"I didn't know he had," the woman said.

Sarah asked a few more pointed questions, and within a couple of minutes she was pretty certain she knew the cause of the man's seizures. "Connie, let's give him another ten milligrams of diazepam IM," she said. Then she turned to the EMTs, who were still there. "If you guys will try to restrain him long enough, I'll see if I can get an IV started. I'll draw blood for electrolytes and a stat blood sugar at the same time. After that, we need to get him to radiology for a CT of the head. My guess is that we'll find evidence of a subdural hematoma."

The hour that followed was jam-packed with action and decisions for Sarah. The IM medication stopped the seizures, although she remained vigilant for their resumption. If seizures went on uncontrolled for as few as twenty minutes, they could result in permanent neurologic impairment. She didn't want that to happen.

It didn't take long to carry out the CT scan of the head, and in the meantime Sarah got back the reports that showed the man's blood glucose and electrolyte levels were within normal limits. A toxicology screen would take a while, but she was pretty certain the cause of the seizures would be revealed by the radiographic studies of the brain.

Sure enough, the CT scan showed evidence of bleeding onto the surface of the brain, what was called a subdural hematoma. There was no way to know when the trauma that caused this occurred, although the swelling and abrasion of the man's scalp seemed fresh. But no matter—he needed neurosurgical intervention as quickly as possible.

Sarah was on the phone to the neurosurgeon on call when Connie interrupted her. "He's seizing again."

"Hold one second," Sarah said into the phone. To Connie, she said, "Give him lorazepam, two milligrams slow IV—over about a minute. If he's still convulsing, give him another two, but slowly."

She finished her conversation with the neurosurgeon, who said he was on his way. "Alert the OR, if you would. And good pick-up," he said.

Only after the patient, whose name was Paul Murchison, was in surgery under the care of the neurosurgeon did Sarah check the time once more. She found that her shift had ended more than an hour earlier. Well, no matter. No one was waiting for her at home anyway.

Kyle Andrews couldn't sleep. His phone conversation earlier with Sarah had been painfully short—it was obvious she was in a hurry. He'd had a few unexpressed doubts about Sarah having a pistol, despite the arguments he made when he initially recommended she arm herself. When she finally contacted him to say she was ready for a gun, those doubts sprang up in his mind once more. Of course, he'd never let her know about his reservations, and he felt better after spending some time with her on the range as she brushed up on gun safety and the use of a pistol. But still, he lay in bed tonight, wide-eyed, wondering if he'd contributed to her safety or set Sarah up for an encounter that would end with her dead.

He looked at the bedside clock, and two minutes later found he'd already forgotten the time, so he checked his watch. Finally he rolled out of bed, slid his feet into slippers, pulled the top cover around his shoulders in lieu of a robe, and headed for the kitchen.

The kitchen clock showed that it was almost midnight. If Sarah's shift went the way he'd heard her describe it when she and Harry double-dated with Kyle and his fiancée, she was often delayed in leaving the ER. If that were the case, she might still be awake, might just be leaving the hospital. But even if he reached her, would Sarah be willing to talk with him?

Finally, he decided that he'd send a text to her cell phone. If she was asleep, she might or might not waken long enough to read the message, but if Sarah hadn't gone to bed yet, perhaps she'd call him. He thought about what to say, and finally sent this text: If U R awake, we need 2 talk.

Kyle put his phone on the kitchen table and wondered whether he should make a cup of coffee. Maybe that wasn't such a good idea when he was already suffering from a terminal case of insomnia. He'd almost decided on a glass of warm milk when a familiar sound made him look down at his cell phone. Sarah had answered his text. Kyle had thought his message was the soul of brevity, but hers made his look positively verbose. Her message was: Sure. Call.

He picked up his phone and speed-dialed Sarah.

"Hello?"

"Sarah, were you about to turn in?"

"No. I've been tied up in the ER with a patient, and I'm about to leave the hospital. But why are you up? And what's on your mind?"

Kyle hesitated. How would Sarah react if he told her he was worried about her? Lately she seemed to resist someone trying to protect her, and that was exactly what Kyle's motivation had been...although not totally out of loyalty to his dead friend, Harry. Finally, he decided on the truth. "I've been worried ever since I gave you that pistol. Part of me thinks it will provide security, part of me wonders if it doesn't just make you more likely to get shot." She started to say something, but Kyle hurried on. "Look, if you're still awake and want to decompress with a friend, why don't you come by for some coffee—decaf if you'd like. I really want to talk with you."

"Decaf or regular, makes no difference to me," Sarah said. "And I guess I can spare another half hour or so. I don't have to go to work tomorrow, so I can sleep a little later...unless my nemesis has something else planned for me tonight."

Sarah noticed that Kyle had turned on his porch light for her. She pulled her car into the driveway and turned off the ignition. Her hand hovered over the pistol, which she'd kept locked in the glove compartment while she was at work but had removed and placed on the seat beside her for the drive to Kyle's. Maybe it wasn't legal to have it out like that, but this late at night she didn't want to take any chances. Now that she was at his house, she locked the pistol inside the glove compartment once more.

When she opened the car door, the interior remained dark. Kyle had told her about switching off the dome light so there'd be no illumination to make her a target as she exited the car. *Keep illumination to a minimum. Never stand with light behind you.* If this situation kept up for much longer, she would be able to give seminars to the staff at the hospital on avoiding being attacked.

Sarah hurried to the front door, which opened before she reached it. She noticed that the living room was dark. "Light in the room behind you shows your silhouette and makes you a better target," Kyle said.

"I know. You told me that."

Once she was inside, he closed and locked the door, turned on a couple of table lamps, and pointed to the sofa. "Would you like to sit in here?"

She answered his question by taking a seat. "Did you make that coffee we talked about?" she asked.

"Coming right up." Kyle left the room, but was back in a few moments with a tray that he put on the coffee table in front of the sofa. On the tray were two thick white china mugs, a carafe of coffee, sugar, sweetener, and a pitcher of cream. He poured coffee and handed the mug to Sarah, then helped himself, adding sweetener to his cup before he sat beside her.

Sarah took a sip, then sniffed the contents of the mug. "Great coffee. What brand is it?"

"It's a Colombian blend I get at a little place near my office. I buy the beans and grind them myself. What do you drink?"

"At the hospital, the coffee in the break room generally stands on the hot plate for hours. I've never asked what brand they use, because by the time I get some it's not recognizable."

"And at home?"

"Whatever's on sale when I have a chance to buy groceries," Sarah said. She leaned back, closed her eyes, and almost fell asleep before she jerked awake. "Sorry. Guess I'm decompressing." She drank more coffee. "What was it you wanted to talk with me about?"

Kyle leaned back, cradling his coffee in both hands as though he were cold and needed the warmth. "A couple of things, I guess. First, I wondered if you'd had second thoughts about owning a gun. I don't want anything to happen to you, but at the same time I want you to realize that a pistol isn't the final answer. I guess I'm ambivalent. Frankly, I'm hoping you don't have to use it at all."

"I'm fine with the gun, Kyle. You didn't talk me into it. The person who's been harassing me, whoever it is, made me change my mind. And I'm grateful that you gave me one and made certain I know how to use it safely."

Sarah waited for Kyle to respond, but he just sat staring into his coffee cup. It was obvious to her that he had something more to say, but for some reason he was having trouble taking the conversation in that direction.

"More coffee?" he asked, lifting the carafe and gesturing with it.

"Sure, you can warm mine." She held out her cup.

Kyle poured for both of them, put down the carafe, took a deep breath, and looked at Sarah. "I don't know how to say this, so I'll just blurt it out. You know I was Harry's friend. He didn't ask me to watch out for you if something happened to him—it wasn't necessary. That was understood between the two of us. And I'm happy to continue to help as long as you'll let me. But I think I may have overstepped my boundaries."

Sarah's mind churned as she recalled Kyle's actions since Harry's death. Had he done something specific for which he was now apologizing? Was he talking about his actions then or more recently? Her memories of the weeks immediately after Harry and Jenny died were still hazy. But as she recalled, Kyle, like everyone else, had been nothing but helpful during the time following the death of her husband and child.

Was he talking about his behavior the past few days? She'd called him right after the fire, asking help because of some sense, probably gained from TV or novels, that a lawyer should accompany anyone giving a statement to the police, even someone against whom the crime had been committed. Of course, after that he'd begun to come on a bit stronger than she was comfortable with. Had Kyle gotten the wrong idea? Or was he apologizing for trying to go too far? Maybe that was what he wanted to talk about.

Kyle had paused during this time, apparently thinking how he wanted to convey his message. Now he broke his silence. "I talked with Steve Farber."

"Our pastor," Sarah said. That reminded Sarah that she probably should talk with the pastor about her efforts to get back on speaking terms with God. She raised her eyebrows, waiting for Kyle to continue. "And..."

"And he made me see that I was sort of pressuring you to react to the deaths of Harry and Jenny the way I did when my fiancée was killed in a freak accident. You know, trust God and move on. Instead, you've been up and down, fragile at times, and sort of estranged from God because you still blame Him."

Sarah simply nodded, but said nothing.

"Dr. Farber told me that everyone reacts differently to tragedies like that," Kyle said. "For instance, he told me how, after his wife, Mary, died of a cancer that their family doctor missed, it took him a long time to get over being angry with God." He set down his cup. "I'm sorry if I've pushed you, Sarah. I promise that from this point forward, I'll try to let you adjust in your own way and your own time. I just want to be there to help if you'll let me."

Sarah realized that Kyle's words carried a subtext, a message left unexpressed. Yes, he'd shown, by his attitude if not his words, that he thought she should get over her resentment that God let Harry and Jenny die. But, more than that, maybe these latest attempts by the unknown person had brought out another emotion that Kyle had kept hidden for some time. And she was going to have to be careful not to encourage that particular feeling in him.

"Kyle, I appreciate your making a point to tell me all this. I'm glad for the help you've given in so many ways. And it's nice to have someone I know I can call on. But let me make something clear to you now. I need to get back to being in charge of my own life, without leaning on Harry...or on you."

"But if there's something I can do—"

"If I need anything, I'll call." *But it's too soon after Harry's death for me to be open to any kind of relationship, so I need to be careful of the signals I send.* Sarah looked at her watch. "Look at the time. I can sleep late in the morning, but I'll bet you have a busy day ahead of you." She put her cup on the tray. "Thanks for the talk. I think maybe it was good for both of us."

"Would you like me to get in my car and follow you to your house?" Kyle asked.

Sarah resisted the urge to sigh and shake her head. Instead, she said evenly, "Kyle, I can't have a bodyguard follow me around until the police catch this person. The pistol you gave me is in my car, and I'll carry it with me into the house. I keep the doors and windows locked, and my house is alarmed. I'll be fine."

"Then call me when you're safely home. Will you do that?"

"Sure," Sarah said. She hurried to her car and drove off, but not before she retrieved the revolver from the glove compartment and laid it on the seat beside her within easy reach. The drive home took less than ten minutes, time spent in reflection about the meeting with Kyle. She was glad he realized that, however gently, he'd been pressuring her to get over her loss. But she also made a mental note to be very careful about the signals she sent Kyle in the future. *Not now, Kyle. Maybe someday, maybe not.*

As she neared her home, Sarah flashed back on something Kyle had said. Their pastor, Steve Farber, had told him about a doctor missing the diagnosis of his wife's cancer. Was it possible that Farber was behind the attacks on her? Surely not. Then again...

Immediately on the heels of that thought she had another, one that made her pulse race. Kyle was never around when any of these episodes took place. Could Kyle be doing them in order to drive her toward him?

She'd need to talk with Bill Larson about this. But could she trust the detective? For that matter, could she trust anyone?

It was after two a.m. The doctor's shift ended long ago. She should be home by now. Multiple scenarios ran through the mind of the man sitting in darkness in Sarah Gordon's bedroom. He touched the button to illuminate the numbers on his watch: two twenty-five. Where was she?

Perhaps she had to work a double shift. Maybe she went home with a friend. It was doubtful she was spending this time with a boyfriend—too soon after her husband's death, you'd think. Then again, maybe she was reacting to the pressure and had decided to stay at a hotel. Perhaps she'd even left town. If she did, that would be too bad. He had more in store for her.

Two thirty. He wanted to stay, to carry this through, but the longer he sat there in the house the more nervous he became. What if he got caught before he did everything he had planned? He had to leave. It was too bad to let such an opportunity pass by, but there'd be others. Meanwhile, maybe he could arrange something that would let her know he'd been here... something to keep up the pressure on Dr. Gordon. And he wasn't ready for the end game. She hadn't suffered nearly enough.

11

As Sarah turned into her driveway, she automatically scanned her surroundings. No lights on in the neighborhood. No people in view nearby. No unfamiliar cars parked at the curb. No suspicious shadows in the bushes and hedges of her yard or those around her. She reached down to the key ring dangling from the ignition and thumbed the button to disarm her security system, used the remote on her sun visor to raise the garage door, and drove in. Still safely locked in her car, she once more remotely lowered the garage door. After she heard the door hit the ground and confirmed it by looking in the rearview mirror, she unlocked her car door and hurried inside the house. There she used the keypad beside the kitchen door to rearm her system, securing all the doors and windows. Now the drawbridge was up. The moat was filled.

She'd carried the pistol with her when she exited her car. She laid it gently on the kitchen table. Now she could relax.

Kyle, once more in pajamas, sat propped up in bed, but the novel in his hand wasn't holding his attention. He supposed the book was interesting enough, but when he turned a page he was hard-pressed to recall what he'd just read. He tried to avoid looking at his bedside clock, but he finally gave in. Sarah had been gone for twenty minutes. The drive to her house should have taken ten. She'd agreed to call him when she got home. Was this simply a case of forgetting, or had something happened to her? Kyle knew his suggestion that he follow her home was probably overkill, but now he regretted not insisting and following through.

Finally, he closed his book and reached to the bedside table for his cell phone. If he called Sarah and she was falling asleep, she might be angry with him. But if he didn't call, only to find out the next day that something bad had happened… No, he had to check on her.

The phone rang four times before she answered, and when she did, it was obvious she was upset.

"Sarah, this is Kyle. Is something wrong?"

She didn't answer for several seconds, and when she did, her voice was tight and pitched a bit higher than usual, as though she were forcing the words out. "Someone's been in the house."

"Did they breach your security system?" He stopped himself. "Never mind, Sarah. I'm on my way. I want you to do two things. First, if you're not already holding that pistol, I want it in your hand when I arrive. Before I get there, if you see something or someone suspicious, shoot. Once you have the gun, call 9-1-1 and report this."

"Should I call Bill Larson?"

"Call the regular police emergency number. They can have a car there in a few minutes. Let them decide whether to notify Larson. But first, get the gun and have it ready. Just don't shoot the police or me when we arrive."

When Kyle arrived, a Jameson police car, its roof lights bathing Sarah's house in flashes of red and blue, was angle-parked at the curb. He carefully kept his hands in sight when he mounted the two steps to her porch. At the open front door, he called, "Sarah, it's Kyle. Can I come in?"

Instead of Sarah, a brawny young man in a police uniform appeared in the doorway, essentially filling it. "Sir, I'm going to ask you to reach into your pocket with two fingers and get out some identification."

"I'll vouch for him. He's...he's a friend." Sarah's voice from behind the policeman sounded a bit better to Kyle than it had minutes ago on the phone.

"That's okay," Kyle said. He produced his wallet and pulled out his driver's license and membership card in the Texas Bar Association. He handed them to the policeman, who studied them, returned them to Kyle, nodded sharply, and motioned him inside.

"Sarah, are you all right?" Kyle asked as he hurried to her.

He saw that her hands were empty and was about to ask about the pistol, but she must have anticipated his question, because she said, "Yes. And in case you're wondering, one of the officers has my pistol. He took it from me when I answered the door."

"You don't need it right now. I'll talk with them when they leave. I'll make certain you're protected, even if I have to spend the night on the sofa in the living room with my own pistol in my hand," Kyle said. "Now what happened?"

"My...my bedroom." She pointed up the stairs.

Kyle asked the policeman, who was still standing with them, "Okay if I go upstairs?"

"If she takes you, it's fine with me. We've checked and there's nobody there now. Meanwhile, I'm going to see if my partner has found anything outside."

At the door to her bedroom, Sarah said, "I didn't notice anything amiss when I walked in. I came straight up here and the light was on. I thought I'd turned it off, but sometimes I forget, so I wasn't concerned. Then I looked at the bed, and..." She pointed.

Sarah had blocked his view into the room as she stood in the doorway. When she moved aside, Kyle saw what she meant. The covers on the right side of the bed were heaped up in a mound as though there were someone under them. "So he—"

"That's the side of the bed Harry always slept on. At first, I thought there might be a person in the bed. When I could see what this represented, I was afraid there was still someone in the house. That's when I ran back down the stairs. Then you called."

Kyle nodded. He stood in the doorway and scanned the room. Nothing seemed out of place except the mass under the covers. He moved toward the bed. As he got closer, he began to see what had happened. Finally, he reached the bed and pulled back the covers. Someone had done a fair job of arranging pillows to simulate a body, even using a smaller pillow to provide a semblance of the head. "So the pillows under the covers made you think there was someone in the bed. Must have been quite a shock."

Sarah nodded. "Initially, yes. But my greatest shock came after that, when I realized someone had gotten past the security system and into my house." She hugged herself. "Every entrance to my home is alarmed. I have to follow a routine so complicated I need a script. And yet someone got into the house, into my bedroom." She looked directly at Kyle. "What else must I do before I feel secure?"

He cruised by Dr. Gordon's house. He'd been gone for about an hour, and apparently she'd come home since he left. There were lights on in every room. Two cars, one of them a Jameson police patrol car, were parked in front of the house. He went by slowly, but couldn't get a glimpse of what was going on inside.

Did he dare go around the block and swing by for a second look? No, he decided not to take the chance. It was obvious from what he saw that his little calling card in her bedroom had produced the desired results. And if she left her security system unarmed once, she'd probably do it again. That was just human nature. When she did, he'd be ready.

He touched the bulge made by the small semiautomatic pistol in his pocket. He'd used it once to frighten her. Soon he'd use it to bring an end to all this... but not before she knew who he was... and why he was doing it.

Sarah was feeling a bit calmer now, although things certainly were far from normal yet. She and Kyle sat on the sofa in her living room, looking up at the two policemen.

The policeman who spoke to her was tall and broad-shouldered, with close-cropped dark hair, a square jaw, and a deep voice. He'd answered the door when Kyle arrived, and the two stripes on his uniform shirt and the way the second patrolman deferred to him led Sarah to believe he was in charge. "Dr. Gordon, my partner and I have been through the whole house. We've searched around your property. We even checked for someone hiding in a neighbor's yard. I can assure you that whoever did this is gone."

"That's good. But the question remains, how did he get in here in the first place?" she asked. "Every door and window is alarmed."

"People can break in and disarm a security system if they're fast enough or for some reason have the code," the policeman said. "But we found no evidence of a break-in. There were no scratches around the locks, no indication of a window being forced open. You say you used your opener to lift the garage door, so the emergency release hadn't been tripped."

"And if it had, that door is alarmed as well," Sarah said.

"Is it possible you forgot to set the alarm?" He apparently saw her about to object, so he hurried on. "It happens all the time. The two main problems with a security system are false alarms and neglecting to set them. And that's especially true if they're fairly new, as I believe you said this one is."

Kyle turned to her and said, "That's true, Sarah. It's tough to get in the habit, and maybe something distracted you when you were leaving, something that kept you from arming the system."

Sarah recalled that when she left she'd received a phone call. Maybe it had distracted her enough that she didn't complete the task of setting her alarm. But was it that simple? She remembered wondering if Tom Oliver had learned the code she assigned, or even put in a second code known only to him, one that would allow him free access. Or, if he was smart enough to install a system, maybe he knew ways to disarm it rapidly enough to keep an alarm from sounding.

And how about the doors? Although she had no certain knowledge of how it was done, perhaps he'd been able to get an impression of the key to her door while he was working on the house. Or maybe, since he did construction, he knew how to get an extra key.

And if Tom wasn't the culprit, maybe he sold the information to someone else. Contractors weren't the wealthiest people in the world. Perhaps he needed money. Or maybe someone put pressure on him. He said he owed Kyle a favor. Who else did he owe? Or, for that matter, was Kyle the one to whom Tom gave the information?

Then there were the workmen. Three men about whom she knew almost nothing had been in her house for a couple of days. Was one of them doing this? Sarah felt as though she was about to scream. Was there anyone who wasn't a suspect? Was there anyone she could trust?

"Sarah, are you all right?" Kyle asked. "It seemed as though your thoughts were a million miles away."

"What... Oh, yes, I was just thinking." She looked up at the policeman. "So what do I do now?"

"You asked about notifying Detective Larson. He'll get our report in just a few hours when he comes to work. I imagine he'll be calling you shortly after that." He took the cap he had tucked under his arm and set it squarely on his head.

"In the meantime, just rearm your system after we leave, and you'll be fine."

"What about her pistol?" Kyle asked.

"Sir, I don't think the doctor has a permit for this weapon."

Kyle stood, dug into his pocket, and once more showed the policeman his ID card for the Texas Bar and his own gun permit. "Officer, I'm Dr. Gordon's attorney. We have reason to believe that her life is in danger. I gave her that pistol, she demonstrated to me that she knows how to use it, and we've started the process for her to receive a concealed-carry permit. Right now she needs the gun for protection, and she has every right to have it in her possession inside her home. I suggest you give it back to her now. If you have any questions, you can call Detective Bill Larson."

The officer shrugged. He turned to his partner and nodded. The other policeman placed the revolver on the table in front of Sarah. The first officer said, "Ma'am, just be careful with this. When people are armed and confront an intruder, most of the time they wind up being the ones shot, rather than doing the shooting. I wouldn't want that to happen to you."

Because Bill Larson had discovered that his work helped him ignore the craving for alcohol he still fought on a daily basis, he generally didn't linger at home once he was awake in the morning. Today was no exception. When he arrived at police headquarters, he headed straight for the squad room and his desk, where he put down the white paper sack containing his breakfast, and glanced at the reports centered on his blotter. The top one immediately grabbed his attention. There'd been a break-in at Sarah Gordon's home during the night. He was actively working on her case, so why hadn't he received a call?

Ignoring the coffee and pastry in the sack, Larson turned away and strode down the hall to the desk of the police watch commander, where Sergeant Dumas was preparing for his daily meeting with the officers who would take over to patrol the city on the day shift.

The detective waved the incident report as he neared the desk. "Sergeant, why wasn't I called when this took place?"

"That's what I asked Carmody. He was the shift sergeant overnight."

"And..."

"He decided that since the patrolmen who responded were two pretty senior men, there was no reason to roust you out when you'd get their full report in just a few hours."

"Don't you—"

"Don't I think that's a decision that should have been left up to you? Yes, I do, and that's what I told Carmody. But it happened, and you know as well as I do that there are going to be slipups like that." He gestured with his coffee cup. "Want some of the world's worst coffee? I think Carmody made this when he came on duty about ten hours ago, so it's got some body to it." The sergeant grinned.

Larson shook his head. "No, thanks. I've got some coffee and an apple fritter waiting for me at my desk." He took a deep breath. "And you're right. These things happen. I presume you set Carmody straight."

"Oh, I'm sure that for a while you'll get called anytime someone involved in one of your cases sneezes," Dumas said.

Larson eased into his desk chair and opened the sack. The coffee was just about right, and he took a healthy swallow from the cup. As he bit into the apple fritter he remembered one of the things he'd read about alcoholics. Sometimes they substituted food—especially sweets—for the alcohol they really wanted. He was going to have to watch that. It wouldn't do to stay sober but die of a heart attack when he weighed three hundred pounds.

He scanned the report Corporal McNaught had filed. It looked as though the patrolman had done everything Larson would have done. He'd even attached a picture of the pillows dummied up to simulate a body in Gordon's bed. When he finished reading the report, Larson agreed the most likely scenario was that the doctor failed to activate her alarm system. That allowed the prowler to go about his business undetected, although Larson would still have to figure out how he breached a door or window to enter the house. But another question remained. Why did the prowler, or stalker, or whatever they decided to call him—why did he leave without confronting the doctor? Did he just want to frighten her? Or had something caused him to leave before completing the task he had in mind?

The detective noticed the report said Dr. Gordon entered her home at about a few minutes before three a.m. That was several hours after she should have gotten off work. He'd need to check that out.

He continued reading, putting himself into the scene, running various scenarios through his mind, compiling a list of questions he wanted to ask the doctor. The apple fritter was gone, the coffee cup was empty, and Larson wasn't ready for police station coffee left too long on the hot plate. He looked at his watch and decided he'd give Sarah Gordon another hour or so before he called. Meanwhile, maybe he'd head over to the coffee shop near police headquarters and get a second cup.

Although he had intentions of taking his coffee back to his desk, Larson encountered some people he knew, so he sat down for what he figured would be a brief talk. That brief talk stretched on, and by the time he re-entered police headquarters it was a little after eight a.m. Since the break-in had been reported less than five hours ago, it was possible a call to Sarah Gordon might wake her, but Larson put himself in her position and decided she probably hadn't slept since the police left her house. Anyway, the sooner he talked with her, the sooner he could resume his search for the person who was behind the activities aimed at her.

He dialed her number, and her answer on the first ring told him he'd probably been right in guessing she was already awake. "Dr. Gordon, this is Bill Larson. I hope I'm not calling too early."

"No, I haven't been asleep. I spent the time after the police left thinking about my intruder, and I've decided the alarm system wasn't a good idea."

Larson heard a man's voice call, "Who's calling this early?"

The transmission sound changed as Dr. Gordon apparently hit the "mute" button to answer. When she returned, she said, "Sorry about that. Anyway, either I failed to set the alarm or the alarm failed. Either way, the system didn't work. So I need to come up with an alternate suggestion."

"I realize security systems are a pain, but what else could you do that might keep you safe?" Larson found himself hoping she didn't say she was relying on her pistol. He still had mixed feelings about that.

"I guess I can keep using the alarm system—after all, it's already installed and I've paid for it—but I think I have an idea that may be even more effective in keeping me safe."

12

AFTER THE POLICE LEFT, KYLE HAD TOLD SARAH, "I'LL STAY here with you."

"That's not necessary. I'll be fine on my own."

Kyle didn't know if this meant Sarah really wanted to be alone, or if she was concerned about his presence in the house. Either way, he wasn't buying it. She'd been through a terrible experience this evening, and the last thing she needed was to be left alone.

Kyle shook his head. "Unless you physically throw me out, I'm going to stay. Why don't you go upstairs to your bedroom and try to get some rest?" he said. "I'll be right down here with my pistol. I'll make certain you're safe."

Sarah shook her head. "I'm not about to try sleeping in that bed," she said. "Not tonight. Maybe never. But I appreciate your offer."

"Do whatever you want," Kyle said, "But I'm not leaving here until morning."

Sarah evidently realized that Kyle was serious, because she didn't argue any further. They had sat together in the living room, alternately exchanging meaningless comments and sitting quietly until the sun illuminated the world once more. Sarah's fear seemed to diminish as daylight dawned, but Kyle wasn't about to leave until he was sure she felt safe.

Sarah rose and moved toward the kitchen. "I think I'll start the coffee." She stopped at the doorway when her cell phone rang.

Kyle edged closer to her. He couldn't hear the other side of the conversation, so he asked, "Who's calling this early?"

Sarah punched a button on her phone long enough to give a one-word answer. "Larson." Then she turned away from Kyle and put the phone back to her ear.

He continued to listen, but none of Sarah's responses helped him decipher what was going on.

Sarah ended the call with, "I'll see you in an hour or so."

"So what's up?" Kyle asked, after Sarah shoved her phone into the pocket of her jeans.

"The detective's read the report about last night's incident. He'll be here in about an hour," she said. "I'm going to put on some coffee and cook some breakfast for us. How do you like your eggs? Scrambled okay?"

"Sure," Kyle said, unsure whether he should follow her into the kitchen.

Apparently, Sarah read his indecision. "You can come in here if you like."

"I can cook, you know," Kyle said. "If you don't feel like it."

"Not necessary," Sarah replied. "I'm not really hungry, but I've learned that I have to stoke the fires if I'm going to keep going. I'll scramble some eggs and make toast. But you can make the coffee."

He opened a few cabinet doors until finally Sarah pointed him to where she kept the coffee. When he had the coffeemaker going, he put butter and jelly on the table and set places for both of them. "That smells good," Kyle said. "I'm afraid my breakfast usually consists of a cup of coffee and a sweet roll or bagel eaten in the car on my way to work."

Sarah put scrambled eggs and toast on their plates while Kyle poured the coffee. When they sat down, he looked at her with upraised brows. "Would you like me to say grace?"

She sighed. "That's something else that's missing around here. Harry and I used to do it with every meal, but since I've been eating alone..." She looked down at her plate. "Yes, please do."

Sarah was putting the plates in the dishwasher when she heard a knock at the door. "Kyle, would you answer that? It should be Detective Larson."

As Kyle headed for the front door, an unsettling thought insinuated itself into Sarah's mind. *Kyle has been with me through the night. He's been my protector. Could he have done this while I was gone to work, then spent some time with me, insisting that I call him when I got home?* She shook her head as though trying to dislodge a particularly pesky fly. *Can't I trust anyone?*

In a few minutes, she walked into the living room where Kyle and Larson stood. "Would you like some coffee?" Sarah asked the detective.

"Yes, if it's not too much trouble. Black."

"Kyle, would you get him a cup? I might as well get started answering the questions I guess Detective Larson has about last night's episode." She pointed Larson to one of the overstuffed chairs, then took a seat on the sofa.

The detective pulled his notebook and a ballpoint pen from his coat pocket and crossed his legs. "Tell me what happened."

"Haven't you seen the police report?"

"Yes, but I want to hear it again in your own words. Sometimes things come out on the second telling—Oh, thanks." He accepted the mug Kyle offered and took a sip before setting it on the table beside him. Then he turned back to Sarah. "Let's start with when you got off work."

Sarah told it once more: the phone call from Kyle, spending longer than she'd planned at his house, coming home to find a light on in the bedroom upstairs, her shock when she saw the pillow-figure under the covers, the call from Kyle, the arrival of the two police officers. "I don't think I've left out anything," she concluded.

"No, I think you've covered it." Larson closed his notebook. "We'll canvass the neighbors this morning. Maybe one of them saw an unfamiliar car here last night. We might get lucky and find an image on a security camera. We've checked before and none of your neighbors has one, but we'll extend our search a couple of blocks. The images they capture can help us identify suspicious vehicles or people. If we come up dry, we'll try a different tack."

"And something else I've thought of," Sarah said. "The security system aside, how did he get into the house?"

"Using an electronic gadget to get past your code and activate your garage door opener, picking the lock on your front door, finding a window you left unlocked—lots of ways," Larson said. "I'm not so much interested in how he got in as I am in who he is."

Kyle had taken a seat on the sofa next to Sarah, and now he asked, "So how do you find that out?"

"We dig, come up with nothing, dig some more, shake off our frustration, and keep working. Most of the time we get the person responsible," Larson said.

"Most of the time?" Sarah shook her head as though in amazement. "That means some of the time you don't. And what if you only solve this case after whoever's behind it decides to stop playing and kills me? I don't think that's going to make me feel much better."

Sarah could feel anger replacing the fear she'd experienced every time her mysterious stalker struck. Maybe that was good. She pointed to the lit panel on the wall by the front door. "I had a security system installed." She patted the bulge in the pocket of her jeans. "I have a pistol now." Sarah did her best to control her voice, but heard it rising with each sentence. "And it didn't do any good!"

135

"Dr. Gordon, I know how you must—"

"No!" she said. "No one can really know how I feel." She looked Larson in the eye. "So while you look for clues that aren't there..." Sarah turned to Kyle. "And while you fuss around like I'm incapable of taking care of myself..."

"But—" Larson started.

"But—" Kyle said.

Sarah ignored them and plowed on. "While you all do what you do, I'm going to take steps to make me feel secure. I guess I'll probably keep using the alarm system, and I'm going to hang onto the pistol, but there's more I plan to do."

Neither man spoke.

"I've been stuck in self-pity since Harry died. But now I'm going to start acting the way I used to—like a mature woman, a doctor who's faced life-or-death decisions in the ER, someone who can take charge."

"What does that mean?" Kyle asked.

"I have some things in mind, but you'll simply have to wait and see what they are."

She saw the questioning look on Larson's face, the hurt on Kyle's. Well, that was too bad. Sarah knew what she was going to do, and she was ready to get on with it. Dr. Sarah Gordon was about to start fighting back.

Kyle closed the door behind the departing detective, turned back to Sarah, and said, "I'm sorry if I've come across too strong. I just wanted to—"

"I know what you wanted to do," Sarah said, "And I appreciate it. But it's time for me to take responsibility for myself. I'd gotten used to being a wife and mother, but both Harry and Jenny are dead. It's just me, and I've been letting this whoever-he-is get the best of me. I suspect that's part of his plan, and I don't intend to let him do it anymore."

"You forget that there's a good chance the final act of his plan is to kill you," Kyle said.

"Oh, I'm aware of that. But I'm not going to let him. If Bill Larson can't find him, I'm going to make the perpetrator—I guess what the police would call the 'perp'—I'll make him come to me. And once I get him out in the open, I'll see that he's brought to justice." She patted the pocket holding her pistol.

"I know Hunter will love you," Harry had said the first time he took Sarah to see his father.

"I'm hoping you like him as well,"

"How long has your mother been gone?" Sarah asked.

"She died three years ago. I tried to get Dad to come live with me, but he adamantly refused. He said he'd lived here on this farm all his life, and he planned to die here. He has his dogs for company, and he's the very essence of self-sufficiency. After he turned down my invitation to live with me, I asked him if I could hire a housekeeper for him."

"And what did he say to that?" Sarah asked.

"He said, 'I can clean, I can cook, I can even sew. Ina taught me what I didn't already know, and I don't want or need to replace her. When I'm too old to do things for myself, we'll talk.'"

Hunter had been delighted to meet Sarah, and the two had hit it off immediately. Her own parents were divorced, living on opposite sides of the continent and not very involved with her life, so Hunter became more of a father to Sarah than her own.

She'd thought about calling Hunter when her stalker started harassing her, but kept putting it off, not wanting to worry him. After all, he'd suffered the loss of a son and a granddaughter. She realized she should have told him about the stalker, but as soon as things began to escalate Sarah figured that if she let Hunter know what was going on, he'd show up on her doorstep with a shotgun.

Maybe that would have been the best course, but now she was determined to stand on her own two feet against her stalker. And to do it, she needed a favor from Hunter. So here she was at his door, about to tell him everything.

Hunter Gordon hugged Sarah, then gently ushered her into his living room. His full head of hair was completely white now, whereas it had been salt-and-pepper when Harry first brought her to meet his father five years earlier. Sarah figured Hunter had to be about sixty-five years old, but his appearance and demeanor were those of a man much younger.

His farmhouse was small and the rooms just the slightest bit cluttered with furniture that had obviously been chosen as much for comfort as for appearance. Although Hunter was a widower, the house was neat and clean, and Sarah knew this was his doing alone.

"What brings you out here?" Hunter asked when they were settled in comfortable chairs in his living room.

"First of all, I need to apologize for not visiting more often," Sarah said. "But after Harry died, I sort of sleep-walked through the next few months. I'm only beginning to get back to whatever this 'new normal' is now that my husband and daughter are gone." She reached out and touched the older man's hand gently. "I should have worried about you. I should have been there for you as you recovered from your own loss. But I had my hands full getting through each day."

"All water under the bridge... or over the dam, or however you want to say it," Hunter said. "But I still wonder what triggered this visit to your father-in-law."

"Some things have been going on since Harry died," Sarah said. "Things I should have told you about earlier, but I didn't want to worry you. I thought I could handle them myself." She went on to relate the series of events that had plagued her over the past several months. "Then there was a fire in my garage. After that, someone took a shot at me when I was going into my house. And last night, the person behind this got past my alarm system and put pillows in my bed to look as though someone was there."

Hunter frowned. "I wish you'd called me. I would have come into town and mounted a guard over you until the police catch whoever's behind this." Whether consciously or unconsciously, his eyes strayed to the mahogany cabinet on the wall to their right where Sarah knew he kept several rifles and shotguns.

Just as I knew you'd react. "I know, and I appreciate it. But I've come to realize I need to meet this head-on, not let someone else fight my battles for me. And that's why I'm here."

This time Hunter rose and moved purposefully to the gun cabinet. "What do you need? Just tell me."

Sarah shook her head and motioned him back to his chair. "No, I don't need a rifle or shotgun. Actually, I have a pistol. You know that Harry had one when we were married, but I made him get rid of it when I learned I was pregnant. Then, after all this started, Kyle Andrews finally convinced me to take a revolver he bought for me."

"I recall Kyle. He was Harry's best man, wasn't he?"

The memory of her wedding caused a brief flashback that brought tears to Sarah's eyes, but she blinked them away. *That was then. This is now,* she reminded herself. "Yes. Kyle was Harry's friend, and he's sort of taken on the task of looking out for me. But now it's time for me to be responsible for my own safety."

"Besides getting a pistol, what have you done?" Hunter asked.

"I put in an alarm system, but either my stalker found a way to get around it, or there was a time when I forgot to arm it. Either way, I've discovered it's not foolproof. And that's why I'm here."

Hunter spread his hands. "Whatever I can do, whatever I can give you, whatever you need—it's yours."

Sarah wondered if she was being foolish or, for the first time in eight or nine months, if she was about to take charge of her life again. In any case, she'd gone this far, and she was committed to her plan of action. "Here's what I have in mind."

13

BILL LARSON WAS HAVING LUNCH AT A LITTLE DELI NEAR police headquarters when his cell phone rang. He chewed and swallowed a bite of Reuben sandwich, wiped his hands on a paper napkin, and punched a button to answer the call.

"Hey, Bill. Where are you?" There was a hint of excitement in Cal Johnson's voice.

"Having lunch."

"Where?"

"At the deli down the block." He looked at his watch. "I can be back in the office in fifteen minutes or so if it's important."

"I've got a better idea," Cal said. "I've been working without a break all morning. Order me a club sandwich and a Dr Pepper. I'll be there in five minutes." His voice dropped to a near-whisper, even though Larson figured he was almost alone in the squad room. "I've found something that may be the key to this Dr. Sarah Gordon thing."

"See you in five," Larson said. He rose, went to the counter, and placed the order for Cal.

It was ten minutes before Cal eased into a chair at Larson's table. His sandwich and soft drink were already waiting there for him. "Sorry. It took me a little longer than I thought to break loose." He reached below the hem of his jacket and made a motion Larson recognized, settling his gun more comfortably on his hip. Once that was done, Cal picked up one of the sandwich triangles and took half of it in one bite.

"I know you're hungry," Larson said, "but if this was so important you wanted to tell me face-to-face, how about sharing what you've found?"

Cal chewed, swallowed, and followed the bite of sandwich with a healthy swig of Dr Pepper. He grabbed a paper napkin from the dispenser and wiped his lips, then leaned over closer, although the deli was almost empty. "Remember we looked at a bunch of people Dr. Gordon had seen in the emergency room."

"Yes, patients and their families. I know."

"And we got zip."

Larson nodded. None of this was new.

"So today I started backtracking Dr. Gordon's late husband, Harry. He was a general surgeon, and his partner is still in practice, which means he still has all Harry Gordon's patient records. I couldn't get them without a court order, but after talking at length to the woman working the front desk at that practice, I eventually got most of what I needed."

"How?"

"She could think of a number of patients that might have grudges against the doctor significant enough to carry forward to his family. In all but one of the cases, the actual patient was dead, so she decided the privacy regulations didn't apply anymore. I finally coaxed six names out of her, and if we hit a wall there, I might be able to go back with a subpoena and get the seventh one. But if you'd like to start working these..."

Larson finished his iced tea, crumpled his napkin, tossed it onto the remains of his sandwich, and stood up. "Give me those names and addresses, and I'll get started."

While Cal dug into his inside jacket pocket to pull out his notebook, Larson wondered if this might be the break that was needed to bring this case to closure. His second thought, following hard on the heels of the first, was to wonder why it mattered so much to him that he be the one to solve it.

Kyle Andrews was standing before the shelf of law books that almost covered one wall of his office when the phone on his desk rang. He'd asked his secretary to hold his calls except in cases of emergency, so this one must be important. *Of course, to Tandra an emergency might be finding that she put on the wrong shade of lipstick this morning.* He stayed standing as he answered. Kyle wanted to finish looking for the citation he needed before the arguments he'd fashioned in his mind fled from him.

"Kyle Andrews," he said, perhaps a bit more brusquely than normal.

"Kyle, I'm sorry to bother you. This is Steve Farber. I...I think I need your professional assistance."

Kyle slowly lowered himself into his desk chair, thoughts of the missing citation displaced by this call from his pastor. "How can I help you?"

"Do you remember when we talked Wednesday night, I mentioned that a doctor failed to diagnose Mary's breast cancer until it was too late? It came up because we were talking about being angry with God."

"I remember," Kyle said. He wondered where this was going, and how it would involve him professionally. But he figured Steve wouldn't call without a good reason.

"Well, when Mary died I wasn't angry just with God. I was angry with her doctors, including her surgeon. He tried to assure me that by the time she saw him and he did the tests, surgical intervention wasn't going to help. She underwent radiation and chemotherapy, but she died anyway...slowly and painfully."

Kyle held his breath, waiting for Farber to say what he feared was coming next.

"I'm afraid I displayed my frustration with that doctor in a number of ways, including a letter in which I said I wished he could watch one of his loved ones die this way." There was a catch in Farber's voice as he continued. "I eventually got over my hurt and frustration, and I apologized to that surgeon. You can probably guess that it was Harry Gordon. And when he was killed, I conducted his funeral. But now the police are looking for someone—"

"Someone who might be doing things to make his widow suffer," Kyle said. "And you're on their list. Right?"

"Another member of our congregation, Bill Larson... Detective Bill Larson called and wants to talk with me. And I wonder if you'd be present during the interview."

Kyle had seen pictures and videos of the machines that were the predecessors of modern computers. The image that came to him now was of cards sorted at lightning speed, eventually producing an answer. His mind went through a similar process, but he had only a couple of cards to scan before making his decision. He was bound, by honor if not by a professional obligation, to represent Sarah's interests. If Steve Farber were the stalker responsible for Sarah's problems, Kyle would face a massive conflict of interest if he represented him. On the other hand, he really couldn't believe the pastor was the man behind the attacks on Sarah.

"I have a potential conflict here," Kyle said. "What I can do is be there to advise you during the questioning. If it becomes apparent that your interests and those of my client diverge, I'll step aside and let you formally engage counsel."

"I presume you're representing Sarah, which makes sense. Please don't let me put you in a difficult position."

"No, what I've described should be okay."

When the phone conversation ended, Kyle took his suit coat from the hanger on the back of his office door, told Tandra he'd be gone for about an hour, and headed out the door. On the way to his car, he thought about the situation.

He'd just implied to Steve Farber that he represented Sarah, but did he really?

Actually, Sarah has never engaged me to represent her. And although she accepted his help and support after the fire at her house, their last time together it seemed she was pushing him away. *So am I her lawyer... or her friend... or both... or neither?*

Detective Bill Larson decided to start at the top of the list Cal gave him. He was startled to see his pastor's name there. Cal's note under Farber's name read, "Threatening letter to Dr. after death of man's wife." *Wow, this one was going to be awkward.* Well, might as well get started.

The pastor seemed to understand when Larson called him. He was apparently unsurprised that the detective wanted to interview him. It was almost as though he were expecting the call. "Certainly," Farber said. "Come on by. I'll be happy to talk with you."

After he rang the doorbell of Steve Farber's home, Larson heard soft footsteps approaching. He was prepared for a housekeeper to open the door. Instead, Farber himself, wearing an open-necked dress shirt and navy slacks, opened it wide and said, "Bill, come in."

Larson stepped inside and the pastor closed the door. "Should I call you Detective, since this is an official visit?"

"No, you know me as Bill, so let's just keep it that way."

"And you can call me Steve, unless it feels awkward." He led the way down a short hall into a room where a desk was almost covered with books, copies of what looked like sermons, and sheets of paper with scribbled notes. In the center of the desk was an open laptop computer.

"Sorry to disturb you," Larson said as he took the chair toward which Farber pointed.

"Just putting together Sunday's sermon." The doorbell rang and Farber turned toward it. "Just a second. I've asked Kyle Andrews to sit in on this."

In a moment, the pastor returned, accompanied by Kyle, who shook hands with Larson, then sat down. "Hope this isn't awkward, but Dr. Farber wanted me to be here."

Larson turned to Farber, who had taken a seat behind his desk. "This is a field interview—nothing more. I'm not going to record it. I didn't bring another detective as a witness. And I'm not going to give you a Miranda warning. All that may come later, but for now I'm just looking for information."

"Fair enough," Farber said. "Please ask your questions."

"You know about the problems Dr. Sarah Gordon has had."

"I knew about some of them. Kyle told me about others," the pastor said. "And you said on the phone that now you're interviewing people who might have some kind of a grudge against Sarah's late husband." He grimaced. "And that includes me because of the letter I wrote."

"I recognize why you might have been frustrated at the time," Larson said. "And who knows but what I might have felt the same way in those circumstances. But we're looking for someone whose anger hasn't cooled down." He reached into the inside pocket of his coat and pulled out a single page of typing. "This is a photocopy of a letter you wrote to Harry Gordon. And, frankly, the writer of this letter is the type of person who'd carry a grudge a long time. I guess my question for you is, 'Are you still holding such a grudge?'"

He passed the letter to Farber, who did no more than glance at it before he rose, walked over to where Kyle sat, and handed him the letter. "I remember this. And to this day I regret writing it."

"And I'm glad you do," Larson said. "But it puts you on the list of suspects. So let's talk about where you were on some of these dates."

Larson consulted his notebook, read off the dates, and watched as Farber consulted the appropriate pages of an appointment book. After a few minutes, it was clear that, since most of the episodes in question had taken place late at night and the pastor lived alone, he had no one to provide an alibi for the times in question.

Kyle decided it was time to speak up. "Detective," he said, "You know as well as I do that many people, when asked about their whereabouts, don't have an alibi. This proves nothing. I hope you don't plan to pursue an investigation that includes your own pastor as a suspect."

Larson shook his head. "Counselor, I've just asked some preliminary questions. There are a lot more to follow. If you asked me right now whether I suspect Steve Farber of these acts, I'd say no. But I have to include him in the list of suspects until we clear this completely."

"Well, I would hope you have more solid leads than this," Andrews said.

The interview went on for another fifteen minutes, but yielded no new information.

As he left Farber's house, Larson had two thoughts. He had a gut feeling that the pastor was unlikely to be the one perpetrating the various acts against Sarah Gordon. But he also wondered if perhaps he shouldn't look more closely at Kyle Andrews's movements during the times in question. He couldn't get past the animosity he felt toward the lawyer.

When the interview was over, Kyle remained seated after Larson left. Farber ushered the detective out, then came back and settled into his desk chair. The pastor looked at Kyle with a neutral expression but said nothing.

Kyle took a moment to gather his thoughts. "I'm sorry I didn't have time to talk with you before Larson got here."

Farber waved it away. "No problem. And as it turned out, he didn't really grill me—just asked a bunch of questions that I answered as truthfully as I could." He reached into his center desk drawer and pulled out a checkbook. "I appreciate you being here, though. Let me pay you for your time."

"No, let's just chalk this up as repayment for our evening together a couple of days ago. And although I doubt Larson will be back with more questions, if it seems this is getting serious, let me see if I can help you find someone to represent you."

"Not you?"

"As I told you earlier, I have a potential conflict of interest, and it's probably best if I don't represent you. I hope you'll understand." *That letter showed me a different kind of person than the one I've gotten used to seeing in the pulpit on Sunday morning. I know you said you'd changed, but until I'm certain you're not the person doing this to Sarah, I don't think I want to represent you.*

Sarah stood at the range in her kitchen, stirring a pot of the soup she was cooking for her supper and thinking. She wondered for probably the tenth time if her new plan was foolish or wise. *Stop second-guessing yourself, Sarah. You've been making life-or-death decisions for years now. You just have to get back in the habit of making them outside the emergency room.*

She'd wondered about whether to set the security system when she returned from visiting her father-in-law. On the one hand... No, enough of that. It was there, so she might as well use it.

And what about her pistol? She—or rather Kyle—had set things in motion for a concealed-carry permit. She was awaiting the routine background check and completion of a mandatory training class for things to become official. Until that time, she shouldn't have the pistol on her person outside her home. But she couldn't very well leave the house without it when someone was out to harm her.

Meanwhile, she would definitely have the gun with her at home. One problem, of course, was keeping it nearby. It would be embarrassing to need it in the living room while the revolver was in a drawer in her bedroom. So, with an empty chamber under the hammer, she had stuffed the pistol in the right front pocket of her jeans, where the unaccustomed weight reminded her almost constantly of the changes some unknown person had forced her to make in her lifestyle.

She tasted the soup, added some salt and pepper, covered the pot, and looked at her watch. Kyle would be home from the office by now. Part of her wanted to call him, invite him over to share her evening meal. She regretted being a bit short with him last night. Sarah had decided that it was foolish to suspect Kyle of being behind the attacks on her. Maybe inviting him to supper would be a peace gesture of sorts. But would that just send the wrong signal about their relationship?

The lid covering the soup jiggled, so she turned down the flame under the pot. Then she turned to her new companion, who to this point had sat silently nearby. "What do you think? Shall I call Kyle, or are we better off keeping news about you to ourselves for now?"

14

SOME NIGHTS WERE BETTER THAN OTHERS FOR SARAH.

Some nights, like the one two days ago, following her discovery of the pillow dummy in her bed, she didn't even try to sleep because she knew it was a lost cause.

Last night was one of the good ones—the first in quite a while. She made sure the doors and windows were locked and the alarm set. She honored her newfound resolution to stay in touch with God by praying, or at least making an effort to do so. Finally, she looked at her new companion and said, "You listen for any sounds of someone trying to get into the house. If you hear them, warn me. I'll take it from there." With that, she made certain her pistol was in easy reach on the nightstand, the barrel pointed away from her for safety. Sarah was asleep almost as soon as her head hit the pillow.

The next morning, she was at the kitchen table eating the last of a bagel spread with cream cheese when her cell phone rang. Sarah took a swallow of the morning's second cup of coffee before answering the call.

"Doctor, this is Bill Larson. Did I call too early?"

"Not at all. I'm just finishing breakfast, then I have to do some things around the house before I leave for work. Do you have something new?"

"We're expanding our search for suspects. Detective Johnson and I spent yesterday afternoon and evening checking out some people who might have a lasting grudge against your husband."

Sarah thought she knew where this was going, but decided to let Larson proceed at his own pace.

"I wanted to go over those names with you to see if any of them strikes a chord. Rather than you making the trip to police headquarters, I'd be happy to come by your house. Would that be all right with you?" he asked.

"Sure. Give me about half an hour to finish getting dressed."

After she ended the call, she turned to her guardian. "Well, you get to meet the detective who's trying to protect me. I wonder what he'll say about you."

Larson started to reach for Sarah's doorbell when a sound from inside the house made him stop and listen. The sound wasn't repeated. Maybe he'd imagined it. Maybe it was a TV program. He pushed the button but didn't hear chimes sound inside the house. Then he remembered—her doorbell was broken. Larson knocked, and this time the same sound he'd heard initially reached his ears once more. Had she... She hadn't mentioned...

The door opened. Sarah Gordon stood in front of him, and from behind her came the unmistakable sound of a dog barking. "I guess I should have warned you about Prince," she said. "Come in." She took a step back from the doorway.

Larson looked beyond Gordon to where a large black and tan German shepherd stood, eyeing him with obvious suspicion. The dog was quiet now, but there was little doubt in Larson's mind that he could spring into action, both vocal and physical, with very little provocation.

"Where did you get him?"

"My father-in-law. Harry's dad lives on a farm about ten miles from here. At any given time, he probably has half a dozen dogs around. He rescued Prince from an animal shelter when he was just a pup and trained him to be a guard dog."

"Is it safe to come in?"

"Sure. You're fine so long as you don't do anything threatening." She led him into the living room, with the dog following her and Larson bringing up the rear. When they were seated, she told Larson, "Put your hand down, fist closed, and let him sniff. After he sees that I'm friendly toward you, he shouldn't give you any trouble, unless I tell him to."

Larson complied. "Is he...? I mean, can he...? That is, I would think that if you were going to get a dog you'd want a dog that could protect you."

"Oh, he is. There's a word I can use that will cause him to attack. And, believe me, you don't want to be on the other end of that if it happens."

"Should you be saying a-t-t-a—"

The doctor smiled. "No, *attack* isn't the word that sets him in motion. Obviously, I won't say it out loud to you. Actually, it's in German, so there's no question of it slipping out in conversation. But be assured that Prince can protect me quite well."

By this time, the dog appeared to have decided Larson was a friend. He gave one final sniff before padding off to lie at Sarah's feet, where he watched with what seemed like canine interest.

"Let's go over that list of your husband's patients," the detective said. He reached for his notebook, but was careful to make the movement slow and non-threatening.

Sarah shook her head. "Sorry I can't be of more help. Harry didn't talk much about his cases," she said. "When he came home, we talked about a lot of things, but he always said we should leave our practices outside the door. So I really don't know anything about any of the people or situations you've mentioned."

Larson stowed his notebook. "That's okay. I'll keep looking. We've been able to clear some people because they were with spouses or other people at the time the various attacks on you took place, even if it was late at night. The ones I just went over with you have no alibi."

"I was surprised to see Dr. Farber on that list. Surely you don't suspect our pastor?"

"We're checking a lot of people," Larson said. "That includes Dr. Farber." He didn't volunteer any reason.

Sarah had noticed another name written in at the bottom of the list. She started to ask why Kyle Andrews had now become a suspect, but decided to let it go for now. If Larson wanted to tell her, if he wanted to warn her about anyone, surely he'd say so.

Larson said, "Well, I guess I'd better let you get on with your day."

"Are you making any progress in the investigation?" Sarah said.

"We're doing a lot of ruling out. And we'll eventually find the person responsible for the attacks on you. Until then, I hope you're taking extra care to be safe."

"I am, but I'm a bit more militant than I was," Sarah said. "Maybe it was because the stalker actually got into my bedroom despite my best efforts to protect myself, but for whatever reason, my attitude has changed."

"What do you mean?"

"After I married Harry, I underwent a subtle change—subtle enough that I didn't really notice it until after his death. I got used to leaving the decisive, take-charge attitude I'd developed as an ER physician at the door, you might say. I was content to let Harry make the decisions for us, which was fine so long as Harry and I were working together as partners. Unfortunately, that passivity continued—actually, was heightened after Harry's death."

"But that's changed?"

Sarah nodded. "Definitely. I've decided I'm through being passive. I'm ready to fight back."

"Thus your acquisition of a dog," Larson said. "And I guess you still have the revolver Kyle Andrews gave you."

Sarah touched the pocket of her jeans. "Yes, and I'm more careful than ever to keep it with me."

"Just remember that you can't carry it concealed—"

"I know," she said. "I plan to follow through until I get my license, but until then I'm at least going to have it with me at home and in the glove compartment of my car. And from now on I'm through running from my attacker. Instead, I want him come after me." Sarah had heard of someone's eyes blazing but had never actually seen it. Now she imagined that if she looked in a mirror, that's what she'd see. "I'll be ready."

It was Saturday. To some people it was a day off, but to Kyle Andrews it simply meant working at home instead of at the office. He looked up at the clock on his study wall and fought the temptation to pick up his phone and dial Sarah's number. About now she'd be changing and gathering things, getting ready to leave for her tour in the emergency room. He wanted to ask her how she was doing. He wanted to see if she was still... *angry* might not be the word for it. But however you wanted to describe it, she seemed to be different when he last saw her. Her attitude—not just toward him, but toward her life in general—seemed to have changed. And, to be honest, he wasn't really very happy about it.

Since Harry's death, Kyle had hung around in the background biding his time. For the past week or so, going back to her phone call right after the fire at her home, he'd assumed the role of someone on whom she could call for help. As things progressed, Kyle was pleased by this new relationship.

He wanted to keep that relationship intact. No, that wasn't right. He wanted to build on it.

But suddenly things seemed to turn around. Sarah had gone from a dependent widow to an independent woman determined to stand on her own two feet once more. He couldn't explain why she'd changed or the exact time it happened, but one of the most notable effects of her turnaround was to push him once more into the background. Right now, he didn't know what to do to get back into her life. But he planned to keep trying.

He tried to apply himself to the brief he was preparing, but in a few moments he shoved it aside. Kyle decided he might as well face it. He wasn't going to be able to concentrate until he talked to Sarah. He picked his cell phone up off his desk and pushed the button that would dial her number.

She sounded out of breath when she answered. "Sarah Gordon."

"Sarah, this is Kyle. Did I catch you at a bad time?"

"No, I just was in the middle of getting things together for work when I remembered I needed to let Prince out in the yard for a bit."

"Prince?" The puzzled look on his face was reflected in that one word.

"Yes. I haven't told you about Prince, have I?"

Kyle listened as Sarah explained about the dog. When she finished, he asked, "Have you given some thought to what you'll need to do to keep a dog?"

"If you mean feeding him, letting him run, stuff like that—Harry's father gave me a short course in taking care of a dog before Prince and I left the farm. I have food for him. I have a dish for his water and a bowl for his food. I've made him a bed with a blanket in the front room and another in my bedroom. I'm going to let him out in the yard before I leave for work and again when I get back. What am I missing?"

"Nothing, I guess." He hesitated. "Is there anything I can do for you?"

Sarah's voice softened. "No, but thanks for asking. And I'm sorry if I offended you and Detective Larson the other night, but it dawned on me that I was becoming so dependent on you two that it was holding me back from regaining my own independence. If Harry were here—" Her voice broke for a moment. "If Harry were here, he'd set me straight. And if Jenny were depending on me, I'd be strong. So I decided to reclaim myself."

Kyle realized he'd effectively been told to back off. Well, she'd need him again. After he ended the call, he sat gazing out the window of his study, wondering how long it might be before that happened and how he could hasten it.

"Okay, Prince. Playtime is over. Time to get back in the house." Sarah tried to recall the command and gesture Hunter Gordon had used to call the dog back. It had seemed so easy when he did it. Fortunately, Prince responded to the tone, if not the words, of her call and trotted back to where Sarah stood holding open the back door of her house.

The dog entered, went immediately to his water bowl, and lapped for what seemed like forever. Then he looked, first at the empty food bowl then at Sarah, with an expression that said, more eloquently than words, "There's no food in here."

"You're going to have to get used to my schedule, boy," she said. Hunter said to feed him twice a day, but she was going to be gone during the time for his evening meal. Sarah had decided to give him some food when she left this afternoon and the rest when she came home tonight. Accordingly, she opened the large sack of dog food, scooped out the appropriate amount, and dumped it into his bowl. "There'll be more later, Prince. I promise."

She could swear that Prince frowned at his bowl for a moment, but soon he was crunching away. When he'd eaten, he looked up at her. Was he expecting more? Probably, but Hunter had warned her about overfeeding the dog.

"They're like children. They don't always know what's good for them, so you have to be a parent," he'd said.

"More when I get home," she repeated.

Prince stared at her for a moment, then trotted to a corner of the room and sat down facing her.

Now came a decision she'd thought about for a while. Should she put Prince into the backyard where he could run and play or leave him in the house? It was summer, and she figured he'd be more comfortable in the air-conditioned house. Besides, how was he going to guard against intruders if he was confined to the backyard? She hoped he could wait nine hours or so for her return. If not, she'd have some cleaning to do. But that was an acceptable trade-off. At least she didn't have to worry about someone breaking into her house. Prince was like an alarm system with teeth.

"I'll be back soon, boy," Sarah said. She picked up her backpack, moved to the door that led from the kitchen into the garage, and gave the command to guard.

The dog sauntered leisurely toward the door where she stood. Then he lay down facing it, seemingly ready to do exactly what she'd asked of him. At least, Sarah hoped so.

As Bill Larson climbed back into his car, he mentally checked the last name off his list. He'd interviewed every person Dr. Harry Gordon's nurse thought might hold a significant grudge against the doctor—significant enough to result in the actions he was investigating. The list now contained an even dozen names, and of those he'd been able to rule out eight through confirming they were elsewhere when one or more of the incidents took place. The remaining four had no alibis for the times of the fire at Sarah's or the gunshot that greeted her return home from work. That didn't surprise him, since both these episodes took place in the middle of the night. The individuals in question might all have been sound asleep in their beds, but if there was no one with them it was impossible to establish their whereabouts for those times.

Larson glanced at the car's clock. It was six p.m. on a Saturday. A line from a song jumped into his mind: *Saturday night is the loneliest night of the week.* Well, for him it was. He didn't want to go home—there was literally nothing there for him. No one was waiting for him to come through the door.

This had been a stressful week, and he didn't see an end in sight anytime soon. But the stress wasn't just from the case. The majority of it was personal. And Larson was tired of fighting it.

He should head for home, but he decided he didn't want to go there. Not now. What he really wanted was to find a dark bar, sit down at a booth toward the back where no one would pay any attention to him, and order a boilermaker—a shot of straight bourbon with a mug of beer to chase it. *And keep 'em coming.*

He could almost taste the liquor flowing across his tongue and down his throat, feel the warmth in his chest as the whiskey found its way into his stomach. He knew that not long after he'd drunk the first shot, he'd start to feel the effects of the alcohol. Oh, it was probably too soon for it actually to work, but Larson knew from long experience that once that first one went down, once he knew there was more on the way, things would look so much better.

Maybe he should eat. That was one of the rules alcoholics learned when they tried to stop drinking: don't get too hungry or too tired. But even thinking about food made him feel queasy. Larson knew of something he could do, though. He could seek out the company of someone who might understand. *If you're tempted to take a drink, call your sponsor.* Well, he didn't have a sponsor, but he knew someone he could call.

Of course, the person he had in mind was on his list of four people who were still suspects—at least, theoretically—in the Gordon case. But somehow, that didn't matter. Right now it was more important to Larson to deal with the urge he felt, one that had become almost undeniable. It wasn't just his need for a drink that was making his heart hammer in his chest. He had to talk with someone about the reason all this had finally overtaken him tonight.

He pulled his car into an almost-deserted strip mall. Larson parked in front of a huge plate glass window covered with "For Lease" signs listing the name and number of a realtor. He withdrew his cell phone from his pocket, scrolled through the names and numbers there, and pushed a button to make his call.

"Steve? Bill Larson. I hope I'm not disturbing you."

"Not at all. I was just putting the finishing touches on tomorrow's sermon. Then I was going to eat some of the casserole I have reheating in the oven. How can I help? Do you need to make an official visit?"

"No, this isn't official, but I'd appreciate it if I could come over." He hesitated. "This one is personal."

"Come on over," the pastor said. "We can talk while we eat. There's enough of the casserole for two. I'd appreciate the company."

"I'll see you in a few minutes." Larson put the car in gear and turned toward where the pastor lived, fighting the urge to turn on the flashing lights behind his grill because, so far as he was concerned, this was an emergency—a personal one.

15

"Slow Saturday evening so far," Sarah said to Connie as the two women passed each other in the ER of Centennial Hospital.

Connie swiped a stray lock of silver hair away from her face. "Just wait."

"I know," Sarah said. "About eleven they'll start rolling in: domestic disturbances, motor vehicle accidents, heart attacks."

Connie glanced at the clock on the far wall. "We'll be lucky to get away without staying over at least an hour. Tell you what. I'll stick around if it's necessary. You can leave on time."

"No need," Sarah said. "I don't have anyone waiting for me at home." Then, as Connie hurried away to check another patient, Sarah realized that statement was no longer true. She did have someone waiting at home for her. Prince was waiting.

Would the dog know if she was late getting home? Did dogs have a sense of time? Or did they simply move from situation to situation while trusting in their humans to provide food, shelter, and a nurturing environment? She guessed that, in that sense, they were like children. As that thought flashed through her mind, Sarah felt tears start to stream down her cheeks. She turned away, hastening to wipe them away before anyone saw. *I had a daughter. Now I have a dog.* There were implications there that Sarah needed to consider—but not now. Now she had work to do.

When she pulled aside the curtains of the next cubicle, she saw a young woman, perhaps in her early twenties, perched on the edge of a gurney. Although she was sitting quietly when Sarah peeked inside, as soon as the doctor entered, the patient squeezed her eyes shut, put both hands to her temples, and began a rhythmic rocking back and forth accompanied by moaning like the keening of a mourner at an Irish wake.

"My head! My head hurts so bad!" She raised her eyes to look pleadingly at Sarah. "Please give me something for it!"

Sarah looked at the clipboard she held. "Darla, I'm Doctor Gordon. When did this headache start? Describe it to me."

"My head! It hurts all over! Please, I need something to make it stop hurting."

Sarah watched the young woman, who continued to sway left and right as she repeated her litany. There was no pallor. She wasn't sweating. Although the overhead spotlight was shining directly in her eyes, the woman didn't look away from it—she had no photophobia. Her words of pain didn't match what Sarah was seeing.

"Have you had these headaches before? Do you have a doctor you've seen?"

"I'm from out of town. My doctor is in Oklahoma."

"What town? Give me your doctor's name. I'll call him."

"You can't," the woman said. "It's Saturday night. I doubt he's available. Please, just give me something to relieve the pain."

Before Sarah could speak, the patient continued. "But I can't take aspirin, or NSAIDs, or codeine. Oh, and I'm allergic to some of the narcotics. What they usually give me is Dilaudid. That works. It generally takes two milligrams IM to stop the pain."

The warning bells that had been sounding in the distance rang louder now in Sarah's mind. A patient coming to the emergency room with a story of pain that couldn't be documented by most tests wasn't uncommon—people did have migraines and other headaches, and sometimes they needed emergency treatment. But in this case there were things that made Sarah suspicious: things like complaints that weren't backed up by physical signs of distress and a physician who was unavailable to confirm the patient's story. The clincher was the woman's claim of allergy or intolerance to almost every common analgesic. Instead, she specified the narcotic and dosage she needed—or, at least, wanted.

Sarah had encountered this many times before, and she'd developed a way to handle situations like it. "I can't give you a narcotic right now. First I need to do some tests, probably starting with a lumbar puncture—what a layperson would call a spinal tap. After all the tests are completed, I'll call one of our specialists, a neurologist, who may admit you to the hospital for a workup and treatment."

The hands went away from the head, the swaying stopped, the moaning went silent. "But I need something right now for pain."

"After the tests, maybe I can order something like ketorolac, if it's needed."

"Oh, I can't take that, either." This came out in a normal tone of voice. All the patient's mannerisms that indicated severe pain seemed to have stopped.

Sarah said in an unemotional voice, "I'm going to get the nurse and a lumbar puncture tray. After I finish with that procedure, you'll need to lie flat for half an hour. Then we'll send you to X-ray for a CT scan of your head. Wait here."

She eased out of the cubicle and stood off to the side, certain of what would come next. Sure enough, in less than a minute the patient, showing no signs of pain or any other problem, eased out from between the curtains, looked around until she saw an "Exit" sign, and hurried toward it.

Like most emergency room doctors, Sarah had a constant fear of turning away a patient with a true need. She'd given narcotics to patients in pain before and would again. Maybe she'd been conned a few times, but her ability to discern between patients who were genuinely hurting and those looking for a "fix" was by now well developed. She was pretty certain she'd gotten it right this time as well.

"Thank you for seeing me like this," Bill Larson said when the door opened.

"No problem," the pastor said. "I'm ready for a break from sermon preparation, and that casserole smells awfully good. I hope you don't mind eating in the kitchen."

"Sometimes I eat standing beside the kitchen sink, wolfing down whatever I've microwaved and hardly tasting it," Larson said. "Sitting down, even at a kitchen table, is sort of like fine dining for me."

Farber opened the oven, donned two oven mitts, and removed a covered casserole dish. "If you'll put one of those pot holders on the table, I'll set this on it."

Larson complied. "No problem. What can I do to help?"

"Dishes are in the cupboard to your left, silverware in the drawer beneath it. Paper napkins are in a holder on the table."

While Larson set the table, Farber removed the lid from the dish and placed a serving spoon in it. "There are soft drinks in the fridge, or you can get ice and cold water from the dispenser in the door." The pastor stopped and looked directly at Larson. "I don't have any wine or beer in the house."

"I...I couldn't drink it anyway," the detective said. "I'm an—"

"I know what you are," Farber said. "You told me the last time we were together. And I'm an alcoholic as well. I presumed from what you said on the phone you were troubled. I suppose I was testing you to see whether you had fallen off the wagon or were teetering on the edge trying to hang on."

Larson filled two glasses with ice and water, then placed them beside the two places he'd set at the kitchen table. "The latter, I guess. I'm sure a lot of people have figured out that I'm an alcoholic. Even though there's an AA chapter here in Jameson, for whatever reason, I haven't attended those meetings. But at times like this I wish I had, because I sure could use a sponsor."

"I haven't gone to the meetings either," Farber said. "Despite the 'Anonymous' in the name, sometimes information slips out. I'd prefer to keep it as much a secret as possible that the pastor of Jameson's First Community Church is a man with a drinking problem. The elders know, and probably some of the congregation suspect, but I don't like to advertise it."

The two men sat down, and the pastor immediately bowed his head. Larson followed suit. After a brief blessing of the food, Farber said, "So you're having problems an alcoholic would understand. Is that about right?"

"I've been clean and sober for over ten months. It never gets easier, but a day at a time I move on. Then tonight... tonight it dawned on me that my wife and son have been gone from my life for almost a year. For some reason that hit me hard—harder than most things. And I wanted a drink as badly as I ever have in my life."

Farber helped himself to a large serving of the casserole, then passed the dish to Larson. Both men tasted their food and nodded approvingly.

"The casserole is good," Larson said.

"One of the women of my congregation brought it over earlier in the week. I think they feel like they can cook their way into heaven by feeding the pastor." He took another bite, chewed, and swallowed. "I'm certainly not going to give them an involved theological explanation of why they can't. But I will be preaching tomorrow on faith and works."

Larson smiled. "I may try to shake loose to come hear that sermon."

Farber's expression became solemn. "Do you want to talk about your divorce...about your family...about how your drinking affects them?"

"I recognize I'll always battle my addiction," Larson said. "I know it was the reason for my marriage breaking up. And I keep hoping that my staying clean and sober will convince my ex-wife to give it another try."

The pastor put down his fork and dabbed at his mouth with a paper napkin. "Bill, you're doing a good thing by staying sober. And maybe it will help heal your failed marriage. But it's possible your ex-wife won't come back. And if she doesn't, it won't be because of a failure on your part. And if she does, you'll still need to stay sober—not for her, but for yourself—to be all that God intended for you to be." He put down the napkin. "End of sermon."

"Thanks...Thanks, Steve. I guess I needed to hear that."

"Good," the pastor said. "Now how about we finish this casserole? And I think there may be half a peach pie in the fridge, from another one of the ladies of the congregation."

Larson smiled. "I haven't paid as much attention as I should, I guess. Are there any unmarried ladies in the church who are good cooks?"

There was a smile on Farber's face and a twinkle that his glasses didn't hide when he said, "One of them made the pie. We'll test it out."

The doctor was supposed to be working in the emergency room tonight, but it never hurt to be careful. When he drove by at eight in the evening there were two lights on in Dr. Gordon's house—lights in what he assumed to be the kitchen and the front room. At ten, those same two lights were on. He could see no movement behind the closed blinds in the front of the house. Time to see if she'd forgotten to arm the alarm system again. True, it was

probably too much to hope for, but he'd check anyway. Sometimes you get lucky.

He parked down the street and strolled casually toward her house. There was no sign of anyone else out and about. He walked up the sidewalk, but before he could step onto the porch he heard a new sound—the low growl of a dog. The growl quickly became a bark, and the barking came closer until he guessed the dog was just inside the front door. No need to test whether that door was locked or the alarm armed—he didn't want to confront the animal that was inside.

As he walked to the side of the home, the barking seemed to follow him. The animal was probably going from room to room, tracking him by the sounds he made or perhaps by his scent. A fence prevented his reaching the back of the house, but he'd seen enough.

The dog presented a new problem. Not one he couldn't solve. Just one he'd need to think about. He pressed the button to illuminate the dial of his watch. Ten fifteen in the evening. The doctor probably wouldn't be home for at least another hour, perhaps longer.

He thought about scaling the fence into the backyard, but that wouldn't help. He couldn't force his way into the house, and if he did, the dog was still a barrier to whatever he might want to do. He thought about what it would take for her to keep a dog. From the sounds he'd heard, the dog was large, so a pet door big enough for it to go out would allow a prowler in. No, she probably depended on letting the dog out into her yard after she came home. If that was the case, he knew just what to do.

He headed back to his car, careful not to run. A man walking in the neighborhood wouldn't attract attention, but one running might. He reached his car without incident, eased into the driver's seat, and pulled away from his parking place. He'd be back— with yet another surprise for Dr. Gordon.

The doctor scheduled to relieve Sarah arrived in the ER on time, and after they spent a few minutes reviewing what had gone before and the patients still waiting for lab work or X-rays, he told her to go home.

"I can stay for a bit and help if you'd like," she said.

"No need," he told her. "Go home and get some rest. I'll see you tomorrow night."

Sarah felt foolish asking the security guard at the ER front desk to walk her to her car, but as before, he assured her he had no problem with it. She unlocked her car, got in, waved to him, and started out for home. As she drove, she thought about the German shepherd waiting for her there. Was this a foolish idea? Would he provide a greater sense of safety, or simply require more effort on her part?

Then her thoughts drifted to the comparison she'd made in her mind earlier—the dog was like a child. It depended on her for things. But she depended on Prince, too. She depended on him to guard her and provide protection. *I guess we're good for each other.*

She disarmed the alarm system, opened the garage door, then reversed the process once she was inside the garage. When she opened the kitchen door, Prince was right where she'd left him—facing the door, looking at her as she entered. She could almost see the synapses connecting. *I was told to guard. This woman belongs here. I won't challenge her.*

"Good boy." What was the command to relax after guarding? Oh, yes. She gave it, thankful she'd been able to memorize the few German words with which Hunter had trained the dog.

In response to the command, Prince rose to his feet, trotted to the back door, and stood patiently. *Well, I guess you deserve some yard time.* Sarah opened the door, turned on the backyard light, and stood for a minute watching Prince tear about. She'd need to exercise him more. Maybe she'd hire a dog walker—but that would mean allowing someone else access to her home while she was away.

Sarah stepped away from the door. She was hungry but didn't know what she wanted. Finally, she picked up an apple from the bowl of fruit on her kitchen table and took a bite. She sat down, chewing thoughtfully, and let her mind wander. In a few moments, she found that she'd finished the apple. However, she hadn't come to a conclusion about how best to take care of Prince.

She rose and went to the door, opened it, and called, "Here, Prince. Time to come in." Instead of the scampering feet of her dog, she heard him barking, loudly and repeatedly. Before Sarah could venture outside to see what was going on, she heard what sounded like a loud pop. Prince gave one high-pitched yelp, followed by soft whining.

As Sarah hurried to the furthest reaches of her backyard where she'd last heard Prince's barks, she thought she heard the sound of running feet in the alley. Never mind that. What had happened to her dog? She scanned the dark area not reached by the light over her door, and finally she saw him. Prince was by the fence that separated her backyard from the alley. He lay on his side, panting. There was blood on his coat. The whining sound he made tore at her heart.

16

Kyle stood at the back of the First Community Church and scanned the congregation. People flowed around him to enter the sanctuary in small groups, filling it with the muted noise of conversations, while a melody from the organ provided a counterpoint. Then he saw her, sitting by herself in a pew about midway from the front of the church.

"I thought about checking to see if you'd like me to come by for you this morning. Unfortunately, I never got around to calling." Kyle slipped into the pew next to Sarah. "Glad you made it. Two Sunday worship services in a row. That's great."

She turned to look at him, and he frowned. Sarah's dark hair was neatly styled, her lipstick was perfectly applied, but there were dark circles under her eyes that her makeup couldn't fully conceal. Her brown eyes were bloodshot. Faint lines radiated from the corners of her mouth. Obviously, there was a problem here.

Kyle debated whether to mention what he noticed. Finally, he said, "You look tired. Want to tell me what's going on?"

"I told you about Prince," she said. "Right?"

"Yes, the dog you got from Harry's father. What about him?"

"I left him in the house when I went to work yesterday afternoon. I was going to feed him when I got home, which I figured would be around midnight. When I came in, I decided to let him out into the yard first. After all, he'd been in the house for ten hours or so. I'm not used to caring for dogs. I didn't know..."

"Take your time," Kyle said. "What happened when you let the dog out?"

"I let him run for a while, and then I heard him barking. That was followed by a noise, sort of a pop. Later I realized it was a gunshot. Anyway, I decided to check on him. I went into the backyard and found Prince lying next to the fence, bleeding."

"That's terrible. What did you do?"

"It looked like he'd been shot in the shoulder. The bleeding was already slowing down, but I couldn't tell the extent of his wound. Whatever it was, I knew he'd require more care than I could give. So I wrapped him in a towel and rushed him to an all-night veterinary clinic."

"Is the dog all right?" Kyle asked.

"The tech on duty called a veterinary surgeon who operated last night to remove the bullet and control the bleeding. They'll probably need to keep him for a few days, but he should recover."

"Did you—"

"As soon as I found out Prince was going to be okay, I called Bill Larson, and he met me at my house with a couple of uniformed officers. They didn't find any clues, but he said he'd be back to have another look in daylight."

Kyle shook his head. "That's tough. But I'm glad you made it here this morning." The choir entered and took their places in the loft. The organ played a bit louder, and the music made him lean closer to her to talk. "Would you like to have lunch after the service?"

Sarah shook her head. "Sorry," she whispered. "I have to meet Bill Larson. I told you he wants to do another search of my yard and the alley behind it. Then I have to go to work."

"If I didn't know better, I'd think you were avoiding me," Kyle said.

Before Sarah could reply, the prelude ended and Pastor Steve Farber approached the pulpit.
Am I pushing too hard? I don't want to do that. But if I don't keep trying, Sarah might slip away from me. Kyle managed to give the appearance of participation as the service progressed, but his mind was elsewhere. It was on Sarah.

Bill Larson didn't make it to worship services at Jameson's First Community Church every Sunday, although he tried his best. Crime, it seems, didn't pay attention to weekends and holidays. This morning he slipped in just before the sermon began and headed, as was his custom, for an aisle seat in a back pew. As he eased in, Bill wondered if he chose this location so he'd be able to leave unobtrusively if he was called away on police business, or if it represented the place he figured he rightfully should occupy—on the fringe of the congregation. Was he still paying, even subconsciously, for the years when he let alcohol control his life?

He'd really fouled things up, Larson thought. His family was in another state. Larson constantly feared he'd receive news that his wife had remarried. He battled alcohol every day. If he didn't, he'd undoubtedly lose his job, and that was the only thing that gave him purpose now—well that and staying sober, hoping it would influence Annie to give their marriage another chance.

Larson made a mental note to call Annie tonight. It had been over a week since he'd talked with her. He wanted her to know he was staying sober. He wanted to talk with his son. Recently, he'd been daydreaming about starting over with someone who was the perfect woman. Then he began to realize that he'd been married to a woman who loved him all along, but his drinking had driven her away. Maybe he could salvage that. If he could, he wanted to make things right, repair that relationship.

As he sat, lost in thought, words from the pulpit penetrated his consciousness and caused him to look up and pay attention. Steve had said he was going to preach on faith and works, but Larson had no idea the message would have such a personal application.

Dr. Steve Farber glanced down at his notes. He didn't read his sermons to the congregation. He simply used the notes he'd prepared to help him keep from skipping important points. This was one of those points.

He looked out at his congregation, and his eyes fastened on Bill Larson. Yes, this would apply to him, as well as to many others in those pews. But when the pastor wrote the words, he'd intended them for himself as much as for any specific member of the congregation. It was a struggle that he and probably many others fought on a regular basis.

"Last night, I said to a friend that some people seem to be trying to work their way into heaven through their actions. I was kidding, but that's not really a joke. There are those among us who keep trying to pile up points with God by their good works. And if they've done something they consider to be terrible, they feel the need to work even harder in order to make up for past sins—to balance things out, so to speak. They say, 'Oh, if I give to the church...' or 'If I do enough good things...' or 'If I can refrain from...' You can fill in the blanks. But, hard as it may be to believe, our salvation isn't something we can earn. It's a gift. And our own good works won't save us...in this world or the next."

Farber looked out at the congregation and saw Bill Larson nodding in agreement. His expression said, "I get it." The pastor hoped he did.

"Now, don't get me wrong," the pastor continued. "Good works are...well, they're good. But they're the offshoot of faith, not vice-versa."

He looked down, flipped a few pages in the Bible that lay open on the pulpit, and said, "Let's look at some Scripture passages and see what they say about that concept. We can start in the third chapter of the book of Romans."

Bill Larson didn't open his Bible—he hadn't brought one. His was lying on the coffee table in the living room of his apartment and was probably covered with a layer of dust. But he followed the words as Steve Farber read them. And it seemed that what the pastor said was aimed directly at him.

It was true. What he'd really figured was that if he could stay clean and sober long enough, God would reward his actions by causing Annie to change her mind and give their marriage another chance. And was his very presence in church today because he felt a hunger for spiritual food, or was it simply an attempt to pile up bonus points with the Creator? Did God really take attendance?

Larson realized he wanted something, but this was different from the desires he had that separated him from the things he loved most in life. Despite the stress he'd been under trying to solve Dr. Sarah Gordon's case, today he wasn't looking for the solace he'd once found in liquor. The shame and hurt of a failed marriage wasn't pushing him toward the relief he'd previously sought in booze. No, right now Bill Larson was interested in the gift his friend and pastor was talking about. It was time for him to put things right with God.

Sarah Gordon relaxed a bit as the final "amen" signaled the end of the church service. Although she'd made it through the past hour, she'd done so despite one particularly difficult flashback to the funeral for Harry and Jenny.

When she had walked out of the church after the funeral, Sarah didn't plan to return—ever. How could she worship a God who'd let something like this happen? A few weeks later, she tried a couple of times, but she found she couldn't stay until the end of the service. Now she'd managed to sit through services for two consecutive Sundays. Maybe this was progress of a sort.

In another indication of progress, Sarah had started reaching out to God. Although it gave her a degree of peace to do so, she'd heard no disembodied voice replying to her prayers. No moving finger wrote directions on the wall for her. And each night when she lay in the dark house in an empty bed, she still felt alone. She was better. But she wasn't well.

As she neared the back of the sanctuary, she saw the pastor standing there, shaking hands with the people exiting. Sarah started to edge into a pew and head for a side door, but two ladies talking blocked her way, and she didn't want to push her way past them like a halfback through a defensive line. She squared her shoulders and followed the crowd down the main aisle toward where the pastor stood. When she reached him, she shook his hand and said, "Nice sermon."

"Sarah, I know how tough it must be for you to be back here. I won't give you any platitudes about things getting better day by day, because I know from my own experience that sometimes it takes many months, sometimes years before you get past an experience like this." He leaned in and spoke into her ear. "If you want to talk, give me a call."

Then he'd turned his attention to the people next in line, and Sarah walked out of the church. As the bright sunshine caused her to blink, she replayed his words. He talked about "his own experience." She didn't recall much about the death of the pastor's wife, although she had a feeling she should. She'd have to check into that. Then she remembered that her pastor's name was on the list of suspects. Surely, Steve Farber wasn't the one who—

"Do you remember that I need to come over for another look at your backyard?" Sarah recognized Bill Larson's quiet voice behind her.

Something about Larson's visits had suggested there was more behind them than just a detective doing his job. Sarah didn't want to lead the man on, but she recognized he did indeed need to see the yard in daylight. Maybe she could handle this in such a way as to make the visit purely professional. "Sure. You can come over right now if you wish."

"I'll stop by somewhere for a sandwich first. Shouldn't take long."

Sarah decided there was no reason fighting it. "I was going to fix a sandwich for myself. I guess I could make one for you, as well."

"Don't go to any trouble," Larson said. "But if we could talk a bit about the case while we eat, maybe this won't take too long."

Sarah figured this was probably the best way to handle the situation. Besides, it would be nice not to eat alone. "Sure." She started to say she'd leave the front door unlocked for him but thought better of it. "Just knock when you get there." She grimaced. "The doorbell is still broken."

Larson finished the iced tea in his glass. It had been a long time since he'd enjoyed a meal this much, even a simple one like a ham and cheese sandwich, chips, and iced tea. The more he thought about it, the more he realized it wasn't just the food—though it tasted fine—but the fact he had company for the meal.

Their conversation was casual and unforced. He asked her how her dog was doing, and she asked if he had any new suspects. Beyond that, their talk was about people they'd both come in contact with, a bit of gossip concerning a local character's latest antics, the status of some of the region's sports teams. In other words, it was normal Sunday lunch conversation—the same kind he and Annie used to have...that is, when he was sober enough to sit down for a family lunch. Unfortunately, those days had become rare toward the end of their marriage.

The barking of a dog in the distance made Larson stop talking and look around.

"That's the dog from down the street," Sarah said. "Ordinarily he's pretty quiet. I don't know what got him barking."

Larson decided it was time to get to work. Although he'd like to continue the pretense of a normal Sunday lunch, this was supposed to be a follow-up on the attack on Sarah's dog. With a sigh of genuine regret, he folded his napkin beside the plate and pushed back from the table.

"Is something wrong?" she said.

"I almost forgot the real reason I'm here. It's time for me to go to work. I need to have another look in your backyard," he said. "I may see something in the daylight that I missed last night. Is this door in the kitchen the only way to get into the yard?"

"From the house, yes. There's also a gate in the fence along the side of the yard, but it's secured with a padlock. And I know what you're thinking—if there were a way into the yard, he could have used a tranquilizer dart or something on poor Prince."

"But since there wasn't, he had to shoot him. Unless shooting him was what he had in mind all along."

"You mean—"

Larson nodded. "Maybe this was another action aimed at torturing you. He didn't want to kill you yet, but he decided that shooting your dog would serve two purposes. It would hurt you and get rid of your guard dog...at least for a while."

"How did he do it? He'd have to be awfully tall to see over the fence, much less shoot the dog from there."

Fifteen minutes later, Sarah stood in the alley and watched as Larson demonstrated how the prowler gained access. "Right here," he said. "See it?"

Sarah moved a step closer to the fence and looked where Larson pointed. Like most such fences, this one was made of panels put together into sections. The boards forming the panels were supported by three sets of stringers or rails constructed from two by fours. These ran parallel to each other at heights of about one foot, three feet, and five feet from the ground. Though they were sometimes on the inside of the fence, in this case the stringers faced the alley. On the bottom and middle rails of one section were two areas where the wood was scuffed and splintered.

Larson turned to Sarah and explained. "Assuming he was of average height, he'd simply need to climb up on the first and second sets of two by fours, lean over the top of the fence, and fire. I'm betting the vet that cared for your dog's gunshot wound will tell me the bullet entered from above. I need to get that slug, by the way, for analysis."

"Can you compare it with the one you dug out of my door frame? You know, ballistics testing?"

"The one from the house was pretty beat up. We may be able to see if the caliber is the same, but that's about it."

"What about fingerprints? He must have grabbed the top of the fence with one hand."

Larson shook his head. "I'll get a technician to check, but there's not a lot of chance we'll get anything usable from wood." He stepped back from the fence. "But now we know how he did it."

Sarah closed her eyes tightly, but although that shut out the scene of the detective standing by the fence, it just made another video run behind her eyelids. In it, she was putting the dog into her car at her father-in-law's house, saying, "I'll take care of you, Prince." Well, she hadn't.

Her daughter had died. Common sense told her she couldn't have prevented it, couldn't have saved Jennifer, but still…Now her dog had been shot, the dog she said she'd care for. Sarah felt the confidence that had been building over the past few days start to fade once more.

As though he could read her thoughts, Larson said, "It's not your fault. And I promise you that, although it may take a while, I'm going to catch this person who's caused you so much pain."

Sarah appreciated Larson's obvious intent to assure her, but what caught her attention was the phrase, "It may take a while." Sure. What if during that time her stalker decided he was ready for the final act in this little drama? What if, instead of making her suffer more, he ended her life?

Larson stopped talking when Sarah's phone rang. He nodded his permission, and she pulled the instrument from her pocket and answered.

Her side of the conversation was mainly short answers: "Today?" and "Can't it wait?" and finally "Okay. See you in half an hour."

He looked at her and asked, "Something important?"

"That was the contractor who did the work after the fire in my garage. He finished everything except replacing the carpet in the hall. He had to order that, so I've been walking on bare flooring in a couple of places for…has it just been a week? Anyway, the carpet came in yesterday afternoon, too late for him to call and install it. He's slammed for the next several days, so he asked if he could send over a couple of his crew to put it down now, even though it's Sunday."

"Well, I think I'm about through, so I'll get out of your way. But I have one more question first."

"Yes?"

"After the accident that…after Harry's accident, what happened to his computer?"

Sarah looked puzzled. "When I finally got around to cleaning up his stuff, I put his laptop in the closet. I guess that one of these days..."

"I'm glad you have it. Because the auto crash was obviously an accident, the police didn't investigate Harry. But now—"

"Now you wonder if there's a clue there about who might be behind these attacks," Sarah said. "You think it could be someone with a grudge against Harry, and now they're directing that anger at me?"

"Right. So, could I see his computer?"

Half an hour later, Larson came down the stairs with Harry's laptop under his arm. In the hall, he passed two workmen laying carpet. They hardly looked up as he edged around them. He found Sarah in the kitchen, removing dishes from the dishwasher and putting them away in the cabinet.

"Find anything?" she asked.

"Battery's dead. I'd like to take this with me and charge it, then see what's on it." He lowered his voice. "Those two men working in the hall..."

"The older white guy is Darrell, the younger black man is Carl. They work for Tom Oliver. What about them?"

"They've worked here since right after the fire?"

Sarah nodded. "Yes. Why do you ask?"

"I can't say more until I check my facts. Meanwhile, just be sure you keep an eye on those two."

17

After the church service, Kyle sat in his car in the almost-deserted church parking lot and brooded. He'd hoped to have lunch today with Sarah, but that had fallen through. He was sorry about that for two reasons: he wanted some time with her, and he hated to eat alone.

During the week he often had a sandwich at his desk, and on more than one occasion he'd finished the food his secretary brought him and couldn't recall what he'd just eaten. There had been a time when Sunday lunch involved relaxation, enjoying both the food and conversation. That's what he wanted today.

He still remembered his Sundays with Nicole. He'd pick her up for church, and afterward they'd either choose a restaurant or go to her apartment, where she'd prepare a light lunch for the two of them. Sometimes there would be a baseball or football game on the TV, the sound muted, with her paying more attention to the score than he did. Mostly, they'd talk. They had it all planned out. After their marriage, they'd move to a house somewhere outside Jameson, where she could raise their children while he continued to earn a comfortable living with his law practice.

But, of course, all that changed when she was killed while on a church mission trip. A beam—a silly piece of wood— had fallen from the top of a chapel the group was constructing in Guatemala. It should have missed her. It might have hit her shoulder or broken her collarbone. But it struck her head, struck it squarely, and according to the doctor who was on the trip she was probably dead when she hit the floor.

Kyle thought about what Steve Farber told him, about how the pastor reacted after the death of his own wife. Kyle hadn't done that. He'd bottled up his emotions after Nicole's death, because he'd heard that was what Christians did. They didn't rail at God. They didn't ask, "Why?" or "How?" He couldn't recall ever being told that in so many words, but someone must have said it to him at one time or another.

Kyle had even gotten frustrated with Sarah because she was letting the deaths of her husband and daughter get to her so badly. She'd pushed God aside, blamed Him for her loss. And Kyle kept trying to correct that.

Then Steve—a pastor, a man of God—had as much as told him that it was okay to shake your fist at God, to be angry, to ask "Why did You let this happen?" He'd assured Kyle that God didn't cause bad things to happen, but after they did, God would provide the help needed to get through them. That was still hard for Kyle to believe. But maybe it was true.

He almost missed seeing the pastor exiting the church and walking toward his car. It appeared that Steve's path would take him right by where Kyle was parked. The attorney lowered his car window, stuck out his head, and called, "Hey, Steve. Do you have plans for lunch?"

Sarah wished she had time to go to the veterinary clinic and check on Prince, but her visit with Larson had taken longer than she anticipated. Then the workers had come to lay the replacement carpet. No, she had to get ready for work, so the visit with Prince would have to wait. Instead, she phoned the vet's office. The tech working this weekend shift told her that the veterinary surgeon, the one who had done the emergency procedure about twelve hours ago, had just checked the dog and said he was recovering satisfactorily.

"Did he say how long Prince would need to stay there?" Sarah asked. She knew about gunshot wounds and emergency surgery for humans, but this was unfamiliar territory to her.

"He didn't say, but usually it depends on how much care the owners can give the pets when they take them home."

Sarah wanted to speak to the doctor. For that matter, she wanted to see Prince. Then again, would he be glad to see her, to hear her voice? Or would he associate her with what had happened to him? After all, he had no idea she was the one who wrapped him in a towel, tried to staunch the bleeding from his wound, rushed him to the twenty-four-hour veterinary facility.

From her surgical experience, she figured Prince would be ready for discharge in two or three days, providing his blood loss hadn't been severe and he continued to heal well. But what about his care afterward? Would she be able to take care of him? She'd have to leave him alone in the house for ten hours or so while she worked. And, in so many ways, she wasn't certain she could give Prince what he needed.

The obvious answer was to see if Hunter Gordon would take Prince back. She hated to break the news to her father-in-law over the phone. Maybe she could do it tomorrow morning. She'd go by the vet clinic and see if she could talk with the doctor. Then she'd drive out to Hunter's. At this point, she wasn't ready to forgive herself for what had happened to Prince. And she wasn't sure if the dog would be forgiving, either.

The room the detectives on the Jameson police force called home was deserted this Sunday mid-afternoon. All three of the desks that occupied the center of the office were vacant when Larson entered. He glanced at the third desk in the room, the one assigned to George Markham. It reminded him that he really needed to check on the detective. His absence on medical leave had left the remaining two detectives stretched a bit thin. Would Markham think Larson was calling because he was anxious for his colleague to return to work? He'd have to be careful not to give that impression.

Larson had his phone in his hand, ready to dial, when it dawned on him. There was something different about Markham's desk. While the detective was out after his surgery, the work surface still contained all the material found on most desktops—memo pads, a cup containing pens and pencils, a phone, a computer. Now all those were gone. The desk was bare. Larson put down the phone, went over and opened each of the drawers. Empty.

As he stood there, pondering this change, Cal Johnson entered the room. Larson hoped Cal had been to church with his wife this morning. If he and Ruth were going to keep their marriage together, Cal's resumption of church attendance would provide a good start.

"Cal, what do you make of the way George Markham's desk has been cleaned off?" Larson asked.

"I guess you didn't hear," Johnson said as he went to his own desk and began thumbing through the pink phone message slips there.

"Hear what? Did the brass and he decide to put him on extended medical leave?"

Johnson shook his head, but didn't look up. "George Markham passed away yesterday."

Larson was surprised by the news. "I'm sorry to hear that," he said. "The cancer really moved fast."

Johnson put down the slips and walked over to stand beside Larson. He put his arm on the shoulder of his fellow detective. "It wasn't the cancer. I guess George couldn't stand the pain and didn't want to die slowly. He took the cop's way out."

"You mean..."

"Yep. He sent his wife on an errand, went into the bathroom, put his service pistol in his mouth, and pulled the trigger."

An involuntary shiver ran down Larson's spine. He knew this was the way some cops chose to end their own lives. The phrase was "eating their guns." Once, when he'd had too much to drink and was deeply depressed, he'd even put his own pistol in his mouth. He remembered the sensation—the cold feel of the barrel in his mouth, the sharp taste of metal mixed with gun oil. On that occasion, thankfully, he'd quickly withdrawn the gun and put it down. That was when Larson made a vow to himself that he'd never take his own life—no matter how bad things seemed. He wasn't certain if it was because it would be an act of surrender or if he had some idea of what it would do to those left behind after such an act. But whatever the reason, he'd never been so desperate as to consider it again.

Larson wondered how much pain Markham had endured to bring him to taking his life that way. He turned away from Cal. "Thanks for telling me," he said. *That could have been me. In my case, it was alcohol, not cancer. But the outcome would have been the same.*

Cal said. "See you in the morning." And he left.

When he was sure the other detective had gone, Larson closed his eyes and prayed—for George Markham and his family...and for himself.

When Sarah finished explaining to her father-in-law how Prince had come to be shot, Hunter Gordon asked only one question: "Are you okay?"

"I'm fine," she said. She saw the security guard walking toward her as she sat in her car in the emergency room parking lot of Centennial Hospital. Without taking her cell phone from her ear, shook her head and gave him an "okay" sign. He turned to walk back into the building.

"Prince is recovering, and he should be ready for discharge in a couple of days. But I'm wondering if I—"

"I know what you're going to say," Hunter said. "You wonder if you'll be able to care for him while he heals, since you have work and... and this other stuff on your plate. Let me stop you right there. Bring Prince back here after he's discharged. I'll take care of him. When he's ready to go back to full activity, you and I can talk about whether you want to give it another try."

"That's great, Hunter. Thanks so much," she said. "And you don't think—"

"I know what you're going to ask. And I don't think you failed in any way," he said. "I think having a guard dog was a good idea. We had no idea Prince would be in any danger. But if this person would shoot a dog, I'm afraid he'll go for you next."

"I'm not going to let him scare me anymore," Sarah said. "I have a pistol and know how to use it." Without conscious thought, she opened the glove compartment and removed the revolver. It felt comforting, sitting on the seat beside her, as she continued to talk with Hunter.

Sarah wondered if she should tell her father-in-law about her plan to use the pistol to try to capture the person who'd been behind the attacks. No, because if she did, Hunter would be knocking on her door, armed with a rifle or shotgun. And she didn't want that much help with this. *Better keep that to myself for now.*

When the conversation ended, she looked at her watch. Time to get to work. She scooped her phone and some other things into her backpack, climbed out of her car, and headed for the door to the hospital. The security guard saw her through the plate glass of the entrance. He stepped outside, put one hand on the butt of his holstered weapon, and watched her approach.

"Thought you might want me to walk you in today," he said as she reached the entrance.

"No, but thanks."

"Well, find me when your shift is over, and I'll escort you to your car," he said.

I may pass on that, but we'll see. Depends on how tired I am and how brave I feel, I guess.

Alone once more in the detectives' room at police headquarters, Bill Larson lifted the lid of Dr. Harry Gordon's laptop and pressed the power button. Nothing happened. He tried again with the same results. He wasn't surprised that the battery was dead. The computer had been sitting unused for many months, and for all Larson knew, the battery was almost depleted when Harry Gordon was killed.

Fortunately, the laptop was the same brand as Cal's. Larson rummaged in the other detective's desk until he found a power cord, which he hooked up to Harry's computer. He'd give it a few minutes and try again.

Meanwhile, Larson began to hunt through mug shots, looking for pictures of the two men he'd seen laying carpet at Sarah's. He couldn't be sure, couldn't put his finger on the details, but his cop sense told him the men were criminals. Maybe he'd seen their picture, maybe he'd seen the men in person, or perhaps it was just a hunch. But it was a hunch he wanted to follow up.

Almost an hour later he found a picture and record for one of them. The younger of the two men, Carl Washington, had been arrested about eight months ago for car theft. After some legal wrangling, which Larson remembered, Washington was charged with and found guilty of theft.

Apparently his lawyer's plea for leniency had some effect on the judge, though, because he gave Washington the minimum sentence for the felony. He served six months, and after his release from jail he had stayed out of trouble with the law—so far. Larson decided that although Washington was a convicted felon, he probably didn't present much danger to Sarah.

Larson searched available mug shots in vain for pictures of the older man, but found nothing for Darrell Kline. Had he perhaps seen that face some years ago when he was a detective in Minnesota? No, apparently not. Finally, Larson did what most people do nowadays when they want a question answered. He did a Google search. And there he struck pay dirt with older stories from the local Jameson paper as well as the larger *Dallas News*.

Darrell Kline had been arrested while attempting to hold up a local bank. After a rather speedy trial, he was convicted of aggravated robbery. The man served six years in prison before he was released. As Larson put it together, he discovered Kline left prison about the time of Dr. Harry Gordon's death.

Larson dug a little deeper until he found more details about Kline's crime and the trial that followed. One of the articles after the sentence was handed down quoted the jury foreman as saying, "It probably took us less than an hour of deliberation to find him guilty." That foreman was a surgeon just setting up his practice in Jameson. His name? Harry Gordon.

18

The emergency room was filling up, but this wasn't unusual for the day and time. Sarah had heard another ER doctor call Sunday afternoon, "Old Dad's day." It was his theory that children visiting their parents at this time would sometimes find that their father or mother had not been feeling well. Whether the problem was chronic or acute, guilt would overcome a few of them to the point they would bring the aging parent to the emergency room, hoping to assuage their feelings by seeking medical attention for the parent before the day ended.

Just as Sarah was about to enter the combination break room–locker room to stow her backpack, Connie emerged. "Typical Sunday afternoon?" Sarah asked.

"Looks like it. I just came on duty. When I checked in with the triage nurse at the front desk, she warned me about the man who's in cubicle three with his father."

"What's up?"

"He visited his father for what was probably the first time in a couple of months and found him on the sofa in the living room. Looked like he'd had a stroke a day or two earlier that left him unable to care for himself, and since he lived alone, he'd been lying there for quite a while and was in pretty bad shape. Rather than calling 9-1-1, the son loaded his dad into his own car and rushed him here."

"I might have done the same thing in the stress of the moment," Sarah said. "I presume the doctor is looking at the father now."

"He would, but the paramedics brought in a patient in cardiac arrest at about the same time. Dr. Crenshaw is dealing with the man who coded, so no doctor has seen the stroke patient yet."

"I'll look at him," Sarah said. "I'll just stow—"

"I want a doctor in here, and I want one now!" The voice came from the area of cubicle three. Sarah looked and saw that the son had pulled aside the curtains and now stood in the open space in front of the gurney where his father lay. He brandished a large, boxy-looking black pistol. "If I don't see a doctor or nurse heading this way in ten seconds, I'm going to start shooting."

Sarah held up her hand and waved. "I'm coming," she said, her voice a bit louder than usual. "No need to shoot anyone. Just give me a second." She held up the backpack, signaling that she wanted to put it away before heading toward him. As she did, she thought it was a bit heavier than usual. Then she realized what had happened. Her pistol had been lying on the seat of her car. When she scooped up the things there and shoved them into the backpack, the gun came with them.

The man with the weapon was looking away now, scanning the ER for anyone moving toward him. Sarah's first instinct was to pull out the gun and fire a shot into his shoulder. She'd been pretty good on the firing range, but was she that good? If she missed, she might hit a bystander. And if the man shot back, he might wound or even kill her or one of the other people in the ER. She actually had the gun out of the backpack, ready to fire, but at the last minute she jammed it back inside and quickly closed the zipper.

Maybe she could calm him down without adding another gun to the mix, without putting anyone in danger. Her decision made, she handed her backpack to Connie. "Put this in your locker for now," she said. Then she began walking slowly toward cubicle three, hands held wide with the palms facing him. "I'm coming," she said in a firm voice. "Put that pistol away. I'm going to need your cooperation and maybe your help. Let's do something for your father."

Two hours later, Sarah and Connie sat in the break room sipping cups of hot tea. "You handled that well. I would have been scared to death," Connie said.

"I was," Sarah said. "But everything worked out okay."

"I like the way you were able to talk the distraught son into putting away his gun. He looked to have enough firepower to clean out the whole ER."

"While I was checking over his dad, I got him talking. The man bragged that his gun was a seventeen-shot Glock, whatever that is. I got the impression this wasn't the first time he'd used it to get his way, either. Anyway, I kept him engaged as I started an IV and got some oxygen going on his father. Then an armed security guard and a policeman, responding to a call from the triage desk, were able to subdue the son and lead him away in handcuffs."

"What about his dad?" Connie asked.

"There's no doubt he's had a recent stroke. We contacted his family doctor, who in turn called in a neurologist. After the man's discharged, he'll probably need to go to a rehab center."

Connie looked around to make sure they were alone. "You know, that backpack of yours seemed a little heavier than usual, and it made sort of a 'clunk' when I put it into my locker. If I had to guess, I'd swear there was a gun in there. Matter of fact, I thought for a second I saw you take one out."

Sarah nodded. "I did. I don't have my concealed-carry permit yet, so I usually lock it in the glove compartment when I leave my car. Today, I inadvertently scooped it up into my backpack with some other things."

"So why did you decide not to use it?"

Sarah had considered that question a dozen times since she approached the man with the gun. "If I pulled out my revolver, I might have shot the man who had the pistol. But if I showed a gun, he could have shot first, and there was no telling who might have been wounded or killed. I didn't think it was the best move, so I decided to try to handle the situation without force."

"And it worked out fine," Connie said. "Does this mean you're going to give up having a pistol with you in case your stalker or whatever you want to call him keeps showing up?"

Sarah put down her cup. "I really don't know." She rose and started for the door. "I'll handle that decision when the time comes. Right now, I guess I'd better get back to seeing patients. I have a job to do."

Before he left his desk, Larson thought about how best to approach Darrell Kline. After a moment's consideration, he decided he probably should start with Kline's boss. The workman was at Sarah Gordon's laying carpet this afternoon, but it was likely he had at least one or two other jobs for today. On the other hand, Tom Oliver was probably at home on a Sunday afternoon.

Larson decided to call first. He found Oliver's Yellow Pages ad under the heading Restoration Services. There was a twenty-four-hour number listed. Larson also found the same number and name, Oliver Construction, under Security Systems and General Repairs. He wasn't surprised. Tom Oliver probably was willing to take on multiple types of jobs, so long as he could get paid. In a mid-sized town like Jameson, Texas, that was what it took to make a living.

He dialed the number and after five rings a man's voice answered. "Tom Oliver."

"Mr. Oliver, this is Detective Bill Larson. You did some restoration work for Dr. Sarah Gordon." Larson didn't make it a question, and Oliver didn't respond. "I need to ask you some questions about your crew."

"Has there been a problem? I told Dr. Gordon to let me know if I need to redo something. Why would the police be involved?"

"This has nothing to do with your performance of the work. It's just that a name has come up in the course of one of my investigations, and I need to ask you about the man."

There was a slight pause. "I'll do what I can to help, but I don't see how—"

"Just a couple of questions, Mr. Oliver," Larson said. "Would you like me to come by your house?"

"No, no," Oliver said. "Can't this be done by phone?"

"Sure," Larson said. "To begin with, how did you come to hire Darrell Kline?"

"Are you going to harass him because he's an ex-con?" Oliver asked. "Look, just because a man's made a mistake, once he's paid his debt to society I think he deserves a second chance. Unfortunately, not everybody feels that way, but I believe it's possible for a man to change. I knew Darrell just got out of prison when I hired him. But he seemed to have turned his life around, and I had no problem putting him to work."

"Mr. Oliver, I don't imagine Darrell answered an ad in the paper. What I'd like to know is if someone contacted you on his behalf."

There was a moment's hesitation before Oliver answered. "I got a call from a friend who explained Darrell's situation and said he needed a job. I told him to send him over. I liked what I saw of Kline, so I hired him."

"And what friend was this who called you?"

"It was the man who defended Darrell Kline at his original trial, the same lawyer who helped my son when he got into trouble. Kyle Andrews."

After lunch with his pastor, Kyle debated going home for a Sunday afternoon nap. Then again, he really wasn't sleepy. Maybe he should catch up on the work that seemed to pile up on his desk faster than he could dispose of it. At home, he searched through his briefcase only to find that the material he needed was at his office. So that's where he went.

After Kyle had been working for a couple of hours, the words began to run together. *That's enough. I need to give it up and head home.* The lawyer figured the balance of his day would involve eating pizza in front of the TV set until sleep claimed him. But the ring of his phone changed those plans.

The call wasn't to his private line into the office, so he knew it wasn't from one of his two law partners or the practice's secretary, the only people who had that number. It was to his cell. That number was known to lots of people, many of them clients, and the caller ID didn't help, since it showed "blocked number." That could mean it was from a telephone solicitor, but it might also mean a collect call from the local jail or from someone he represented who preferred not to have their number displayed. As an attorney who often did criminal defense, Kyle expected calls like that.

"Kyle Andrews," he said.

"Mr. Andrews, this is Detective Bill Larson. Do you have a moment to talk?"

There was nothing in the detective's words or even his tone of voice to betray what was behind the call. Had the detective perhaps come up with a clue to the person behind the attacks on Sarah? And, if so, why would he be calling Kyle? There was one way to find out. "Certainly. How can I help?"

"I have some questions for you, and I wonder if it would be convenient for me to talk with you."

When he worked at his office and no one was around, one of the first things Kyle did was slip off his shoes. He did that primarily so that he could put his stocking feet on the desk without his secretary fussing at him the next day for scarring the mahogany surface. Even though the detective couldn't see him, the lawyer shoved his feet back into his shoes and sat up straight at his desk. Then he said, "Sure. Fire away."

"I'd rather not do this over the phone," Larson said. "Would you like me to come to your home? Or perhaps it would be better for you to come down to the police station."

The average citizen might have been scared by the last sentence that Larson seemed to have tossed in carelessly, but Kyle had been a practicing attorney for too long to be frightened of either police or their place of business. On the other hand, if Larson came to Kyle's office, the attorney might have what he thought of as a home field advantage. "I'm in my office, and that will do fine. Just knock on the door when you get here, and I'll let you in."

Kyle sat up, letting his feet hit the floor with a thump. As he tied the laces of the wing-tips he'd worn to church that morning, he wondered what Larson wanted. He retrieved his coat from the hanger on the back of his office door and straightened his tie. He made sure the door from his private office to the waiting room was wide open, then reseated himself at his desk to wait for the detective. What did he want? No telling. But whatever it was, Kyle was certain that years of experience in a courtroom had prepared him to handle anything Larson might throw at him.

Bill Larson read the words inscribed in black paint on the glass-paneled door: "Andrews, Gilmore, and Stark, LLC. Attorneys at Law." He tried the knob and found the door locked. He rattled it a couple of times, then raised his hand to knock, but before he could tap on the door, it opened.

"Come in," Kyle Andrews said. "Forgive me for not leaving the door unlocked, but I think you can see why that wouldn't be a good idea for a criminal attorney alone in his office on a weekend."

"Quite all right," Larson said. "Thanks for seeing me."

Andrews closed the door and locked it behind Larson. Then he led him into an inner office and pointed to a sofa in one corner of the room. "Why don't we sit there? It's a lot more comfortable than the client chairs."

Larson eased down onto the leather upholstery. He wondered how many times the attorney had stretched out for a nap on this comfortable bit of furniture. It was probably a good thing that no such convenience was available at the police station. If the detective wanted to snatch a couple of hours' sleep while putting in late hours on a case, he had to use a small cot in a back room, one that seemed to have been designed by the same people who devised the rack and other similar devices of torture. If something like this were available to him, Larson figured he might spend all his time napping on it.

Andrews crossed his right leg over his left. He straightened the cuff of his trouser leg, but not before the detective saw the small revolver in an ankle holster. Might as well get that out of the way. "I presume you have a carry permit for that revolver," Larson said.

"I do," Andrews said. "I can show it to you if you'd like. As a practicing attorney, I've made a few people angry, and some of them are the kind who like to put actions to their feelings."

"I'll take your word for it," Larson said. "Anyway, that's not the reason I'm here. I'm working to find out who's behind the harassment of Sarah Gordon. Right now I'm looking into the past history of her husband, Harry, and I find that he was foreman of a jury that convicted a man who's now—"

"Let me interrupt you, because I see where you're going," the lawyer said. "You discovered that when Darrell Kline was released from prison I recommended that Tom Oliver hire him. Right?"

"Right. Now I haven't connected the dots completely, but would you care to explain how it was on your recommendation that a convicted felon with every reason to hold a grudge against her husband is now working in Dr. Gordon's home?"

"Sure. I don't know if you noticed the name of the lawyer who represented Darrell during his trial."

"Not really. I was looking for a connection to Harry Gordon."

"Well, the attorney originally representing Darrell Kline had a massive coronary on the first day of the trial. It was my turn to do some *pro bono* representation, so the judge named me to step in. I asked for some time to prepare, but Darrell wouldn't let me ask for a continuance. He said he'd made the decision to pay for his crime and get on with his life. I talked to him about changing his plea to guilty, but for some reason, he wanted the whole thing to play out. He had some idea of getting it all out in the open, I guess. The trial went quickly, the verdict was a foregone conclusion, but what I managed to get for Darrell was a lighter than usual sentence."

"So..."

"When he was released from prison, Darrell came back to Jameson and contacted me. I warned him he'd be better off starting over in a new location, but he said he'd grown up here and wanted to show the people who knew him that he'd changed. So I called Tom Oliver. If you've talked with Tom, you know he doesn't mind hiring people like Darrell if they've really turned their lives around."

"Didn't Dr. Gordon tell me that you were the one who recommended Tom Oliver's crew to repair the fire damage?"

"Yes, but I had no idea Darrell would be one of the workers on that job. Once I found out about it, I started to tell Sarah, but decided she had enough to worry about. After all,

Darrell had convinced me he was a changed man. However, I did ask Tom to keep an eye on the workmen, especially Darrell, while they were at Sarah's. So far, he hasn't reported anything unusual going on."

Larson stared at the attorney for a long moment. Then he looked at his watch. "I've taken enough of your time. I think I'll drop by Darrell Kline's apartment on my way home for a little chat."

As he walked toward his car, Bill Larson ran through what he'd learned in the last half hour. Could it be that he was finally zeroing in on the person responsible for the harassment of Dr. Sarah Gordon? Part of him hoped that was the case, but another part—one he'd tried to suppress just as he suppressed his desire every day for a drink—wanted things to continue for a bit longer, because he liked being around this attractive woman.

Maybe it was because her dark good looks reminded him of his ex-wife. Perhaps his near-fascination with her was part of his subconscious desire to start over with someone else, to prove he could do it right this time, and she epitomized the type of woman he sought. But for whatever reason, since the beginning of this case a new temptation had been added to his life.

19

When Sarah arrived home around midnight on Sunday, she went through her usual routine with the alarm system and garage door, a routine that still required conscious thought. On the other hand, although Prince had only lived at her house for a day, she half-expected to see him waiting for her return when she entered the kitchen from the garage.

She wanted to find time tomorrow to go by and visit him in what she now thought of as the "doggy hospital." When he was well enough to leave, Sarah would need to take him to Hunter. She had severely mixed feelings about Prince going back to his original home, but she knew that Hunter would take better care of a convalescing dog than she could. When Prince had fully healed.... Well, she'd see.

Sarah was ready to make her final trip around the house for the day, checking that the doors and windows were secure. She started to pick up her pistol and carry it with her, then put it down, but after a dozen steps she turned back and retrieved it.

When that chore was done, she was about ready to shower and don her pajamas. Then she decided there was one more thing she should do. She sat on the side of the bed—Sarah wasn't comfortable with kneeling, but figured that God didn't care what her posture was when she talked with Him—and began to pray.

"God, thank You for Your protection today. Please give me the strength I'll need tomorrow and the days after that. Keep me safe. Lead me and help me follow. In Your name, Amen."

She put her pistol on the nightstand. That night, despite the absence of her new companion, she slept well.

On Monday morning, Bill Larson watched while Cal Johnson added cream and two spoonsful of sugar to his second cup of coffee. The waitress dropped the check between the two men and walked away.

Larson carefully scanned the tables around them at the cafe. When he was satisfied that the conversation was secure, he said, "I may have made some progress in finding the person responsible for the attacks on Dr. Gordon."

"Good. Tell me about it."

Larson moved aside the plate holding crumbs from his order of wheat toast. He sipped from his mug of coffee, set it down, then said, "I was suspicious of a couple of guys, part of Tom Oliver's crew working in the doctor's house."

"Did you recognize them or something?"

"No, I guess you could call it cop's intuition," Larson said. He went on to explain what he'd found out about Kline. "I was going to go by his apartment yesterday evening, but I was worn out. So I checked on him this morning, and it looks as though Darrell's skipped out."

"Why do you say that?" Cal asked.

"The furnished apartment he rented was empty. Most of his clothes were gone, and there were no toiletries in the bathroom. Apparently, he left in the middle of the night."

"Did his boss know anything about this?"

"I hadn't gone by Kline's apartment when I talked with Tom Oliver the first time. I'm going to call him again later this morning. It's interesting that Kline disappeared after I'd talked with both Oliver and Kyle Andrews about him."

"You think one of them tipped him off and he ran?" Cal said.

"I don't know. I'm just making an observation right now."

"Do you think Kline's responsible for the attacks on the doctor?"

"He's the best suspect I have so far. What are you working right now?" Larson asked.

"I'm pretty clear. The defendant in the case in which I was going to testify took a plea deal over the weekend. I have a couple of cold cases I'm working, but I'd be happy to help out on yours. What do you need?"

Larson finished his coffee and wiped a few drops off his upper lip. "I have Harry Gordon's laptop. I wanted to see if there was anything on it that would point us to anyone else besides Darrell Kline as the culprit."

"I'll go through it," Cal said. "And I presume you're going to try to find this Kline guy."

"Yeah. The fact that he ran off doesn't necessarily mean he's guilty."

"But it doesn't do a lot to show his innocence," Cal said. He drained his coffee cup, and pushed the check toward Larson. "I think it's your turn to buy breakfast."

"Prince is—excuse the expression—a lucky dog." Dr. Brad Selleck, the man who operated on Prince, sat with Sarah in his office at the veterinary hospital. She figured Selleck was about her age. He wore a white coat over jeans and a Jimmy Buffett tee shirt. He smiled, displaying previously hidden dimples. "Sorry, but I've been waiting for months to use that."

Sarah noticed that Selleck wore no rings. Then again, lots of professional people, like a veterinary surgeon, didn't wear theirs, especially at work. There was no doubt that, despite herself, she felt an attraction for this tall, dark, articulate man. Of course, maybe it was just gratitude for what he'd done for Prince. "You can make all the jokes you want. I'll never complain. After all, you saved my dog's life," Sarah said.

"Not sure I saved his life, but I think we repaired the damage pretty well," Selleck said. "The shot came from above Prince, but either it came while he was moving or the shooter wasn't very accurate. The soft tissue injury was in the area where a human's left shoulder would be. There was bleeding, which I managed to control. A bit of clean muscle injury, but the bones and joint weren't injured. A little more toward the center, though..."

"I know. I'm a physician," Sarah said. "Sometimes a few centimeters with a gunshot can make a critical difference."

"We'd like to keep Prince another day or two. I gave him one transfusion to replace his acute blood loss. He should build up his blood count on his own now, but we need to change the dressing and watch for infection. Can you leave him here a bit longer?" He shook his head. "Sorry. I'm used to talking to average pet owners. I mean, as a doctor you could watch for infections and all that. You may want to take him home earlier."

Sarah looked down at her feet. "No, I'd rather leave him here. I live alone, and I hate to think of leaving him while I'm at work." *Besides, when he leaves here, I'm going to take him to someone who can give him the care he needs.*

Selleck nodded his approval. "He'll be fine with us. But you can come by any time to visit him...or me, for that matter."

She looked up into his caring eyes. Was he reading her mind? "That's very kind of you. And, just so there's no misunderstanding, I've only recently become a widow. My husband died almost nine months ago. So I'm not—"

"Sorry. I didn't mean to put my foot into it," Selleck said. "I guess it takes some people a long time to get over a loss such as yours." The expression on his handsome face remained neutral, but his eyes smiled at her. "I realize you're not ready to date again, and that's not what I'm suggesting. But if you'd like someone to talk with...I know a bit about loss."

"Oh, did your wife die?"

"There's no wife, and my former fiancée is alive and happily married...to another guy. So, yes, I know about loss...just not what you've suffered." Selleck pointed to a door. "If you want to see Prince, I'll take you back. And the offer to come back to visit still holds—him or me or both of us."

Kyle Andrews left the courthouse Monday mid-morning, wondering why he didn't feel happier. He'd done his best for his client, a man who was obviously guilty. Upon repeated questioning by the police, the man finally admitted embezzling five thousand dollars from the auto dealership where he worked. Kyle had managed to cut a deal so his client would get a year's probation, plus repaying the money with interest. All things considered, it could have been a lot worse.

As he began walking toward his office, Kyle wondered if his being down might be because he was tired of defending people who were lawbreakers. He had known, even before he started law school, that our Constitution guarantees everyone, whether guilty or innocent, legal representation in their defense. And he and his partners had built quite a nice practice providing that. But it was beginning to wear thin.

Then again, maybe he felt guilty because of Larson's visit yesterday. But how could Kyle have behaved differently? Darrell Kline appeared to have undergone a change for the better during his trial and subsequent incarceration. It was evident when the man, fresh out of prison, contacted the attorney and asked for his help in finding a job. Before his arrest, Kline had done construction of various types, moving from job to job, never putting down roots. He was ready to settle down. But a job for a convicted felon was tough to come by.

"In prison, I was lucky," Kline had said. "The skinheads wanted me, but I managed to avoid them. Instead, I sort of fell in with a group of new Christians. It wasn't long before I found the Lord. I've changed. Can you help me find a job here?"

Until Larson's visit yesterday, Kyle figured Darrell Kline was backing up his words with actions. Once or twice, right after the ex-convict began work, Kyle had checked with Tom Oliver, who reported that the man was a dependable, hardworking member of his crew. But it had been a while since Kyle inquired about his former client.

His mind still miles away, Kyle entered his office, picked up his message slips from his secretary, and slipped out of his coat. When he was seated behind his desk, he decided to call the detective and see if there was any further word about Kline. After all, he felt sort of responsible for putting the ex-con in a position where he could get that close to Sarah. Maybe he could help.

"Larson."

"Detective, this is Kyle Andrews. I wanted to call and see if I could help you further with Darrell Kline. You know, maybe set it up for you to talk with him so he doesn't get skittish and disappear."

The silence went on so long that Kyle pulled his cell phone from his ear and looked to see if he'd lost the connection. Finally, Larson said, "You're serious, aren't you?"

"Why wouldn't I be? I know you policemen don't much like attorneys, but I thought—"

"Kline is in the wind."

"He's what? What do you mean?"

"I went by Kline's apartment early this morning, and he was gone," Larson said. "His toiletries and most of his clothes were missing. The landlord didn't know anything about it. The rent was paid for the rest of the month, and Kline gave no indication he was leaving."

"I...I don't know what to say," Kyle said.

"Do you know where he might go?"

"No, but I can check my records and see if there's anything there that might help you."

"You do that," Larson said.

Kyle started speaking again, but stopped when he heard the beep signaling Larson had ended the call. He pushed the intercom button on his phone console. "Tandra, would you get me the file on Darrell Kline? It will be in the inactives."

The desk where Cal Johnson was working was close enough to Bill Larson's in the detectives' office that it wasn't necessary to raise his voice. Cal looked up from the laptop that sat on his desk and said, "If they ever award a prize for a computer with the least interesting material on it, this one would take it hands down."

"Nothing to suggest who might want to take revenge on Harry's wife?"

"Nothing to suggest the man was anything but a complete straight arrow. His browsing history is mainly for medical sites. His personal correspondence was primarily about church. And the Quicken folder shows that he lived within his means, both before and after his marriage."

"Well," Larson said. "We had to look."

"Remind me again why no one had a look at his computer after he was killed?"

"Because there was no question about why or how he died," Larson replied. "He and his two-year-old daughter were killed when another driver ran into them head-on."

"Yeah, I guess there was no reason to investigate that," Johnson said. "How about the other driver. Did he survive?"

"It was a woman, and no, she was dead at the scene as well."

Johnson closed Harry's laptop and unplugged his power source from it. Then he rose and took the computer to Larson's desk, where he deposited it. "I'll let you take this back to Dr. Gordon. Sorry it didn't help."

Larson sat for a moment, something the other detective had said still tickling at the back of his mind. He ran through their conversation again, then snapped his fingers. "I'm an idiot."

"Not necessarily, although you're going to have to be more specific."

"Is it possible that the family of the woman killed in the crash that took the life of Harry and Jennifer Gordon somehow blamed the doctor for her death? We haven't even considered that. What if the husband is still alive? What if he's been seeking some sort of revenge?"

"Do you want to look into it?"

Larson picked up a pen, pulled a pad toward him, and scratched a note. "We need to follow up on that, but I don't want to let go of this end of the string yet. Let's see if we can track down Darrell Kline. I still think he's our best suspect. Harry Gordon was the foreman of the jury that found him guilty. He got out of prison about the time the phone calls to Sarah Gordon started. He's been in her house, and there's no telling what that might have done to stir up feelings in him. And, of course, while he was there he could have made a duplicate key to her door, figured out how to bypass the alarm system...whatever was needed."

"But didn't you tell me he convinced Kyle Andrews that he changed while he was in prison?" Cal said. "And he gave the appearance of having turned his life around."

Larson shook his head. "Maybe it's just the cynicism I've developed after years of police work, but I keep thinking about my own experience. I've seen a number of people convicted of terrible crimes, while their neighbors said things like, 'He seemed like such a nice person,' and 'I never suspected anything.'"

"Okay," Cal said. "Why don't you check with Kline's parole officer while I run down some of his known associates. Let's see if we can't locate this guy."

It had been a fairly average Monday so far in the ER of Centennial Hospital, meaning that it was possible to keep up with the patient flow, although sometimes just barely. When it came time for their supper break, Sarah and Connie retreated to the break room to eat the sandwiches they'd brought from home.

"Would you like some hot tea?" Connie asked as she pressed the tap to fill her mug with hot water.

"No, I think I'd like a Dr Pepper," Sarah replied. She pulled one out of the refrigerator, popped the tab, and took a long swallow.

"Anything more from the person who is...I started to say harassing you, but since he's set a fire, then shot at both you and your dog, I guess it's gone beyond harassment. Anything more about whoever's behind the attacks on you?"

Sarah took a small bite of her cheese and tomato sandwich, chewed, and swallowed. "Not since he shot my dog, Prince, in my backyard."

"How's your dog doing?"

"He's recovering well. I'll probably go see him tomorrow. He should be ready to leave the vet's soon." As Sarah took another bite of sandwich, thoughts came unbidden into her mind, thoughts not of Prince but of Brad Selleck. There was no doubt the veterinary surgeon was handsome. She kept picturing that one curl of dark hair hanging over his blue eyes. And she figured, from what she'd seen so far, that he'd be fun to be with. That was one of the things she always enjoyed about Harry. If she went to see Prince...

"Earth to Sarah. Come in Sarah," Connie said.

"I'm sorry. I was daydreaming," Sarah said. She drank more Dr Pepper. "Connie, do you think I'll ever get over losing Harry and Jennifer?"

Connie chewed on her own sandwich for a moment before answering. "I don't think you get over a loss like that. You get through it, but things are never the same. But eventually you get used to the new normal. Why do you ask?"

"No reason, I guess."

"Well, I have one bit of advice for you. Harry and Jennifer are gone from your life. The good memories will crowd out any bad ones, and that's as it should be. But remember that although they're dead, you're still alive. There's no need for you to remain in mourning forever."

"I thought I was supposed to...I don't know. 'Mourn' isn't really the word I want, but I thought I should observe at least a year of widowhood before thinking about moving on."

Connie wiped her mouth with a paper napkin. "I have one question for you—one you should ask yourself. The answer will dictate what you ought to do."

Sarah looked at her friend with raised eyebrows. "Yes?"

"Would Harry want you to mourn for a year, or two years, or whatever arbitrary length of time you choose? Or would he want you to be happy?"

"I think—"

Connie held up a hand. "You don't have to answer to me. Ask yourself that question. Answer it in your heart. Then you'll know what you should do next."

20

Judge Atkins's clerk called Kyle while he was skimming Darrell Kline's file. Could the attorney come to the courthouse? The judge wanted Kyle and the opposing lawyer to sit down and try to hammer out a compromise in a civil suit set for trial in his court. The other attorney had indicated he'd be willing to do this, and the judge hoped Kyle would likewise be amenable to it. If they could come up with an agreeable compromise, the judge could clear the trial off his calendar, always desirable in this day of crowded dockets.

The two lawyers worked for several hours, butted heads on a few points, agreed on some others, and eventually reached a settlement they thought their clients would accept. The men retreated with their cell phones to opposite ends of the conference room where they'd been working. When Kyle ended his call, he looked at the other lawyer, who also appeared to be on the tail end of a prolonged conversation. Kyle gave him a thumbs-up, and he, in turn, nodded to signify that his client was willing to agree to the terms they'd hammered out.

They moved back to their positions next to each other at the conference table. "I'll call the judge's clerk in the morning to let him know we succeeded," Kyle said. "Want to check your schedule to find a time when our clients can sign the agreement?"

"I'll have my secretary type up the settlement agreement tomorrow. Then we can play dueling datebooks and get this thing signed." The other attorney pulled back his sleeve and consulted his watch. "I need to get going. My wife expects me not only to go hear the symphony in Dallas tonight, I'm supposed to act like I enjoy it." He smiled ruefully. "Too bad this couldn't have run about an hour longer."

The two men shook hands and left the courthouse. Kyle climbed into his car and pulled out into the street. The clock on his dashboard said six p.m. He considered going back to the office and studying Darrell Kline's file, still lying on his desk. Then again...

He put on his signal and made an abrupt turn. He'd look at the file in the morning, then call Detective Larson if he found anything of significance. Actually, there was only one phone call he wanted to make tonight. Kyle wheeled into a half-full mall parking lot, pulled out his cell phone, and used the speed dial function.

He almost never called her at work. If he waited until she got off, it might be too late in the evening. Well, if she were too busy to answer right now, maybe she'd call him back. Besides—

"Hello?"

"Sarah, I'm sorry to call you at work. Do you have a moment?" Kyle asked.

"Actually, I do. I'm just finishing my supper. Is something wrong?"

"Not at all. I just wanted to see if I could get together with you some time tomorrow—maybe for lunch. We really need to catch up."

"I...I'm going to the vet's tomorrow to see Prince," Sarah said.

"Prince...Oh, yeah. Your dog. How is he?"

"Improving. Anyway, I thought I'd go tomorrow morning late, so I imagine lunch is out. But thanks for asking."

Kyle didn't miss a beat. "Why don't I drive you there? We can both see Prince, then have some time afterward to visit. I know a great little restaurant not too far from the veterinary hospital."

The response came so quickly he wondered if she'd even thought about it. "No, no. There are some other things I may have to do. But we'll get together another time. Look, I have to go now. Thanks for the invitation."

Kyle ended the call and sat slapping the phone into his palm, thinking. Sarah hadn't just declined his invitation to lunch. She'd almost run to get away from it, even when he'd made it pretty open-ended. He could think of two explanations. Come to think of it, both were variants of the same thing: either she had plans she didn't want him to know about or she simply didn't want to see him.

He checked his calendar and found that it was open from mid-morning until mid-afternoon. It wouldn't be difficult to wait outside the veterinary clinic and see where Sarah went when she left. Kyle rose from his chair and was reaching for his coat before he stopped. *What am I thinking? I'm about to stalk Sarah.* Wouldn't that be great? Sarah's friend and lawyer arrested for stalking.

But it was eating at Kyle that Sarah might be meeting another person. He wondered who it might be. And why.

He returned to his desk and tried to concentrate on some papers there, but his mind wouldn't turn loose of the question—what was Sarah doing? And why didn't it involve him?

When Sarah arrived home, the lamp in the living room was lit, courtesy of the timer she'd set, but the rest of the house was dark. The usual vehicles were parked in front of her neighbors' houses, with none in front of hers. There was nothing to arouse her suspicion, but the exercise of caution was becoming second nature to her. She went through what was by now a familiar ritual—disarm the security system, raise the garage door, lower it, open the door from the garage into the kitchen, rearm the system. Sarah was surprised to find that she already missed being greeted by Prince. Maybe after this was all over she'd talk with Hunter about the German shepherd coming to live with her once more.

Sarah tossed her backpack onto a chair in the living room and began what had become her nightly routine. She went from room to room, checking doors and windows. She looked in closets and—even though it made her feel silly— she knelt beside each bed in her house, lifted the bedspread, and checked to make sure no one was hiding there.

Just when she was certain she was alone and safe, Sarah noticed the blinking light on her phone. There was a message waiting for her. It had to be a telephone solicitor. No one ever called her land line. She only had it because hospital regulations required that she have one, so they could contact her in case her cell was for some reason inoperative.

Well, better see what this was. She hit the button to play back the message, but when she heard the message Sarah dropped into a chair, deflated like a balloon that was losing air. The voice was soft, with a mechanical quality as though it were being sent through a filter of some kind. The message was brief, but was enough to send chills up her spine. "What happened to your dog could happen to you, too."

Sarah replayed the message twice, each time feeling the pit of her stomach clench a bit more. Her first thought was to call Bill Larson, but before she could dial the number she doubled over, then ran to the bathroom, where she fell to her knees and clutched the toilet bowl as she retched. She didn't know how long she knelt there, at first bringing up the sandwich and soft drink, then just dry heaving. When she finally was able to get back to her feet, she thought again about calling the detective. Then the roiling in her stomach started all over again.

Part of her wanted to call Bill Larson, if only to get some reassurance that he'd be able to catch the person behind these episodes. But the rest of her wanted to put the whole thing aside for at least a few hours. After all, what could Larson do tonight that would make any difference? She'd call him first thing in the morning. He'd probably fuss at her about the delay, but she couldn't stand any more of this tonight.

Sarah prepared for bed, walking through the motions with her mind on the person who continued to make her life miserable. As she sat on the edge of the bed, her prayer was brief but fervent. *Please protect me. And let this be over... soon.*

"You should have called me last night," Bill Larson said as soon as Sarah opened her front door to him.

"And good morning to you, too," she said. "How am I? As well as can be expected. And thanks for asking."

The sarcasm in her voice didn't escape Larson, and he regretted his actions. "I'm sorry," Larson said as he stepped into her living room. "It's just that... This guy has really gotten under my skin."

"Well, join the club," Sarah said. "And for your information, I thought about calling you last night. Then I asked myself what you could do at that time that you couldn't do eight or ten hours later. So I went to bed. Didn't sleep well, but at least I tried."

Larson held up his hands in surrender. "I apologize. Let me get right to it. Which phone did he call?"

"My land line," she said, pointing to a phone sitting on an end table in her living room.

"Do you use this for outgoing calls?"

"No."

"Get many calls on this line?"

"It's listed in the phone book, but the only time it rings is a call from a telephone solicitor. My friends use my cell number."

"Then why do you—"

"Hospital regulations require me to have a land line as well. But I'll probably have the number changed and make sure the new one isn't in the phone directory. I probably should have done it when I got those calls after Harry died."

Larson picked up the receiver but didn't dial. "Do you have caller ID on this?"

"No," she said. "I never saw the need to spend the money, since I never get calls on that line."

Larson nodded. He checked to make sure there was a dial tone, then punched in star sixty-nine. He heard a series of clicks, then the buzzes indicating the number was ringing. It rang a dozen times with no answer and no indication of a voicemail box. He hung up the phone. "I'll check to see what number called you last night, but dollars to donuts it was a disposable cell phone—what we call a burner."

Sarah turned away from him and dropped onto the sofa. "I'm sorry I snapped at you," she said. "Do you think there'll be more of these calls? Can you trace them? Should you have a recorder on this line?"

"I don't know," Larson said. "I'll talk to the tech people at the department about putting in a recorder, but that would only help if he calls again. And tracing is probably going to be impossible. So all we can do—"

"I know," she said. "All we can do is wait."

Sarah parked her car in front of the Ashton Veterinary Clinic, but didn't get out. She wanted to see Prince again, but three fears were holding her back. The first was that the dog's recovery had progressed to the point that it was time to return him to her father-in-law, a visit that, despite Hunter's reassurance, she dreaded because it would make her feel sad. The second was akin to the first. Would Prince know in some dog-instinctive way that she'd put him in harm's way, was actually responsible for his being shot? And her third fear, the one she didn't want to recognize even existed, was that when she saw Brad Selleck, the veterinary surgeon, she'd feel the same attraction to him, the same feeling that hit her on the previous visit.

She was an intelligent woman, a professional, a physician. Maybe she could figure out why she was attracted to Brad. Was there a physical similarity to her late husband? Their build was about the same, but any resemblance stopped there. Brad had dark hair, Harry's had been blonde. Their features were nothing alike. Actually, Kyle looked more like Harry than Brad did, and despite what she figured were his best efforts, Kyle hadn't stirred any romantic feelings in her.

But Brad was like Harry in an important way. He always seemed to be smiling, if not with his lips then with his eyes. His whole attitude seemed to be, "Let's find the best in all this and enjoy it." She'd felt comfortable with Harry. She'd relaxed in his presence. She'd felt a similar vibe from Brad, and maybe that was responsible in large part for the attraction she felt.

Enough of this dithering. She wanted to see Prince. And she needed to see Selleck, if for no other reason than to find out if the feeling she'd experienced at their first meeting was still there. What was the worst that could happen?

Ignoring that last question, Sarah emerged from her car and walked with rapid footsteps down the sidewalk to the front door of the veterinary hospital. She opened the door and was greeted by a cacophony of barks, from high-pitched yips to *basso profundo* growls. There was also a smell, one she hadn't paid much attention to on her last visit, but which now was quite evident—the smell of animals. She was pleased to realize she didn't find it off-putting at all.

The receptionist recognized her name and reacted positively to it. "Doctor Gordon, I'll bet you want to visit Prince." She smiled as she pulled a folder from a stack sitting on her desk, glanced inside, and said, "He's doing quite well. Dr. Selleck says here he could be discharged in another day or two. If you want to see him—"

"I'll take Dr. Gordon back," came a voice from the doorway to Sarah's left.

She turned and saw Brad Selleck standing there. Today his crisp white coat covered a clean pair of jeans, topped by a bright red polo shirt. Just as it had the last time she saw him, a curl of dark, almost jet-black hair hung over his forehead. And, just as before, she felt a sensation she hadn't experienced for a long time. Sarah couldn't put a name to it, couldn't describe it, but there was no doubt in her mind about the feeling.

Connie had asked Sarah to consider whether Harry would want her to be happy. She'd thought about it and was pretty sure she knew the answer, but it wasn't until she first met Brad Selleck that it became clear to her. The answer was yes. And this encounter underscored it.

Kyle Andrews balanced his phone between his left ear and shoulder while he paged through the file that was open on his desk. His call continued to ring, and just as he was about to hang up he heard, "Larson."

He reached up to take the phone with one hand just before it slipped and fell. "Detective, this is Kyle Andrews. I finally got around to studying the file we have on Darrell Kline."

"What took you so long?"

"Hey, as surprising as it may be to you, I work. That work involves a number of clients, and when I get a call from one of them, it's often a matter that requires my immediate attention. Anyway, I scanned the file yesterday, but had to go into a conference before I could study it carefully." Kyle took a deep breath. "I think I may have found something that would help you."

"Good. And I'm sorry if I came down on you. It's just that—"

"I know. We're all doing our best to find the person who has his sights set on Sarah Gordon. Anyway, as you've discovered already if you looked into it, Darrell Kline was released after six years, his sentence having been reduced for good behavior."

"Yeah. I found that out," Larson said.

"Parole wasn't required—he was a free man. That meant there was no need to report to a parole officer, not even a requirement that he give an address when he left prison."

"Tell me something I don't know," said Larson.

"I'm getting there. I looked for next of kin, but he didn't show any. Then I thought of looking in another place on our forms."

"Where?"

"When clients fill out papers in this office, we ask for next of kin. Kline left that blank. But the line after that asks for the name of someone to notify in case of emergency. Of course, that's really someone who can help us locate him if he tries to disappear."

"And—"

"And he listed a friend. Do you want the name and address?"

"I think Prince is glad to see you."

Sarah Gordon had dreaded the reception she'd get from what she'd already come to think of as "her" dog, but it wasn't what she feared. Either Prince didn't blame her the way she was blaming herself for the gunshot wound inflicted on the German shepherd, or the dog had a very forgiving nature.

Either way, it was obvious that Prince was glad to see her. "The feeling is mutual," she said as she knelt in front of the dog.

After a few minutes with Prince, she turned to Selleck and said, "Thanks again for what you did for Prince."

"I didn't do anything you wouldn't have done—actually, what you do on a regular basis in your profession."

"How about getting rousted out at midnight to do emergency surgery?"

"No problem," Selleck said. "Part of my practice. Besides, I didn't have anyone waiting for me at home."

Sarah added that to what she already knew about the man. No wedding ring, a fiancée who'd married someone else, the man now living alone. Her curiosity wanted one more piece of the puzzle, but she didn't know how to go about getting the information without being too direct. "Well, anyway, thanks." Sarah started to turn away, but the veterinarian's next question stopped her.

"You don't recognize me, do you?" Selleck said.

The question made Sarah frown. She began to run scenarios through her brain. Had she seen him in the emergency room, either as a patient or accompanying one? Did their paths cross at a store in some fashion? Had she encountered him in a parking lot when their grocery carts bumped?

"After your husband and daughter were killed in that auto crash, you pretty much stopped attending church, but I joined right before all that happened. My first thought was that maybe you'd started attending somewhere else. But now I figure that wasn't the case. I'm guessing you just stopped going to church altogether. Was that it?"

Sarah nodded.

"Well, I was glad to see you back in church last Sunday," he said. "It's important, after a loss like you've suffered, to let God back into your life. I hope you're doing that now."

And in those few, brief sentences, the last bit of information Sarah wanted about what seemed at first like a chance encounter fell into place. There was very little doubt left in her mind. Her meeting with Brad Selleck wasn't really a chance circumstance. It was what Harry had liked to call "a God thing."

Now what am I going to do about it?

21

LARSON FOUND THE APARTMENT HE WANTED WITH NO trouble. He shrugged to settle his shoulder holster a bit more comfortably under his sport coat, then knocked. The man who opened the door for him was probably in his sixties. His hair, what there was of it, was silver. He wore what appeared to be the pants to an old suit, a rumpled and stained dress shirt, and a look of pure disdain. "Yeah?" he said.

"I'm Detective Larson," Bill said, holding up the badge wallet containing his gold shield. "You have a tenant here named Jerger?"

"Apartment 3-B. But he works nights, so I don't think he'd want to be disturbed."

Larson resisted the temptation to respond with a sarcastic remark. Instead, he said, "Thanks for your help," and looked for the stairs.

A few minutes later, the detective was knocking on the door of 3-B. He wondered once again if he should have called his fellow detective or a uniformed patrolman to provide backup. No, he simply couldn't imagine a scenario where this man—or Kline, for that matter—would give him any trouble. Besides, and this was probably the real reason he was here alone, this had become his personal quest, and he wanted to be the one to end it.

Larson increased his knocking to a pounding, then a voice within the apartment responded, "Yeah, yeah. I'm coming." The man who opened the door was wearing a Dallas Cowboys tee shirt and a pair of sweatpants. He was barefoot. His hair was mussed, and there were bedding wrinkles along his right cheek.

"Larry Jerger?"

"Yeah, what's so important that you woke me up?"

Larson held up his shield and identified himself. "Is Darrell Kline a friend of yours?"

"Sort of. We were in the same classes in high school. We go out together to eat once in a while, have a few drinks. Why?"

"I'm trying to locate him. Do you know where he might be?"

The man ran his fingers through his disarrayed hair without much effect. "Yeah. He called early yesterday morning and asked me to get his mail and check on his apartment while he's gone. Hang on. I've got the address here somewhere. I think he gave me the phone number, too."

"Your eleven thirty appointment had to reschedule," Kyle's secretary said.

"Thanks," he replied. "Then I'm free until one. Right?"

"Yes sir."

Kyle released the intercom button on his phone and swiveled to look at his two partners, who sat across the desk from him. He noted that each had a yellow legal pad with notes on it. Sometimes he thought lawyers were born with those pads and would be laid to rest clutching them. "Anything else we need to discuss?"

The male partner, Jerry Gilmore, spoke first. "I think that wraps it up." He looked at the woman sitting next to him. "Ann?"

"Just one thing," Ann Stark said. "Remember that I'll be on vacation next week. I don't have any cases coming up soon, but if that will has to be probated—"

"I'll do it," Kyle said. "You enjoy your time off with your husband."

In a moment, he had the office to himself. He reached for the phone, drew back his hand, reached once more, and finally picked it up and punched in Sarah's number. She'd turned down several invitations to see him, but he intended to keep at it. Maybe his persistence would pay off.

"Hello?"

There was noise in the background, but he couldn't identify it. For reasons he didn't fully understand, Kyle reached for a switch located in the kneehole of his desk. "Sarah, this is Kyle. Do you have a moment to talk?"

"Uh, sure, I guess. What's up?"

"I know you planned to go to the vet's, but I was wondering, if you're through there, if you'd like to reconsider my invitation to lunch." When there was no response, he hurried on to say, "If you tell me where you are, I could meet you. Anyplace you choose." *C'mon, Kyle. Don't push it so hard. You sound like a sophomore asking the Homecoming Queen out for a soda.*

"Kyle, when you called earlier I thought I told you that I wouldn't be able to get together and have lunch with you. I know that you want to take care of me now that Harry's not around. But I'm starting to get my life back on track. I really need some space now."

"Sure, sure," he said. "Just know that the invitation's there. Give me a call anytime."

"I will." Her voice softened a bit. "And thanks, Kyle. I appreciate your concern, and I know Harry would be grateful."

After he ended the call, Kyle flipped a switch next to the phone console, and in a moment the conversation replayed through the speaker. As an attorney, he often needed to record a phone conversation. This was perfectly legal in Texas so long as one of the two parties involved knew about it. He wasn't sure why he'd decided to record this one—but he was glad he did, because he wanted another chance to hear the background noise on Sarah's side of the call.

He listened twice more before he was certain. What he'd heard was the buzz of voices and the clatter of dishes typical of a restaurant at lunchtime.

"He was at his mother's?" Cal Johnson asked.

"Yep," Larson said. He and Cal stepped off the elevator at police headquarters and moved toward the parking lot.

The two men climbed into Cal's car. "Well, don't keep me in suspense. Tell me about it."

"I got the address and phone number from the friend he'd listed on his registration form when Kyle Andrews represented him. I took a chance and called the number, and Kline answered."

"He answered the phone at his mother's house?"

"Yep. He was staying there. Kline wasn't running. He said he got a phone call late Sunday night from her neighbor that his mother, who lives about twenty miles away, had suffered a stroke and was in the hospital. Kline packed his things and took off but didn't say anything to his landlord or his boss. I think his mind was on his mother's stroke, and he just wanted to get there as quickly as possible."

"I thought you told me he left the 'next of kin' line blank on Andrews' form," Cal said.

"He did. He and his mother were estranged at the time, but they made peace while he was in prison. He's called her regularly since getting out. Even spends some time with her."

"Does he have alibis for the times when our mysterious Mr. X set the fire at Dr. Gordon's house or took a shot at her or any of the other things he's done?"

Larson pulled a notebook from his inside coat pocket and flipped a couple of pages. "I'll want to check these out, but he spent the night at his mother's house on two of those occasions."

"You said she had a stroke. Is she able to speak?"

"She's still rocky, but the doctor is supposed to call me when she's well enough to talk." Larson stowed the notebook back in his pocket. "But for now, it looks like Kline may not be our man."

Cal wheeled into the parking lot of his favorite barbecue restaurant. "Well, we have more people to investigate. Remember that you mentioned looking into the woman driving the other car in the wreck that killed Harry and Jennifer Gordon?"

Larson unclipped his seat belt but stayed seated. "Yes?"

"While you were talking with Kline this morning, I did a little computer work in that area." He grinned. "And if you're willing to spring for a plate of ribs, I might be persuaded to share what I've found with you."

Sarah looked around the crowded restaurant. For some reason, she was relieved when she failed to see anyone she knew. "I shouldn't have agreed to have lunch with you," she said.

"It's not like it was a date or anything," Brad said. "You came to see your dog, who's recuperating after I did surgery for his gunshot wound. We talked, found that we had some common interests, and that talk carried over to lunch. No big deal." He took a sip of water. "Happens all the time."

Sarah shook her head. "After the fire at my house, Kyle took me to lunch a couple of times. Other than that, this is the first time I've had a meal out with another man since Harry died." She lifted her glass of iced tea to her lips, surprised to find that the mention of her late husband's name hadn't caused her to tear up. "And I have to admit, I'm feeling a little guilty about it."

"Look, I won't say I know what you're feeling. Losing a spouse and a child must be devastating. My break-up with my fiancée was tough, but nothing like what you're going through. But I'm pretty sure you don't have to feel guilty about enjoying yourself every once in a while."

Sarah wanted to believe what Brad was telling her. And she wanted to feel good about having lunch with someone else—not just with a handsome man, that was a bonus, but with a person who could make her smile, even laugh. Yet she still felt a bit of guilt about these few minutes of enjoyment. Maybe she'd get past it—she hoped she could. Right now, though, she was willing to take what she could get.

Brad looked at his watch. "I've got to get back to the clinic, and I suspect you need to head back home to get ready for work." He covered the check with his hand and pulled it to him.

Sarah reached for her purse. "Please, let me pay for this. You can call it my thank-you for saving my dog's life."

"We can split it if it would make you feel better, but it bothers me not to pay for a woman's meal. It sort of undermines my masculinity, I guess. Would you humor me?"

Sarah smiled. "If you insist. And perhaps you can come to my place and let me cook for you to sort of even things up."

"It's a date," Brad said. Then, apparently realizing what he'd said, he hurriedly added. "I mean, I'll look forward to it."

As they left the restaurant and climbed into Brad's car for the ride back to the clinic, Sarah wondered if the shiver she'd felt at Brad's choice of words was because she felt guilty, or was it a by-product of her anticipation of what would be, despite whatever words they chose to use, a date?

Bill Larson watched Cal gnaw the last morsel of meat off the rib and add it to the pile of bones on his plate. "I can see why you like to come here," Larson said.

"Got to be true to my Southern heritage," Cal said. He tore off a long piece of the paper towel the restaurant placed on the table in lieu of traditional napkins, and wiped his mouth and hands. "Now I suppose you want to know what I found out about the other driver in the Harry Gordon accident."

"I think I've been exceptionally patient," Larson said. "Now give."

Cal dug into the inside pocket of his sport coat, which was hanging on the back of his chair, and pulled out his notebook. "The driver of the car was Mrs. Rena Hawkins. She was pronounced dead at the scene. Her husband, John M. Hawkins, was a CPA. He tried to go back to work after the accident, but either quit or was fired from his job within a couple of weeks."

"Children?" Larson asked.

"No. According to one brief paragraph in a follow-up story, the fact that Jennifer Gordon was killed in the accident was a source of great anguish to Mr. Hawkins. He and his wife had wanted children but had been unable to have any. Then the accident took the life of someone else's child."

"So, do you have an address for John Hawkins? I'll talk with him this afternoon."

"I doubt that. Hawkins took his own life three weeks after his wife died in the car crash."

22

Kyle Andrews couldn't stop thinking about it, trying to figure out where he stood. When someone tried to burn down Sarah's house, Kyle was the first person she called. When she was frightened, Sarah actively sought him for counsel and support. As it became apparent that whoever was behind this meant to harm her, she'd taken the revolver he offered—even let him help her learn to use it. It seemed that, as the stress mounted, he was becoming more and more a part of her life, someone she could lean on.

But then she'd begun to distance herself. Oh, not in a rude fashion, but certainly one that indicated—at least, to him—that Sarah was trying to stand on her own two feet, to become the independent woman she'd once been. And that meant that she needed Kyle's support less. Unfortunately, as Sarah had come to depend more on him, Kyle had noted his feelings for her getting stronger. But now her part of it was changing. This wasn't the way it was supposed to go.

His latest conversation with Sarah, the tape of which he'd just replayed for perhaps the fifth or sixth time as he sat in his office, seemed to confirm his suspicions. Not only didn't Sarah appear interested in him as anything more than a friend, she was starting to see someone else—the person with whom she had lunch. *Isn't it a bit too soon after Harry's death for her to start dating? And when she does, shouldn't I be first in line?*

It didn't take long before another small voice in his head chimed in, though. *Trying to make Sarah dependent on you isn't working. It's going to take a more direct approach. You have to tell her straight up you have feelings for her.* But what were those feelings?

Kyle shoved the papers on his desk aside and put his head in his hands. Had his feelings moved to the point of obsession? Was this a rebound thing, as buried feelings for his dead fiancée surfaced? Did he want Sarah? Was he just trying to step into Harry's shoes because he'd seen the happy family they had? What did he really want? The questions went on and on.

What he needed was another opinion, an objective one, but where could he turn for it? He was unwilling to talk directly to Sarah about his feelings—at least, not yet. His law partners were unlikely to be of help in a matter like this. And when he searched his brain for the name of a friend he could ask, he came up empty. Well, maybe there was one person he could talk with about his problem. Kyle reached for the phone, hesitated, then finally lifted the receiver and dialed.

"Pastor...uh, Steve? This is Kyle Andrews. Could I drop by this evening after work? I need to talk with you about something."

"Certainly," Farber said. "One of the ladies of the church brought over some spaghetti and meat sauce today, and there's enough to feed a small army. If you come after five, we can talk awhile, then eat."

"Sounds good," Kyle said. Now if he could find the courage to tell Steve everything that was on his mind.

Sarah's mind was elsewhere as she changed into the scrubs she'd wear for work. She folded the slacks and blouse she'd worn to visit the vet's and placed them on a chair in her bedroom. Sarah didn't want to admit that, rather than throwing on her usual attire for running errands—a pair of jeans and a tee shirt—she'd dressed with care. She'd even sprayed on some cologne, an unusual act for her when she was just going out. Face it. She had been looking forward to seeing Brad Selleck. And although she wanted to deny it, even before leaving her house, she knew her encounter with him would end in lunch together.

Harry, is it too soon for me to be interested in another man? You and Jenny have been gone for almost nine months. Should I wait a year? Should I ever date again? I need some help here. If Sarah was looking for a sign, something to help answer her questions, she was disappointed. Then she thought of what Connie had said. "Would Harry want you to mourn for a year, or two years, or whatever arbitrary length of time you choose? Or would he want you to be happy?" Sarah knew the answer—she just had to convince herself to accept it.

Moving from her bedroom down the stairs, through the living room, into the kitchen, Sarah unloaded and reloaded her backpack. When she tossed it onto a chair in the kitchen, ready for her to pick it up as she left, she heard the "clunk" it made and froze. She'd forgotten the pistol inside. She recalled Kyle's assurance that, with an empty cylinder under the hammer, the pistol was safe from accidental discharge. Sarah wasn't sure whether she believed it or not and reminded herself to be more careful in the future.

How long am I going to have to carry that gun? How long will this go on? Surely by now Bill Larson has found the person responsible for doing this to me. She reached for her cell phone and hit the speed dial for Larson's number before she could change her mind. She needed some reassurance.

"Detective Larson."

"This is Sarah Gordon. I just wanted to check..." Sarah hesitated. Asking for reassurance would put her back to where she'd been a month ago, dependent on others to protect her. But she'd made the call. She needed to think of an excuse, fast. Then her eyes lit on the phone in the living room. "I wanted to see if you had any word on getting a recorder on my phone at home."

"I put in the request, but command staff is sort of jammed up right now. It may be another day or two. You've only had that one call this time—right?"

"Right," she said. Then, as though it was simply an afterthought, "Is... is there any progress in tracking down the person responsible?"

"No, but there are a couple of us working on it. I'll keep you posted."

She could tell he was in a hurry, even though he tried not to betray it. "I'll let you go. Thanks for your efforts."

Sarah ended the call, then slumped into a kitchen chair. She reached over to her backpack, unzipped the outer compartment, and removed the pistol. It fit comfortably into her hand. It was lighter than the one Harry used to have. Strange, how such a small instrument could be so lethal. Could she really shoot someone with it? Then she thought of everything the unknown person had done to torment her—the phone calls, the stalking, the fire, the gunshot, the wounding of her dog. And Sarah knew, just as certainly as though it had been written out for her, that the next event would be an actual attempt on her life.

She nodded to herself and shoved the pistol into the backpack. Yes, she'd definitely use the gun, if it came to that. Matter of fact, she sort of hoped she'd have the opportunity soon.

The call from Sarah Gordon had been a welcome interruption, but now Bill Larson turned back to his computer. He could remember when detective work was done mainly on the streets—knocking on doors, talking to people, investigating and following up. Now it seemed that much of his day was spent at his desk, usually consulting one or another of the law enforcement databases, sometimes talking on the phone. He wasn't sure if this was truly progress, but that was the way it was now.

He wished he could simply go to the NCIC—the National Crime Information Center—and enter a search term like "person harassing Sarah Gordon." Unfortunately, it wasn't that simple.

One of the first things he'd done after returning from lunch with Cal was check on the late John Hawkins. It wasn't that he didn't trust Cal's research—truth be told, the other detective was more computer literate than Larson. But he couldn't believe there wasn't some connection between Mrs. Hawkins, the woman involved in the accident that killed Harry and Jennifer Gordon, and the current attacks on their wife and mother.

Larson had to wade through several layers to be certain he was checking on the right man, given the common name, but it wasn't long before he found the information he wanted. A matter of weeks after Rena Hawkins died in the car crash, her husband, John Hawkins, committed suicide. He was found inside his garage, in his car with the engine running and a hose going from the tailpipe into the auto. The police hadn't found any evidence of foul play, and the medical examiner ruled it suicide. Case closed.

What about other family members? Larson knew Cal had investigated this possibility also, but he double-checked. Both Rena and John were only children. Their parents were dead. They'd been childless. So far as he could tell, there was no one left to mourn the Hawkins' passing except a few friends. Dead end.

Cal had already looked for anything in Sarah Gordon's life that would explain the harassing attempts, and come up empty. Not that he doubted Cal's work, but Larson rechecked, with the same results. Then he'd searched for connections with Harry Gordon but could find nothing suggesting a person who might be responsible for all the things Sarah had suffered. Larson had followed every lead he could think of, and they all were dead ends. And that left him with one possibility—these were the random crimes of a deranged person, with no motivation outside the sick workings of his brain. And such people were almost impossible to catch.

The detective wanted to bang his head against a wall in frustration. No, that wasn't right. It dawned on him that what he really wanted was a drink...or two...or five. He could almost smell the aroma coming off the glass as he raised it to his lips, could taste the alcohol stimulating his taste buds, could feel the calming effect of a few drinks. Previously, no matter how frustrated he'd been, no matter how difficult the problem with which he dealt, it had always worked. And he had no doubt that it would now...for a while.

Of course, there was always the after. He'd experienced that as well. And it had kept getting worse and worse until one day he'd awakened in the drunk tank in his own jail. His gun and his shield were gone, of course. When he called Annie to explain, she told him his captain had already contacted her. And rather than asking a lawyer friend to bail him out, she'd simply said, "No. He might as well get used to sleeping alone. I'm leaving."

Larson didn't want that to happen again. But if he started drinking, something he fought every day, he knew it was only a matter of time before he'd once more be stripped of his gun and his shield—and the last shred of self-respect to which he clung.

He knew he could fight the temptation to drink, but Larson thought of something that might be better than going down this road alone. He dialed a number, praying the party on the other end of the line would be available.

"Hello?"

"Pastor? Steve? This is Bill Larson."

"Bill, how are you?"

"I've been better," the detective said. "Are you going to be home for a while?"

On Tuesday, Pastor Steve Farber usually gave himself permission to relax. He had a couple of sermon topics in mind for this coming Sunday. Tomorrow, he'd pull out some references, do a bit of Bible study, and make a final decision. But today—ah, today was going to be given to reading for pleasure, taking a long walk, getting some things done around the house. That is, it was until he started getting phone calls. Ah, well. What was it he'd heard so many times in his life? *If you want to hear God laugh, tell Him your plans.*

The doorbell rang. Farber pushed himself out of the comfortable chair in his study, moved slowly to the front door, and made certain he was smiling when he opened it. "Bill, come in. Come in."

Bill Larson shook hands with the pastor. "Thanks for seeing me on short notice. I suspect you know why I'm here."

"One of two reasons, I suspect," Farber said. "One is that you're here to arrest me for all the terrible things I've done to Sarah Gordon because I hate doctors after one let my wife die."

The detective shook his head.

"Well, in that case, we'll go with my other guess," the pastor said. "Since you don't have an AA sponsor, you need some support to avoid drinking." He led the way into his study. "Why don't you take that chair there? I think you'll find it a comfortable place to sit while you tell me what's caused this latest crisis in your life."

The detective poured out his story, and Farber found he could identify with the frustration Larson felt. *All of us, no matter what our profession or station in life, can hit walls like this.* But although he waited and watched for Larson to mention one particular problem, it never made it into the conversation.

When Bill seemed to have run down, Farber said, "Feel better?"

"I guess so. I'd still like for all my problems and frustrations to go away, but that's not going to happen. Instead, I have to deal with them. I need to suck it up and move on."

"So you're not likely to drink?"

"Not today."

"Right answer. That's what we have to hang our hats on—one day at a time." Farber fiddled with the papers on his desk, wondering how to phrase his next question. Finally, he decided to speak plainly. After all, Bill had called him, not the other way around. "I keep waiting for you to mention your personal situation. Doesn't your divorce, the miles that separate you from your wife and son, bother you?"

Bill nodded. "Of course. But I think I've finally reached the point where I realize I can't get Annie and Billy back just by not drinking. My sobriety is necessary, of course, but ultimately it's her decision whether we get back together."

"But you're still staying in touch with your ex-wife? You call her regularly?"

The pastor watched as Bill thought about that. He could see him going over the past few days in his mind. Then he shook his head.

"I...I usually call Annie every week or so. You know, ask about Billy, see what's new with them, that sort of thing. I've intended to do that this weekend, but, come to think of it, I didn't."

"Why do you think that is?" Farber asked.

"I guess I've just been too busy."

"Is that it... or have thoughts of reuniting with your ex-wife been replaced in your mind by a plan for you to marry someone else—someone like Sarah Gordon?"

Kyle Andrews hurried up the walk to Pastor Steve Farber's house, the aroma from the wrapped loaf of fresh French bread he held drifting up to his nostrils and making his stomach rumble. He looked forward to dinner with Steve, but when he thought of the conversation he needed to have first, his hunger threatened to vanish as quickly as it had manifested itself.

He had his hand poised over the bell when the door opened, and he almost ran into Detective Bill Larson. Larson's head was down, his mind obviously elsewhere, and it was only quick work on Kyle's part that prevented a full-on collision. The detective looked up at the last minute, stopped in his tracks, and said, "Sorry. I guess—"

"Yeah, I know. Your mind was a thousand miles away. Been there."

Larson hurried to the curb, trailing one last word of apology after him.

Steve Farber appeared in the doorway Larson had just vacated. "Come in, come in." He reached out and took the loaf of bread. "I'm going to wrap this in foil and put it in a low oven to keep it warm. You know where my study is. Make yourself at home."

Kyle eased into the club chair, figuring from his prior visit that the pastor would take a seat in what appeared to be his favorite chair, leaving the two men facing each other.

Sure enough, Farber headed straight for the wing chair. When he was seated, he said to Kyle, "Well, what's on your mind this time? Still having trouble letting Sarah deal with her grief in her own way?"

"No, I've pretty well reconciled myself to that," Kyle said. "After meeting with you, I made an effort to pull back and stop pressuring her to get over it, the way I did. For a while, she was leaning on me a lot, and frankly, I enjoyed her dependence. But lately she's started acting more independent, to the point of not really needing me anymore."

"Isn't that what you want?" Farber said.

"I'm not sure. There's something else going on, something I guess I ought to share with you."

Farber nodded but remained silent.

"I've had feelings for Sarah since Harry's death... maybe even before then, after I lost Nicole. These feelings—I don't know if you'd call them love or need or what—but they've driven me to do some crazy things."

"Such as..."

"Well, most recently I recorded one of her phone conversations with me. And I've seriously considered stalking her."

Sarah had no sooner gone through the sliding glass doors that marked Centennial Hospital's emergency entrance than her cell phone began to ring. She looked at the display and saw that the call came from inside the hospital. She was at least half an hour early for her shift. Did the ER need her now? Would she have to stay a bit late? She moved to a quiet area at the end of the registration desk and answered the call.

"Dr. Gordon, this is Madge in the hospital administrator's office. Can you come here now?"

"Is this something we can handle over the phone?" Sarah said. "I'm just about to go on duty in the ER."

Sarah heard a male voice in the background.

"Hang on a second," Madge said. Then her voice was replaced by what passed for music on hold at the hospital.

Sarah was about to hang up when she heard the same male voice, this time talking directly into the phone. She hadn't heard it much lately, but when he identified himself she had no reason to doubt him. "Dr. Gordon, this is Reginald Archer. I need to see you in my office right now."

"Mr. Archer, can this wait? It's almost time for me to go to work in the ER."

"That's what I wanted to tell you face-to-face, but since you seem to be forcing my hand, I'll tell you on the phone. You're not going on duty. You're suspended."

23

Steve Farber wondered sarcastically if perhaps there was something in the water. Or maybe it was the phase of the moon. Two men had come to him for counseling today, and the crux of both visits was either infatuation or love for the same widowed doctor in his congregation. *They certainly didn't talk about this in seminary.*

"Do you think you've always had feelings for Sarah?" he asked Kyle Andrews.

"I've tried to sort it out, and I'm not sure," Kyle said. "If I did while Harry was alive, I must have buried them pretty deeply. After all, they were happily married."

"So what you're experiencing now came on after Harry Gordon's death."

"It's been gradual, I think. When someone tried to set her house on fire, I'm the one she called. When that same person took a shot at her, she phoned me—although, come to think of it, she also called Detective Larson."

"And did that make you jealous?" Farber asked.

"I...well...maybe a little, I guess."

"Why were you jealous? A crime had been committed. Larson's job is to investigate."

Kyle didn't have an answer for that. He shook his head.

"Do you think competing with Larson affected your feelings toward Sarah Gordon?" Farber asked.

Kyle frowned and was quiet. The pastor didn't break the silence. *Let him think. He's intelligent. He'll see it in a moment.*

Kyle sighed. "I guess it intensified the attraction I felt. And I haven't mentioned this to you yet, but I think she's seeing someone else now."

"And if she starts dating anyone at this point, it should be you. I mean, after all you've done, it's only fair. Is that what you think?"

After a prolonged silence, Kyle melted like a schoolboy who's just had his theories smashed by a patient but authoritative teacher. "I see what you're saying," he said.

"And what do you plan to do with your newfound insight?" Farber asked.

"I really don't know."

"Let's talk about it some more," the pastor asked. "And then maybe we should pray about it."

"So I'm suspended?" Sarah worked to keep her voice down, but it was all she could do to maintain a halfway civil tone. "Care to tell me why?"

"Doctor, I wanted to avoid an outburst like this, which is why I asked you to come to my office. Unfortunately, you had to hear the news over the phone, and I'm sorry about that." The hospital administrator pointed to the chairs across from his desk. "But now that you're here, please sit down and give me a chance to explain. When I'm through, I believe you'll understand."

Sarah dropped her backpack on the floor beside her, grabbed both wooden arms of one of the chairs opposite Archer, and slowly lowered herself into a sitting position. Her actions throughout were deliberate, but when she looked down she saw that her knuckles were white as her hands gripped the chair. What she really wanted to do, she thought, was vault over the desk, grab the lapels of the administrator's gray pinstripe suit jacket, and shake him.

Archer leaned back in his executive swivel chair, tented his fingertips, and said, "First, let me say that I and all of us here in administration understand the stress you're under, not just with the deaths of your husband and daughter, but the events that have taken place in the past week or more."

Sarah bit down so hard she felt her jaw pop. Obviously, the hospital's gossip network was working well, even though she'd tried to keep the knowledge of what she was going through confined to a few people. *And what does it matter if he knows? Don't look for another fight to pick. You have enough to worry about, Sarah.*

"I've heard from the ER personnel about the way you handled the man who pulled a gun down there on Sunday. It was very brave of you to face him, then to distract him until the security guard and a policeman could subdue him. You're to be congratulated."

"Thanks, I guess. But I didn't ask for a medal. Matter of fact, I had thoughts for just a moment of pulling a gun and trying to shoot the man instead of reasoning with him."

"I realize that," Archer said. "You had a revolver in your backpack, and for a brief moment you had it in your hand. Unfortunately, that was the cause of the problem we now have."

Sarah shook her head as though trying to drive away a bothersome fly. "What? I don't know what you mean."

"As you may know, we have signs at every hospital entrance saying that it's against the law to bring guns onto the property. This, of course, doesn't apply to sworn law officers and our security people, but—"

"But the man with the gun broke the law. I realize that. I imagine he'll pay a fine or get some jail time."

"He will, but you also broke the law. And, unfortunately, an older couple was in the ER awaiting treatment of the husband. They saw you with your pistol and reported it to the police and to this office. The police were willing to ignore your possession of the gun, given the outcome of the incident. I met with the people who made the complaint and finally convinced them to drop the matter, providing I counseled you and suspended you for two days."

"That's—"

"I discussed this with Dr. Crenshaw, your supervisor in the ER, and he's arranged for someone else to cover your shifts. You'll be off for two days, but they'll be treated as additional vacation, so you'll still be paid. I look forward to seeing you back here..." He looked at the calendar on his desk. "I'll see you on Thursday. Please check in with this office before you go on duty."

Sarah wasn't sure how to react, but as they both rose and Archer extended his hand to her, his parting words effectively silenced any further arguments she might have. "Oh, and although I didn't mention this to the couple who complained, I suggest you continue with the application process for your carry permit. But don't bring the pistol to work, even when it's legal for you to have it with you."

Sarah was in her car, almost home, when her cell phone rang. Had something come up in the ER that made them put out an "all hands on deck" call? Did Chuck Crenshaw want to talk with her about her suspension? Could he be calling to tell her not to bother coming back? *Stop imagining things, Sarah, and answer the call.*

"Dr. Gordon."

"Sarah, this is Brad Selleck. I couldn't remember what time your tour of duty started. Can you talk?"

"Sure." *Actually, I have lots of time.* "Is something wrong with Prince?"

"Not at all. As I told you earlier today, he's healing quite well."

"When will you want to take out the stitches?" Sarah asked.

"You didn't notice because of the dressing covering the wound, but I used subcuticular sutures to close the incision I made when I explored the wound. There's nothing on the surface for him to scratch and no sutures to remove. I was calling to see if you'd like to bring him home tomorrow."

"As it happens, I'm off tomorrow. Why don't I come over sometime around mid-morning? We can visit a bit, and then I'll take Prince home." *Home to where he came from—home to Hunter Gordon—because I don't know if I can take care of him anymore.*

When Sarah ended the call, she thought back to her first encounter with Brad Selleck. Certainly she'd felt gratitude for the work he'd done to treat Prince, but there was more to it than that. Brad caused her to have feelings, feelings she hadn't experienced since Harry's death. She struggled to put her finger on exactly what was causing those feelings... and what they represented.

When she was with him, Sarah felt comfortable. That was the simplest way to put it. Sure, there was some physical attraction as well. She couldn't deny it. But the way she felt around Brad was the key. Could it be...? No. She wasn't ready to name this feeling, to call it by the "L" word. But she definitely was ready to explore it further.

Maybe her survivor guilt was lessening. Perhaps the dark night that had engulfed Sarah since her husband and daughter were killed was lifting. Or maybe this was the message she'd been seeking, one that said, "It's okay to live again. Harry would want you to. And, by the way, do you see the person I've prepared to step into your life?"

Kyle Andrews leaned back in his chair and resisted the temptation to ease his belt out a notch. Dinner with Steve

Farber had been relaxing, as well as delicious. Now, as he sat at the pastor's dining room table with a cup of coffee and the crumbs from a piece of homemade pie in front of him, Kyle wondered if they were going to take up their conversation where they'd left it.

"Thinking about what we were talking about earlier?" Farber asked.

"You certainly know how to make a person examine his motives," Kyle said. "Surely they don't teach counseling like this in seminary."

"They teach some, but not like this," the pastor said. "I have to confess that I've learned more about counseling by observing and talking with my congregation than I did from books and lectures in the seminary. It's strange. Once you look at it closely, the human condition never really changes much. For instance, your feelings toward Sarah Gordon aren't much different than those described in the book of Second Samuel. Like King David, you saw a beautiful woman who appeared to be in love with someone else, so your own feelings toward her increased."

"You're talking about the story of David and Bathsheba," Kyle said. "Well, I hope I don't let my yearnings make me go as far as he did."

Farber emptied his coffee cup before he spoke. Then he very deliberately put it down on the saucer, pushed away the dishes, and said, "I hope so, too."

It was dark, although not late enough for Dr. Gordon to be home. Nevertheless, his route took him by the house and, as was his habit, he slowed so he could look at it. A light shone through the front window as usual. She undoubtedly had the lamp on a timer, something homeowners often did to give the appearance someone was home.

There was no car at the curb, nor was one visible in the driveway. When Dr. Gordon came home, she used the garage now. That, among other things, was a change he'd noticed since he began what he liked to think of as his campaign of terror.

He was about to speed up when he caught movement out of the corner of his eye. Had someone or something moved past the living room window? He thought he knew her schedule, and right now Sarah Gordon should be on duty in the hospital emergency room. Was she ill? Had there been some change?

At first, he thought about driving on by. Before, he'd always thought out his moves well in advance. He didn't like the idea of doing something spontaneously. That was one of the things that could easily compromise an otherwise well-thought-out plan. On the other hand, perhaps fate was handing him an opportunity he should seize. His hand patted the Beretta in his waistband. Maybe this would be the day.

No harm in checking. He parked a block farther down the street, made certain the pistol was securely under his belt and his shirt tail covered it, then walked casually back toward Gordon's house like a man out for an after-dinner stroll. When he was almost past her home, he quickly looked around, then darted down beside the house and flattened himself against it. He was near one of the windows in the living room, and he could hear her voice coming clearly from inside.

She was on the phone with someone named Connie.

"Yes, Connie. I'm going to be okay, but I appreciate your call. Are things going smoothly in the ER?"

She was silent as she listened, then she said, "Well, I'll only be off tonight and tomorrow night. I'll see you again on Thursday."

She'll be home again tomorrow night. That would give him time to fine-tune his plan. He crept away from the house before anyone could see him. "Enjoy tonight," he muttered. "I wanted you to suffer like we all suffered. But now I think it's time to end it. Tomorrow night, you die."

24

SARAH STOOD BEFORE THE OPEN DOOR OF HER CLOSET AND debated what to wear today. *Don't make a big thing of this. You're just going to pick up Prince from the vet's.* But this trip would also mean seeing Dr. Brad Selleck, and she wanted to look nice. She still wasn't certain why. This was a new sensation for her. Could she be turning the corner, thinking about moving on with her life? Was the widow ready to enter society again?

Sarah carefully counted the months since Harry's death—almost nine. Everything she'd heard, everything she'd read, said she shouldn't make any important decisions until at least a year had gone by since her loss. Sarah knew her emotions were still subject to rapid changes, triggered by things as simple as hearing a song she and Harry used to like or seeing a child that reminded her of Jenny. Her feelings were settling down with the passage of time, but they were still unpredictable enough that she knew she had to move cautiously.

But what if she decided not to move forward right now? What if she didn't start dating again? Would that door close? Would it remain shut for who knew how long—perhaps forever? Could this be her one chance?

If she were going to start dating someone, there were three men—all of whom were members of her church—who'd expressed an interest in her one way or another. There was

Kyle, whom she'd known the longest. Since Harry's death, Kyle had shown himself to be someone she could depend on. In the midst of the stress that accompanied her tormentor's actions, it was Kyle to whom she turned. She'd noticed lately that he seemed to want to be more than a friend, but that was the way she thought of Kyle—as a friend, but not as a potential husband.

What about Bill Larson? He'd definitely shown more than just a professional interest in her case, and in her. He was divorced, probably because of the alcoholism that seemed to be common knowledge in the community. As best Sarah could tell, Larson was winning the fight against his addiction, but she wasn't sure whether he was trying to reestablish a connection with his former wife. She was no psychiatrist, but Sarah figured Larson's attraction to her, if indeed there were one, was something like a rebound phenomenon.

That left Brad Selleck. She'd only met the man recently, yet there'd been an indefinable attraction, almost an electric tingle when she was around him. More than that, she felt comfortable in his presence. There was something about Brad, something she couldn't quite put her finger on, that made her want to see more of him. Well, it couldn't hurt to explore the relationship. And, frankly, she was looking forward to seeing him again.

With one last look into her closet, Sarah pulled out a skirt and blouse and tossed them onto her bed. *After all, it's not the clothes, but the person wearing them that's important.* But then she put back that outfit and selected another. *This is ridiculous. You're acting like a teenager going on her first date.*

Sarah was rescued from the throes of indecision by the ring of her cell phone. She retrieved it from the charging cable at her bedside and answered the call.

"Hey, how are things going?"

The caller didn't identify himself, but Sarah had no problem recognizing the voice of Harry's father, Hunter Gordon.

She'd planned to phone him anyway, but he'd beaten her to it. "Hunter, I'm so glad you called," she said.

"Is everything okay with you? And how's that dog?"

"I'm doing well, and they tell me that Prince is recovering nicely. Matter of fact, I'm going to pick him up today and was planning to bring him to the farm so he could convalesce there."

"I'll be glad to see you, and I'll take care of Prince if you want me to, but I hope you'll take him back as soon as he no longer needs any post-op care."

"I...You know dogs, Hunter. Tell me truthfully. Prince was shot while in my yard. He'd been guarding me. Do you think he'll be hesitant to be back here, to be around me? I mean, is it likely that Prince will blame me for his getting shot?"

"You haven't had a dog before, have you?" Hunter asked.

"Not really. But I've been around them some. We seem to get along."

"None of us really knows what goes through a dog's mind, but I don't think there's any chance Prince can connect the dots and associate you and your place with the fact that somebody shot him," her father-in-law said. "My guess is that he'll be glad to see you and happy to be back in what he probably already considers his new home."

"So you don't think he'll associate getting shot with me and this location?"

"It's more likely that Prince will be sorry he hasn't been there to fulfill his function as a guard dog." She heard the sound of Hunter's deep breath before his next words. "Tell you what. Why don't you go ahead and bring Prince home with you? What time do you have to go to work this afternoon?"

"I...I'll be off for the next couple of days." *No need to tell him why. That was a bit embarrassing.*

"I'll come by late this afternoon, then. We can have dinner together, my treat, and discuss where we go from here with Prince."

"Sounds okay," Sarah said. "But instead of going out, let me cook for you."

"I won't argue. There's nothing I'd like better than visiting with you over a home-cooked meal," he said. "I'll see you later today."

After the call ended, Sarah sat on the edge of the bed and thought about what Hunter just said. Maybe she'd been beating herself up for nothing. Perhaps Prince would be happy to be back with her. Well, in a few hours she'd know.

Meanwhile, Sarah wanted to seek the counsel of someone who might shed some light on the problem with which she was currently wrestling.

Steve Farber looked around the crowded Starbucks coffee house and finally spotted Sarah Gordon at a table for two in the corner. He signaled that he'd seen her, then gave his order at the counter. In a few moments, he was seated across from her, blowing across his *grande* Caffé Americano to hasten the cooling process.

"Thank you for coming," she said.

"Happy to do it." He looked around. "Would you like to see if one of the tables outside would give us more privacy, or is this okay with you?"

Sarah shook her head. "I'd prefer not to sit outside."

"Weather?" he asked. "It is a bit windy."

"No, I just feel too much like a target," she said, gazing into her coffee cup.

So, she was still worried about the stalker. Well, maybe that would soon end. "So, what's on your mind?"

Sarah stared into her cup. "Harry's been gone for almost nine months now. I've been warned against making any major decisions during this first year after his death."

The pastor nodded. He was familiar with this bit of conventional wisdom. He'd received that same advice from numerous friends after his own wife died. Like most such advice, he'd found that it held true in some instances, not in others. Everyone had to decide the best timetable for them.

"What makes you ask?" the pastor said.

"Let me say up front that I haven't been looking to replace Harry. Even if I marry again, the man won't be a substitute for the person I lost. But recently I've met someone in whom I'm interested."

The pastor sipped his Caffé Americano, both to enjoy the coffee and to buy time before he responded. He leaned closer to Sarah. "Is this someone you know fairly well? Or someone you've been thrown together with in some sort of situation?"

She surprised him with her answer. "Actually, I just met him less than a week ago."

Farber's raised eyebrows must have caught Sarah's attention. She hurried on. "I know. It's crazy. But I liked him the first time I met him. I felt at ease with him. And, strange as it sounds, I wondered if God was directing me to him."

Is there an epidemic of this sort of thing? "Sarah, I'm sure you're familiar with the 'rebound' phenomenon. It's not confined to men and women who latch onto someone quickly after a relationship breaks up. It happens to people who are widowed, or those whose fiancé dies. Are you certain this isn't what's happening?"

"I guess it could be, but somehow I don't think this is a rebound. And if it were, there are two men whom I know better than this man, men who have shown definite signs they're interested in me. I think I'd be drawn to one of them."

Interesting. I wonder if she's talking about Kyle Andrews and Bill Larson. "So, your question is what?"

"I wonder if it would be okay to date him. I don't mean to get serious. I'm not ready to remarry. But I really want someone to talk with, to sit down to an occasional meal with, to... to share with." She looked up at the pastor and her eyes glistened with unshed tears. "I was hoping you could give me some advice. And I guess the real question in my mind is should I wait longer? And if it's too soon, how long should I wait?"

Farber put down the Starbucks cup he'd been holding and folded his hands on the table. "Let's look at it this way. How long were you and Harry married?"

"Almost four years."

"And were you happy?"

"Very much so. Oh, there were times when I wanted to shake him until he rattled, because he frustrated me. And I'm sure the reverse was true. But those instances were rare. Yes, I believe we were happy in our marriage."

"Do you think Harry would want you to be happy again?"

Sarah was silent for a moment. "You're the second person who's asked me that. And, yes, I'm certain he would."

"Then all the other questions become moot. If God's presented you with a gift in the form of a man you like, someone with whom you can share, someone to talk with—take the gift. See where it goes. And never mind what the calendar says."

All the way to the Ashton Veterinary Clinic, Sarah replayed her conversation with Steve Farber. If Harry would want her to be happy, then by all means she should take the opportunity for happiness when it was presented. Her own feelings, after Harry's death, of course, were a mixture of grief for loss—both his and hers—and guilt that she was left behind. Sarah recognized that since that time she'd lived each day with an overtone affecting all her actions and feelings, one that said, "He's gone. I'm here, but I shouldn't enjoy it, because he can't."

She knew about survivor guilt. She'd counseled people about it. But she had tried to ignore her own. *And what would Harry have to say about that?* When she had tough decisions to make, difficult things to do, she'd thought about Harry's voice, saying, "Go ahead, Sarah. You can do it. You're strong."

But this time, she heard a different message. Just as clearly as if he were speaking in her ear, Harry said, "Just because I'm gone is no reason for you to roll over and die. God has given you this day—enjoy it."

I will, Harry. I will.

She parked her car in front of the veterinary clinic and hurried up the walk. The receptionist greeted her with a smile. "Hi, Dr. Gordon. I think Prince will be glad to see you. Do you remember how to get to his kennel?"

Sure enough, Prince welcomed her with a couple of yips, followed by enthusiastic wagging of his tail. She noted that the incision Brad had made to explore the gunshot wound and control bleeding was no longer covered by a dressing, and it appeared to be healing cleanly. Now she could see for herself that there were no external stitches to remove, or for Prince to gnaw at. It appeared the dog was indeed ready to leave the hospital.

"Looks pretty good, doesn't he?"

Sarah turned and saw Brad coming toward her. As usual, he wore a knee-length white coat covering casual clothes. He stopped about a yard away. "I notice that you got here around noon again. Did you come prepared for me to buy your lunch?"

"Aren't you getting tired of taking me out to lunch every day?"

"Not at all," Brad said. "But I don't want to come off too strong, either. If you'd rather not—"

"No," Sarah said. Then she added, "I was sort of looking forward to it."

Around them, the noon rush of the restaurant provided a curtain of noise that shielded their conversation from anyone more than a few feet away. Despite this, Brad and Sarah were quiet. Usually, they found a great deal to talk about, but today seemed different. Brad Selleck knew why.

He kept his eyes focused on his salad as he used his fork to move the same piece of lettuce from the right edge of his bowl to the left and back again.

"If you really enjoy stirring vegetables around, you can play with my salad, too," Sarah said. "You haven't eaten more than a bite or two since we sat down. Is something wrong?"

"Wow, I can't put anything past you, can I?" Brad said. "I guess I'm trying to decide the best way to say this."

Sarah put down her fork and pushed her dish away. "The way you put it, it sounds like bad news. I've always found the best way to deliver news like that is to get it out there quickly, sort of like ripping off a bandage." Her tone was light, but the expression on her face was serious.

"Okay," he said. "Here goes. You're a beautiful, intelligent woman who happens to also like dogs. In other words, you're three for three on my rating scale."

"I sense a 'but' coming," Sarah said.

"No. Well, maybe. I guess so. Remember, I told you I'm also a member of the First Community Church, so when you came here the first time, I knew you'd become a widow less than a year ago. I wanted to get to know you better, but because of your situation I tried to hang back, not be too forward. It was difficult—actually, almost impossible for me—because I sensed some interest on your part. And that made me hopeful. But I kept wondering if it wasn't too soon for you."

Sarah nodded, but remained silent.

Brad drank half his glass of iced tea, but his throat still felt dry. "We haven't known each other very long, and you may not be ready to move ahead with dating anyone, but…"

Sarah raised her eyebrows and leaned forward. Apparently, she wasn't going to make this easy on him.

"But when you are," Brad said, "I'd like to be a part of your plans."

He wasn't sure how Sarah would take his declaration. It had taken courage for him to say what he had just voiced, and he'd tried to prepare himself for almost any reaction to his declaration—rejection, disappointment, anger, happiness—but what he saw took the wind out of his sails completely.

Sarah pulled a tissue from her purse and gently wiped away two tears that slowly wended their way down her cheeks. Despite the tears, she wasn't sobbing. Matter of fact, there was a hint of a smile on her face. After a moment, she reached out and covered his hand with hers. "I've wrestled with this situation since Harry died. For the first several months, I was certain I'd live alone for the rest of my life. After all, I'd lost my husband and baby daughter. How could I ever be happy again?"

"I think I understand," Brad said softly.

She continued as though he had said nothing. "Then someone—we still don't know who or why—but someone began to harass me. His actions became increasingly violent, and I leaned on one of Harry's friends for support. But when that man started giving off signs that he wanted to be more than a friend, my first reaction was wondering whether moving forward with my life would be..."

After a moment of silence, Selleck completed her sentence. "Disrespectful to your late husband's memory."

Sarah nodded. "Maybe that's it, although I don't think I used those words. But at any rate, I didn't think seriously about dating again until I met you. Then I really began wondering if it was too soon"

"And what did you decide?"

"I received the same counsel from two people I asked—ignore the calendar and ask myself if my late husband would want me to be happy. I've thought about it, prayed about it, and I think the answer is 'yes.'"

"So..."

"It's too soon in our relationship to get serious, but it would be wonderful to have someone to talk with, someone I could share with. And, if you agree, I want that someone to be you. And as things progress...who knows?"

Prince lay quietly in the back seat of Sarah's car, looking right and left as though he might be asked to describe the scenery or even guide her back to the veterinary clinic. When she had finally left there after a chaste hug from Brad and a promise to talk later, Prince trotted at her heels to the car. True, he'd moved a bit slowly, as though testing the strength of his surgical wound, but there'd been no hesitancy in his following her. Maybe he didn't associate her with the shooting—or perhaps he'd forgiven her for any role she might have had in it.

As Sarah turned down the last street before home, Prince sat up and gave a low growl. He didn't bark, didn't cower in a corner of the car's seat. Rather, he seemed to sense trouble ahead and was warning her of it.

"That's okay, Prince," she said. "The last time you were here, you encountered a prowler, and he hurt you. But he's not here now. And I'm not going to let anything bad happen to you. I want you to know that. Just as you've been trained to take care of me, I'll watch out for you, too." She looked in her rear view mirror and noted that Prince had once more assumed a position lying in the center of the seat, turned toward the side of the street on which her house sat—a true guard dog position.

Sarah went through the routine to which she'd almost become accustomed—disarm her security system, open the garage door, pull in, close the door, exit the car and rearm the system once she was inside the house. Prince came out of the car without coaxing. Once he was inside he took a quick tour around the kitchen, sniffed once at his now-empty food and water bowls, and then settled into a position facing the door to the garage.

"Good dog," Sarah said. "And when you need to go outside, I may go out with you." She lifted her purse and felt the reassuring heft of the revolver in it. "And this time, I dare our mystery man to come around."

Kyle Andrews had worked through the lunch hour, nibbling at a sandwich of indeterminate composition while plowing through a stack of legal papers. When he made the last note on the last page of the contract, he tossed the document into his "out" basket, leaned back, and heaved the contented sigh of a man who has just completed a task he's been dreading for far too long.

The clock on his desk, a handsome timepiece mounted in a mahogany square, had been a gift from some group to which he'd spoken—he couldn't recall which one, and he didn't want to lean forward far enough to read the inscription. He could see just enough to determine that the time was about half past three. Kyle had been doing a lot of thinking since his evening with Steve Farber, and some of his soul-searching hadn't made him feel very good about himself. Now it was time to pass on that information to another person. And he dreaded this even more than he'd dreaded the legal work he'd just completed.

He should have called Sarah earlier, but the time had slipped away from him. Kyle tried to remember her schedule. Ordinarily, she'd just be getting started on her shift about now. On the other hand, if she were off today, this would be a good time to call. Well, either she'd answer or she wouldn't. He'd let her response dictate his.

Kyle picked his cell phone off the desk and chose Sarah's number from his short list of "favorites." She answered on the third ring.

"Sarah, this is Kyle. Not working today?"

"I'm... that is... no, I'm off today. Can I help you with something?"

"I was wondering if I could come by in a few hours to talk with you, maybe take you to dinner. I have some things I need to discuss."

She hesitated for a moment, then almost blurted out her answer, as though she had to hurry before changing her mind, "I think I need to tell you some things, too. Why don't you come to my house about six? I'll fix us a bit of supper, and we can talk."

Sarah's phone rang about five thirty. Was this Kyle, saying he'd be late... or not coming?

"Sarah, this is Hunter Gordon. I'm sorry to call so late, but when I told you I'd come by I completely forgot I had an obligation this evening that I can't skip. Would it be okay if I come tomorrow about mid-morning? That is, if you still want me to bring Prince back here to the farm to continue his convalescence."

She closed her eyes and shook her head at her forgetfulness. When Sarah invited Kyle to come for supper, it had slipped her mind that her father-in-law was going to come by and pick up Prince this evening. Oh, well. This would be better. "Sure. Prince will be glad to see you then, and I'm sure he and I will do fine this evening. I'll see you tomorrow."

"Thanks for understanding. Put on a fresh pot of coffee about mid-morning. I'll see you then."

Sarah went back into the kitchen, and as soon as she came into the room Prince slowly got up, walked to the door leading to the backyard, and stood there, looking up at her. His expression clearly said, "I'm glad you remembered me. Now would you please open this door?"

She did just that, then hurried to the living room and grabbed her pistol out of her purse. Sarah felt foolish holding the pistol at her side when she stepped into the backyard, but she figured she'd feel even more foolish if her stalker chose that moment to come by and take another shot at Prince.

The dog moved a bit more slowly than usual, but otherwise showed no evidence of his recent injury. Prince took a few moments to accomplish his business, strolled around the yard a couple of times as though to make certain nothing had changed, and then headed back inside.

Back in the house, Sarah dropped the pistol inside her purse, but before she could decide what to do next, there was a knock at the door. Was Kyle early? Had Hunter decided to come anyway?

She opened the front door and said, "This is a surprise." She was about to say more, but stopped when she saw the gun pointed at her.

25

Sarah's voice showed the surprise she felt. "Tom, what are you doing with that gun?"

Tom Oliver edged past her and closed the door behind him. He gestured with the pistol he held. "I'm going to kill you, of course. But first, why don't we go into the living room? I think that will be a good place for what I have in mind."

"Tom, why are you behaving this way? I've never seen you act like this before."

"That's all you've seen," he said. "Acting. I put on a great performance so you'd never suspect me."

"What do you mean?"

"Actors have what they call 'method acting.' They talk about 'motivation.' Well, that's what I've had. That's why I've been able to act like a normal contractor for the time I've been working at your house. I've had motivation."

Sarah wasn't sure how to handle this, but for now she wanted to keep the man talking. That way she could buy a few more minutes of life. "I don't understand. What motivation? Why are you doing this?"

"Revenge, of course."

"Revenge for what? You can't be angry about my drawing the blood alcohol on your son."

"Oh, no. That has nothing to do with this. My son got straight after that little incident, and he enlisted in the Marines." Tom used his gun to wave her to the couch. "Why don't you move over there? I think it will be better, and—"

"Wait," Sarah said. "I've seen the car my stalker drives, and it's a dark sedan. You drive a red pickup. Where did the dark car come from?"

"My wife's," he said.

"You mean she knows what you've been doing?"

"Oh, I suspect she understands. So does Tommy. So does the Hawkins family."

"What do you—"

"Sarah, are you here?" Kyle's voice moved closer with every word. "No one answered my knock, and the front door was open."

Perhaps she could warn Kyle before he walked into the room. Sarah raised her voice as much as she dared. "Tom, please put that gun away!"

Over Tom's shoulder, Sarah saw Kyle appear in the doorway. He dropped to one knee and reached down for his ankle holster. At the same time that Kyle moved, Tom whirled and fired at him. Kyle's change in position turned what would have been a bullet in the attorney's body into a shot that hit his left shoulder—not a fatal wound, but enough to put him out of commission for the moment.

Blood began to flow from Kyle's left shoulder, leaving a dark stain on his suit coat. He straightened up in a series of jerks and grabbed the injured area with his right hand, pressing to hold pressure against the wound.

"Tom, please. Don't shoot again," Sarah called.

Tom's voice was flat. He showed no emotion. It seemed as though he were outside the scene, observing the action. "Well, this complicates things a little, but I can improvise. That's what marks a good actor, you know. I can improvise, handle any situation."

Sarah moved toward Kyle. "You need to let me look at that wound," she said. A wave of Tom's pistol stopped her. She almost shouted, "Don't you realize he could bleed to death?"

"It doesn't matter," Tom said with a strange smile. "You're both going to die anyway."

"Tom—" Kyle said in a weak voice.

"Shut up!" Tom snapped. He motioned with the gun. "Get over there by the doctor," he said. "I wish I could have strung this out a bit longer, but I think it's time to end it. All it will take is three shots." He pointed with his free hand— first at Sarah, then at Kyle, then at himself. "After that, none of us will have any worries."

Sarah heard a faint sound from the kitchen. As Kyle moved toward her, still holding his bleeding shoulder, she edged to her right to get a better view of the doorway.

Prince stopped and crouched there in a position of readiness. The fur on his neck was standing up. His mouth was slightly open, his teeth bared, but he made no sound. The dog stared at Tom Oliver, and Sarah could almost hear him asking if he should attack, begging for her to give the command. Could she do that? Could she ask him to risk being shot once more? She decided she had no choice.

In a sharp voice, she called, "Prince. *Fass.*"

With two giant bounds, the dog, showing no evidence of his recent gunshot wound, leaped at Tom's gun hand, clamped his teeth onto it, and tugged. Tom tried to turn the pistol on Prince, but the German shepherd was too strong.

While this was happening, Kyle released the pressure he was holding on his shoulder wound long enough to pull his pistol from its holster on his right ankle. But when he extracted the pistol, Sarah saw that Kyle's right hand was visibly shaking. He was going into shock from blood loss.

Fearing that Kyle was about to drop the revolver, Sarah took it from him and pointed it at Tom. "Drop the gun, then kick it over here."

Tom hesitated only a moment before he complied. "Get this dog off me," he called.

Sarah stooped and picked up Tom's semiautomatic pistol. Now, with a gun in either hand, she spoke again in a firm voice. "Prince. *Aus*." Upon that command, the dog released his hold. Tom immediately cradled his injured right hand under his left arm.

"Prince, *Wache*."

Prince assumed a guarding position. Tom kept his eyes fixed on the dog, but made no movement.

"Hello? Anyone home?" Bill Larson came through the door of the living room. As soon as he took in the situation, he crouched and drew his gun, but didn't seem sure at whom to point it.

"Bill," Sarah said. "Tom Oliver tried to kill both of us. Prince made him drop the gun. Cuff him while I call an ambulance for Kyle."

When Larson approached Tom to handcuff him, Prince growled. After Sarah gave the command *Lass*, the dog relaxed and backed away, but remained watchful.

"There's a word in German I'm supposed to use that means 'good dog,' but I forget what it is," Sarah said.

"I think the tone of voice will let him know what we mean," Larson said. After he'd cuffed Oliver, the detective reached a tentative hand toward Prince's head, patted him, and said, "Good dog."

Sarah went around her kitchen table, pouring coffee for the three men sitting there. She filled her own cup and turned back to the counter where the coffee maker sat. This was Saturday morning—fifteen days since the fire, twelve days since the first shot was fired at her, less than three days since Tom Oliver came very close to killing her and Kyle. So much had happened in her life in the past few weeks. Most of it was bad, but now things seemed to be looking up.

Hunter Gordon lifted his cup and blew across the surface. To Hunter's right was Bill Larson, a thin manila folder before him. Across from Hunter sat Kyle Andrews, his left arm in a sling, looking a bit wan. Sarah replaced the coffee pot on its warming plate, then took the remaining chair at the table.

"I'm glad you asked me to be a part of this meeting," Hunter said.

"I thought we should all get together so everyone knows what happened and why," Sarah said. She turned to Larson. "Do you want to start the explanation?"

The detective tapped the folder that lay unopened in front of him. "Cal Johnson and I spent a couple of hours questioning Tom Oliver after I arrested him. I gave him the standard Miranda warning, but he said he didn't want a lawyer. I told him he had the right to remain silent, but it seemed he couldn't wait to tell us what he was doing. He seemed proud of the way he managed to fool everyone."

"The man's insane," Hunter said.

"Of course, it's going to be up to a psychiatrist to determine whether he knew what he was doing was wrong, but Oliver laid it out like it made perfect sense to him."

"I can't believe he'd do something like this," Sarah said.

"No one did," Larson said. "He put on a great act for everyone. I'm sure he seemed like a perfectly nice guy. He did to me."

"He had me fooled, and I probably knew him as well as anyone...or thought I did," Kyle said.

"Why didn't he go after me while he and his crew were working in the house?" Sarah asked.

"His scheme involved inflicting as much emotional pain on you as possible," Larson said. "If he simply shot you without making you suffer first, his whole idea of revenge went out the window."

"Revenge for what?" Sarah asked. "I still haven't figured out that one."

"The revenge was for the deaths of Mr. and Mrs. Hawkins."

"I don't understand," Sarah said. "Harry didn't kill Mrs. Hawkins. She killed him...and Jenny. And Mr. Hawkins committed suicide."

"It doesn't make sense," Hunter said.

"What was his connection with those people?" Sarah asked. "I thought you said the Hawkinses didn't have any family."

"According to Tom Oliver, his father died when he was in junior high. Because his mother worked long hours, Tom went home from school each day to the home of their neighbors, the Hawkins family," Larson said. "Rena Hawkins fed him supper. John Hawkins helped him with his homework while they waited for his mother to pick him up. Mr. and Mrs. Hawkins were like family to him. He even called them Aunt Rena and Uncle John."

"I still don't see the reason behind all this," Sarah said.

"I can hazard a guess," Kyle said. "It probably began when Tommy was killed. Oliver's son enlisted in the Marines after I got him out of that scrape where his friend was driving drunk. Tommy had just finished a tour in Afghanistan and was about ready to come back to the States when an improvised explosive device—an IED—killed him. Oliver had figured his son would carry on the family name. His death was a terrible blow to the man. I think that loss left him a bit unhinged."

"So that was what set him off?" Sarah asked.

"No," Larson said. "That set the stage, but then something else happened that made things worse for Oliver. His wife died of ovarian cancer. After that, he was alone in the world except for Aunt Rena and Uncle John. He leaned heavily on them. Then, after they died—first Rena in the car crash that killed Harry, then John, who committed suicide—Oliver had no one. That's when he decided to take his own life. But first he wanted to exact revenge."

"But the accident wasn't Harry's fault," Hunter said.

"For some reason, Oliver decided it was. And since Harry was dead, he decided to get revenge on Harry's widow." Larson looked at Sarah. "After he'd made you suffer, he was going to kill you, then take his own life." He looked at Kyle. "When you came on the scene, Oliver simply decided it would be easy enough to kill you as well."

"What will happen to him?" Hunter asked.

Kyle looked at Larson. "I presume he's already had an arraignment."

"Yes, and he's been remanded for psychiatric evaluation," the detective said.

"Part of this depends on the outcome of that evaluation," Kyle said, "But I can assure you all that he'll be in some sort of confinement, either in a psychiatric hospital or in prison, for a long time."

Hunter Gordon looked at his watch. "Well, I think I'd better be heading back to the farm." He looked at Sarah. "You've had Prince here for a few days. Do you still want me to take him with me?"

Sarah shook her head. "I don't think so. It's been good to have him with me... to know there's another beating heart in the house."

"What about your work schedule?" Hunter asked.

"I think he and I can make enough adjustments for things to work," she said. "And thanks for training him so well. Those German commands were tough to memorize, but I'm glad I knew them."

"Well, it all came out okay," Larson said. He pushed his chair back from the table. "Now, if you'll excuse me, I need to go, too."

"Work?" Hunter asked.

"No, I need to make a phone call—one that's long overdue."

Kyle stood up. "And I guess I'll go to the office and work a bit," he said.

"Now that I won't be calling on you for help, you should get out of that office more," Sarah said. "Enjoy life a bit."

Kyle nodded and shrugged. "I'll try."

Hunter Gordon was the last out the door. He hugged Sarah and said, "I'm glad you're safe. Now you can get on with your life."

"I'm going to do just that. Thanks." *And I'll start this evening.*

When she heard the knock at the door, Sarah rose from her chair and put down the magazine she was holding but not reading. She paused in front of the mirror in the front room and touched her raven hair. Sarah smoothed away nonexistent wrinkles from the skirt she wore—a red-and-white print that contrasted nicely with her white blouse. *Here goes.*

She opened the door and stepped aside. "I tried the doorbell, but it doesn't seem to be working," Brad said.

"No, it's been out of commission for several months." She wondered why she didn't say Harry had never gotten around to repairing it...and why she didn't tear up at the memory. Maybe what friends told her was right. Maybe the pain did get better with the passage of time.

"I can't believe we're doing something besides hurrying off for a quick lunch," Brad said. "I have reservations at a nice place for dinner."

"Sounds great," Sarah said. "It will give us a chance to talk...to get to know each other better."

"That's what we both need," Brad said. "I realize it's going to take some time, but I'm willing to spend it if you are."

Sarah nodded, but before she could say anything, Prince ambled in from the kitchen.

Brad stooped and ran his hand over the dog's head, being careful to avoid the shoulder where the animal had been wounded. "Prince, it's good to see you. You're not used to seeing me in this place, are you?"

Prince moved beside Sarah and nudged her. Brad stood still until Prince repeated the maneuver with him. After a couple more nudges, the two stood side by side. Then Prince moved back a few feet and settled into a comfortable position on the floor facing them.

"Can dogs smile?" Sarah asked Brad.

"I'm not sure," he answered. "But if they can, that's exactly what Prince is doing." He put one arm across her shoulder. "And I must say I agree. Because I am, too."

Group Discussion Guide

1. Dr. Sarah Gordon was an intelligent, capable physician until the death of her husband and daughter changed her. What changes do you see from the person she apparently used to be? Do you understand them? Why do you think she felt that way?
2. Kyle Andrews is fighting a battle within himself. What forces are pulling him? What do you think will happen next in his life?
3. Detective Bill Larson is a recovering alcoholic. How does this affect his professional and personal life?
4. We can only infer what caused the break-up of Detective Cal Johnson's first marriage. What do you think might have been done differently to save it? Do you think this one will be different?
5. Pastor Steve Farber is also a recovering alcoholic. What are the good and bad points about that? Do you think people with such an addiction should be in the pastorate? Why?
6. Is there a chance Bill Larson will be reunited with his family? Are there things he can do to enhance his chances?
7. What do you think of Connie's approach to witnessing? Would you do it differently? If so, how?
8. What was your take-away message from this novel?

Want to learn more about Richard L. Mabry, M.D.
and check out other great fiction from
Abingdon Press?

Check out our website at
www.AbingdonPress.com
to read interviews with your favorite authors,
find tips for starting a reading group,
and stay posted on what new titles are on the horizon.

Be sure to visit Richard online!

http://www.rmabry.com

We hope you enjoyed *Medical Judgment* by Richard L. Mabry, M.D. and will continue to read his novels of medical suspense. Here's a sample of *Fatal Trauma*, also available from Abingdon Press.

1

DR. MARK BAKER SWEPT HIS STRAW-COLORED HAIR AWAY from his eyes, then wiped his forearm across his brow. He wished the air-conditioning in the emergency room was better. Patients might complain that it was cool, but if you were hurrying from case to case for eight hours or more, it was easy to work up a sweat.

"Nobody move!"

Mark spun toward the doors leading to the ER, where a wild-eyed man pressed a pistol against a nurse's head. She pushed a wheelchair in which another man sat slumped forward, his eyes closed, his arms crossed against his bloody chest. Dark blood oozed from beneath his splayed fingers and dropped in a slow stream, leaving a trail of red droplets on the cream-colored tile.

Behind them, Mark could see a hospital security guard sprawled facedown and motionless on the floor, his gun still in its holster, a crimson worm of blood oozing from his head. Mark's doctor's mind automatically catalogued the injury as a basilar skull fracture. *Probably hit him behind the ear with the gun barrel.*

The gunman was in his late twenties. His caramel-colored skin was dotted with sweat. A scraggly moustache and beard framed lips compressed almost to invisibility. Straight black hair, parted in the middle, topped a face that displayed both fear and distrust. Every few seconds he moved the barrel of the gun away from his hostage's temple long enough to wave it around, almost daring anyone to come near him.

The wounded man was a few years older than the gunman—maybe in his thirties. His swarthy complexion was shading into pallor. Greasy black hair fell helter-skelter over his forehead. His face bore the stubble of several days' worth of beard.

"I mean it," the gunman said. "Nobody move a muscle. My brother needs help, and I'll kill anyone who gets in the way."

Mark's immediate reaction was to look around for the nearest exit, but the gunman's next words made him freeze before he could act.

"You the doc?"

Now the gun was pointed at him. Mark thought furiously of ways to escape without being shot, but he discarded each plan as fast as it crossed his mind. "Yeah, I'm the doc."

The gunman inclined his head toward the man in the wheelchair. "He's...he's been shot." He snatched two ragged breaths. "I want you to fix him, pull him through." He punctuated his words with rapid gestures from the pistol. "If he dies...if he dies, I'm going to kill everyone in here." The gunman turned back toward his hostage. "Starting with her."

Mark's eyes followed the gun as it traversed once more from him to the nurse pushing the wheelchair. To this point his attention had been focused on the gunman, but now that he recognized the hostage, he knew the stakes were even higher. Although her red hair was disheveled, her normally fair skin flushed, there was no mistaking the identity of the woman against whose head the gunman's pistol lay. The nurse was Kelly Atkinson—the woman Mark was dating.

Kelly gritted her teeth against the pain of the gun barrel boring into her temple. Her stomach clenched and churned with the realization that her life was in the hands of this crazed gunman. Her lips barely moved in silent prayer.

Mark's voice seemed remarkably steady to her, considering the circumstances. "I can see that he needs help, and I'll give it, but stop waving that gun around." He nodded toward Kelly. "First of all, I'm going to need some assistance, and the nurse certainly can't help me with you holding that pistol against her head. Why don't you put it down and step away? You can wait over there, and I'll let you know—"

"Shut up!"

Suddenly the pressure on Kelly's temple was gone. Out of the corner of her eye she saw the gunman turn his weapon and his attention once more to Mark. If she was going to act, now was the time. She looked down at the man in the wheelchair and put all the urgency she could muster into her words, "Doctor, I'm not sure he's breathing! He may be in arrest."

Ignoring the gunman, Mark took several steps forward and squatted in front of the wheelchair. He touched the wounded man's neck with two fingers, then placed his stethoscope on the man's chest. In a few seconds, Mark pulled back his bloody hand, straightened and said, "We need to get him into one of the trauma rooms. Right now!"

Ignoring the gunman, Kelly started pushing the wheelchair toward trauma room 2. "What will you need?" she asked over her shoulder.

She hoped Mark's reply would communicate the urgency of the situation and further distract the gunman's attention. He didn't disappoint her. "I need to intubate him and start CPR. Start a couple of IVs with large bore needles so we can push some Lactated Ringer's into him until the blood bank can cross-match him for half a dozen units."

After an emphatic gesture from her, Bob, one of the ER aides reluctantly fell in behind Kelly. Bob's ebony skin couldn't show pallor, but he was sweating profusely. As he followed Kelly, he murmured under his breath, "What does the doctor think he's doing?"

Kelly's answer was a hoarse whisper. "I think he's trying to save everyone's life."

"Hold it right there, Doc," the man with the pistol said. "You don't move unless I tell you to."

Mark watched as the gunman's finger tensed on the trigger of his weapon. He fought to keep his voice steady. "Every second you keep me standing here makes it less likely I can save your brother's life."

The gunman gestured at the door through which Kelly was disappearing with the wounded man. "Okay, but I'll be right behind you." He glared, his brown eyes seeming to bore a hole through Mark. "And remember—if my brother dies, everyone in that room dies—the nurse, you, the aide—everyone."

Out of the corner of his eye, Mark saw the curtains flutter at the ER cubicle he'd recently left, and a faint spark of hope arose in him. To set this up, he had to move. After a split-second's hesitation, he strode swiftly to the open door of the trauma room where Kelly and the aide were already moving the wounded man onto the treatment table.

Despite the sweat that poured out of him a few minutes ago, now Mark felt a chill that went deep into his bones. He probably had one chance to make this end well, but to make that happen, everything had to work perfectly. Otherwise, he and several other people would die.

"Start some oxygen," Kelly said to the aide. "I'll get IVs going."

"Help him, Doc," the gunman snapped.

Mark, at a shade over six feet and a hundred seventy pounds, was larger than the gunman. But the pistol in the man's hand was a great equalizer. Besides, when he looked into the brown eyes of the man holding the gun, Mark saw a fire that was due to zeal for a cause or the effect of drugs or maybe both. It took every bit of courage he had to keep his own eyes from showing the emotion he felt—fear.

Mark turned to the gunman and said, "I'll help him, but we need some space. If you're determined to watch, at least step back." He jerked his head to the side. "Stand there by the door. You can see everything, but you'll be out of the way. I need to start CPR on this man."

"But—"

Mark's voice carried all the authority he could muster. "Move! Now!"

The pistol came up, and Mark felt his heart drop as he waited for that trigger finger to tighten one last time. Then the gunman shrugged and backed up until he was against the door. "Okay, but remember—I'm watching." His pistol traced a circuit from Kelly to Mark and back. "Get cracking."

Mark reached down even further for courage he didn't know he had. "Okay." He moved to the side of the wounded man, where his fingers felt the neck for the carotid pulse. He took a deep breath and looked up at Kelly. "Got those IV lines in yet?"

"Just finished one," she said. "About to start on the second."

"No time. Let it go," Mark said. "When you started the IV, did you get some blood to send to the bank for T&C?"

She patted the pocket of her scrub dress, producing a glassy tinkle. "T&C for six units, stat hemoglobin and hematocrit, everything. Got the tubes right here."

"Bob, take these to the lab—"

"Nobody leaves the room!" the gunman snapped.

Mark started to argue, but decided it would be fruitless. "I'm going to start chest compressions now." He glanced at Kelly. "Hook him up to the EKG so I can see if there's any activity. We may have to shock him."

Mark looked down at the man on the treatment table. The aide had cut away the patient's shirt, revealing three puckered entrance wounds where bullets had pierced his chest. They were grouped tightly right above the man's left nipple, close enough together that a playing card could cover them all. Now the bleeding had completely stopped.

Why wasn't he here by now? How long would it take? Mark had to keep going. "I'm going to start CPR now." He put one hand over the other, centering them on the patient's breastbone. He wasn't sure how long he could keep this up, though. *Come on. What are you waiting for?*

The door crashed open, sending the gunman staggering forward onto his knees.

"Police. Drop the gun!" The policeman held his service pistol in a two-handed grip. "On the floor! Now!"

Instead, the gunman, still on his knees, twisted to face the policeman, his own pistol extended. The next seconds were filled with gunfire.

When he heard the first shot, Mark reached across the patient and shoved Kelly to the ground. "Get down," he screamed.

It seemed to Mark that the gunfire went on for a full minute, but he knew better. It always seemed that time either sped up or slowed to a crawl in emergency situations like this. His ears were still ringing when he raised his head and looked around. The gunman lay sprawled on his back, open eyes unseeing, his gun a foot away from his outstretched hand. Mark had seen enough death to know the gunman no longer presented any danger.

The policeman was crumpled in the doorway, one hand clenched over his abdomen, a fountain of blood issuing from between his outstretched fingers. The other hand still clutched his service pistol. He was breathing, although his respirations were labored.

Mark took in the scene in less than a second. He jumped to his feet and called to Kelly, "We need a gurney. We have to get him to the OR, stat." To the aide, he said, "Stick your head out the door. Have them call for help. Alert the OR I'm coming up."

"He looks familiar. Who...who's he?" Kelly asked.

"Sergeant Ed Purvis. He brings patients here sometimes. I'd just finished with one when all this started." Mark moved to the side of the wounded policeman. "Now help me get him onto a gurney."

"What...what about the wounded man already on the table?" Bob asked over his shoulder as Kelly and Mark slid their hands under the fallen officer.

"Don't worry about him. He was dead by the time Kelly wheeled him into the ER."

2

IN THE OPERATING ROOM, A GERMICIDAL SOLUTION splashed on Ed Purvis's abdomen by the circulating nurse turned the pale skin bronze. The scrub nurse hurriedly placed sterile green sheets around the operative area. While the anesthesiologist was still injecting medication into the patient's IV line to relax him, Mark, now clad in a sterile gown, reached out a gloved hand for the scalpel and made a vertical incision that opened Purvis's abdominal cavity wide.

"Is one of the surgeons on the way?" Mark asked.

"We've put out a call," the circulating nurse said.

"Guess it's up to me until one shows up," Mark said. He looked to the anesthesiologist at the head of the table. "Can you give me more relaxation?"

Dr. Buddy Cane nodded. "Coming up. You've got a pretty good head start on me, you know."

Mark worked on, assisted by the scrub nurse. His attention was riveted on the operative field when a husky contralto voice from across the room said, "Tell me what we've got."

Dr. Anna King stood in the doorway, dripping hands held high in front of her. The scrub nurse turned away from the table to help the surgeon gown and glove.

For a moment, Mark had almost forgotten that Anna was a surgeon. In his mind, she was an attractive blonde he'd dated occasionally. Of course, he'd heard rumors... Never mind. He wanted help and now he had it. "Multiple gunshot wounds of the abdomen," he said. In a few sentences, he related how Purvis had been shot. "He's hanging on by a thread. I think we need to—"

"I've got it, Mark. Thanks." This was a different Anna King from the one with whom Mark had shared dinner just a week ago. That one was funny, easy-going. This one was, in every sense, the surgeon. The attitude was "I'm in charge," and Mark had the feeling that if he crossed her, he'd regret it. He was already wondering what a long-term relationship with her would be like. Never mind. He'd deal with that later.

Within less than a minute, Anna was gowned and gloved. She moved to stand at the patient's right side, and Mark slid around to a position opposite her. Anna readjusted the self-retaining retractor and held out her hand. "Let's get some suction in here. Adjust that overhead light."

For a few minutes, the OR was quiet except for the murmured conversation of the surgeon and assistant as they bent over the operative area. Once, the circulating nurse darted in to mop Anna's brow with a cloth. When she eased up behind Mark, he shook his head and she backed away.

"How many units of blood?" Mark looked toward the head of the table.

The anesthesiologist checked his notes. "Six." He paused. "More coming. But his vitals keep slipping."

Mark's deep breath resonated inside his surgical mask. "Let's—"

"Mark, you called for help. I'm here. Let me be in charge, would you?" There was no anger in Anna's words, just a simple statement of fact.

Mark nodded, but didn't reply. He'd have to be careful not to cross Anna while she was in this mode.

His mind moved from the Anna he'd known socially to the surgeon, Anna King. So far she seemed to be doing fine. There were too many smells in the operating room for him to pick up any scent of alcohol drifting through her surgical mask. Still, Mark wondered...

Anna spoke without taking her eyes from the operating area. "Mark, I know you feel responsible for this patient, but you did your part by getting him up here as quickly as you could. Now it's my responsibility." She held out her hand and the scrub nurse slapped a hemostat into it. "We'll do our best. But we can't save every patient."

"I got him into this," Mark said, clamping off another bleeding point. "It's my fault he got shot."

"No," Anna said. "Like every police officer, he knew the risks the first day he put on that uniform. You took the only chance you had to save the lives of three people."

"And it cost the life of another one," Mark said.

"Not yet," Anna said. "Now, if you're going to assist, don't focus on assigning blame. Just help me."

Anna King pushed her surgical mask down to hang beneath her chin. She stripped off her latex gloves and tossed them in the designated waste receptacle, then turned around so the nurse could unfasten her surgical gown. "I'm sorry, Mark." She balled the gown into a mass and threw it after the gloves. "We did what we could. We just couldn't save him."

Mark opened his mouth, then decided he had nothing to say, so he simply shook his head. Let her assign whatever meaning she liked to the gesture.

Anna paused with one hand on the operating room's swinging door. "I'll see if his family's here yet."

"No!" Mark hadn't meant to bark the word, but, considering the state of his emotions at this point, he wasn't surprised at the way it came out. "No," he said more softly. "Let me go out there and talk with them. They need to know more than that he was shot dead." He swallowed hard. "I need to tell them that he saved my life."

"Mark, you can't take this personally. You see gunshot wounds in the emergency room all the time. Some of those patients we can save, some not. What's so different about this one?"

Mark knew what was different, but he wasn't prepared to say the words. Not yet. Instead, he snatched the surgical cap off his head and held it in front of him like a penitent presenting an offering. "When they come into the ER—makes no difference which side of the law they were on when the bullets hit them—when they reach the ER, they're mine. I'm going to do my best to save them. Some I do, some I don't. I accept that." He looked at the body of Ed Purvis, now covered by a sheet. "But this wasn't someone who showed up with a gunshot wound. This was a man I knew—admittedly, not well—a man that I literally asked to put his life on the line to save mine." Mark bowed his head.

Anna put her hand on Mark's shoulder, probably the closest she could come to a gesture of tenderness in this situation. "And he responded the way you hoped he would. He did what law enforcement officers do every day in this country. He did what he'd signed up to do, and in doing so he saved your life." She opened the door. "Come with me if you like. I know his family would appreciate it. But don't take the responsibility for his death on yourself. And don't think you have to spend the rest of your life making up for it."

"Thanks for doing this, Steve," Kelly said. "The adrenaline from what happened has about worn off, but I just couldn't be alone...not for a while, at least. Besides, I...I think it might help if I sort of talked this out, and you're a good listener."

Before he took a seat in the booth opposite her, Steve Farrington, pastor of the Drayton Community Church, handed Kelly one of the two steaming cups he'd obtained from the service counter at this all-night fast food establishment. "No problem, Kelly." He blew across the surface of his cup. "When I heard about the gunman in the ER, I headed for the hospital. I found out you were one of the hostages, and after you were freed I stuck around to see if you needed anything." He took a sip of coffee. "But, to be clear, did you want me here because I'm your pastor or your friend?"

"Both, I guess," Kelly said. "So you can wear whichever hat you want...so long as you stay here with me for a while."

"I'm happy to sit and talk with you, but don't you need to call anyone else? Family, maybe?"

Kelly thought for a moment. "No. My family wouldn't understand or even care."

He looked into his coffee cup but didn't drink. "Why don't you tell me about it?"

Kelly leaned across the table. "I was at the triage desk in the emergency room tonight when a man came in, supporting a gunshot victim. I was about to call for an aide to get a gurney for the patient when the first man grabbed a wheelchair and told me to push his brother back into the ER. I started to argue. Then he pulled a gun..." She bowed her head, closed her eyes, and took several deep breaths. "Sorry. He pulled a gun, held it to my head, and said, 'Take my brother back there and get a doctor to fix him up, or I'll kill you.'"

"Obviously that was frightening," Steve said. "So what happened then?"

Kelly worked her way through the explanation of the next few minutes, ending with the shooting of the gunman by Sergeant Purvis. "We rushed the policeman into the elevator and wheeled him into the OR. The night crew had just finished an emergency case, and they took over. I went back down to the ER and spent the next hour or so talking with the police."

"How do you feel now?"

Kelly shook her head. "I'm still shaky, but it's getting better. Talking about it helps, I guess." She looked down. "Now that I have time to think about it, during that time I was as worried for Mark as for myself."

"About what?"

Kelly stared into her cup. "I didn't want him to die."

"Why is that? Is it because Mark isn't a Christian?" Steve asked.

"I...I'm not sure where he stands. I've broached the subject a time or two, but Mark always deflects the conversation. I get the impression he doesn't like to talk about religion." She drained the cup and shoved it aside. "He says he got too busy for all that when he was in medical school." Kelly patted her lips with a paper napkin. "I think talking about religion embarrasses him."

"You and Mark have been going out for a while, haven't you?"

"Several months," Kelly said.

"Is it serious?"

"It's not exclusive for him, I guess—he went out with one of the surgeons from the hospital last week—but I haven't dated anyone else since I started seeing him."

Steve started to stand. "Would you like some more coffee?"

Kelly shook her head.

He sat down again and took a sip from his cup. "Is Mark's spiritual status the main reason you were concerned about him?"

"I..." Kelly shook her head.

"This probably isn't the time for you to talk with Mark about this, but that time will come soon. I think you'd better try to sort out your feelings before then." He reached over and placed his hand on top of hers. "Until then, maybe you should pray about it."

Kelly nodded silently. *Yes, for both Mark and me... because I didn't tell you the rest of the story.*

Mark struggled to keep his voice steady as he stood face to face with Dr. Eric McCray in a relatively quiet corner of the emergency room. "Tough night," Mark said. "Thanks for taking over down here."

"No problem, man. When I got the call from the hospital about what happened, when they told me you had to go up to the OR to try to save the policeman's life, I jumped into my car and headed here, praying all the way." He pointed around the ER. "Everybody pitched in. Jim's coming on duty in another hour, but I think I'll stick around to help him clear out the backlog."

"No need. I'm okay to get back to work."

"Forget it," Eric said. "I don't have anyone at home waiting for me. You need to clear out of here."

"I...I appreciate it."

"Listen, how's Kelly doing?"

Mark shrugged. "I don't know yet. The ER people told me she'd left as soon as the police were through with her. I wanted to talk with her, but they grabbed me when I got down from the OR."

"Well, give her my best, and tell her I'm glad she's okay." Eric clapped Mark on the back and walked away.

Mark's pulse still wasn't fully back to normal when he collapsed onto the sagging couch in the break room, holding in one hand a Styrofoam cup of what had to be the world's worst coffee. He'd retrieved his cell phone from his locker, but right now it was still in the pocket of his scrubs. He should call Kelly, but he wasn't quite ready to talk with her.

Mark thought about everything that went through his mind when the gunman first entered the ER. He was ashamed of his first reaction. Fortunately, it had all worked out in the end. Thank goodness the gunman believed his friend was still alive and might respond to treatment. Of course, that only worked because Kelly picked up on the idea immediately. Matter of fact, as Mark thought more about what happened, Kelly might have had the idea first.

If she hadn't...don't go there, he reminded himself. He'd survived, and so had Kelly. The gunman was on his way to the morgue to lie alongside his brother. As for the policeman who'd killed him...Mark pushed thoughts of Ed Purvis aside. Anna was right. The man knew the risks. And despite what his heart told him, Mark's head reminded him he couldn't save everyone.

As soon as Mark returned to the emergency room from the OR, the police had grabbed him for questioning, asking the same things again and again. No, he had no idea of the identity of the gunman or the patient. No, he'd never seen them before. No, he was pretty certain the gunman fired first, but it all happened so fast. Yes, Sergeant Purvis identified himself as a police officer and ordered the gunman to surrender. And on and on and on it went.

Actually, Mark had some questions of his own. Who were the men who'd invaded the emergency room—both the gunman and the wounded man? How did the shooter get past the metal detector at the ER door? What was the condition of the hospital security officer the gunman struck down? After his first couple of questions went unanswered, Mark decided the police weren't interested in giving out information. Maybe he'd learn more eventually.

The questioning was finally over, but Mark had the feeling there'd be more. But, for now, he was alone. He crumpled his empty cup and flung it toward the wastebasket in the ER staff lounge, missing by a foot. It lay amid two other cups and a wadded candy wrapper, a testament to poor aim by staff called away before they could pick up their trash. Mark started to get up to clean up the mess, then decided he'd do it in a moment. He leaned back on the couch and looked at his cell phone as though it could provide the answer to his frustration. Come to think of it, perhaps it might, if Kelly would only answer.

Kelly was relaxing—or at least, trying to relax—in a hot tub when she heard the ring of her cell phone. Her first instinct was to get out of the tub, wrap herself in a towel, and trudge into the bedroom to answer the call before it rolled over to voicemail. After all, that's one of the first reflexes instilled into medical personnel. It could represent an emergency. The hospital—or, in this case, the police—might need something.

Then again, the call might be from Mark. After it was all over, she wanted to hug him, tell him how brave he'd been, to say how glad she was that he was alive, to pour out her heart to him. But now Kelly wondered if that talk should wait until they both calmed down some more. She hadn't even dared share with her pastor what she'd really thought tonight. Maybe neither she nor Mark was ready for this conversation right now.

Kelly turned on the tap to run more hot water into the bath. She needed to relax muscles that were tense as bowstrings. She sighed, eased back into the water, closed her eyes, and went over the events of the evening for what must have been the twentieth time. Her pastor had been right. What happened tonight was a natural springboard for a conversation she needed to have with Mark. But there was more there than the pastor knew... and she wasn't certain she was ready to tell Mark everything.

Mark's call went to voicemail. His message was brief: "Kelly, this is Mark. I'm sorry I couldn't see you right after the shooting. Please call me." But she didn't. Finally, after waiting as long as he could, he called again... and yet again. The results were the same, except that he didn't bother to leave a message on those occasions, although perhaps the chip responsible for voicemail picked up the sound of his grinding molars.

Even though Kelly, like Mark, relied on her cell phone, she had a landline number. He tried it now, but there was no answer. Many hospital personnel, including Mark, complied as inexpensively as possible with the hospital's requirement they have a landline by using a "voice over Internet protocol" or VoIP phone. Most of the calls Mark received on that line were either wrong numbers or telephone solicitors, so usually he simply ignored the phone when it rang. Maybe Kelly was doing the same thing. After what they'd been through, he certainly couldn't blame her.

Common sense told him to give up, go home, try to get some rest. But he wasn't in a mood to rest. He was as jittery as the cook in a meth lab right now, and he knew there was no hope of his getting to sleep until he came down from his nervous high. He could call Anna King—she'd probably still be awake—but for some reason he wasn't ready for another conversation with her. Mark wondered if their conversation in the OR hadn't revealed too much of her already.

He had a few friends, most of them doctors, but Mark hated to wake them up. His parents wouldn't understand, and his call would only upset them. He tried to think of someone else to whom he could talk, but Kelly's name kept coming to the forefront.

Mark knew that some of his colleagues drank to relax after a particularly difficult case. Anna was a case in point. Maybe he should call her, perhaps drop by her home to wind down with a drink. He squelched the thought as soon as it popped into his mind. That wasn't any kind of a solution. It would only make matters worse.

He couldn't escape the feeling that what he and Kelly went through tonight had somehow tightened the bond between them. What did that mean about his relationship with Anna King? Maybe tomorrow he'd think about it. He had to take things one step, one day at a time.

The clock on the wall in the break room hadn't worked since the Reagan administration. Mark abandoned the practice of wearing a watch when he started working in the ER. He looked at the time displayed on his cell phone and discovered that it was almost one A.M. He shrugged into the white coat he wore to cover his scrub suit as he went to and from work, pulled his car keys from the pocket, and headed out the door. Common sense dictated that he drive directly home, maybe stopping at an all-night fast food place for a burger or malt. But he knew that wasn't going to happen. There was no doubt in Mark's mind what his next stop would be.

Finally, Kelly could put it off no longer. She crawled into bed, but sleep eluded her. All she could do was lie there and stare at the ceiling. She tried closing her eyes, but the images kept coming. A hot bath and a bowl of Blue Bell vanilla ice cream with chocolate syrup was her usual bedtime prescription for nights when sleep wouldn't come, but tonight the remedy hadn't worked. She read a Bible passage, but the words kept running together, and she got no comfort from them. Her prayers were a jumble of thoughts and incomplete sentences stemming from emotions running rampant in her brain.

She'd seen the "missed call" messages on her cell phone: three calls from Mark. While she was in the tub, still winding down from her ordeal, she hadn't been ready to talk with him. Afterward, when she started to call him back, she couldn't bring herself to press the button. Was it too late? Or was she just not ready for the conversation? In either case, the call went unmade.

Now Kelly tossed and turned, seeking sleep that wouldn't come. She was about to get out of bed and turn on the TV, usually her last resort, when she heard a car pull up outside her house. That was unusual at this time of the morning in her neighborhood. The occupants of the homes around her were mostly older couples whose children had long since left home, and by this time of night the street was quiet and empty.

Kelly eased from her bed, wrapped a robe around her, and slid her feet into worn, comfortable scuffs. She tiptoed to the front room and parted the blinds far enough to see the white sedan parked in front of her house. The lone occupant sat unmoving, shrouded in darkness, for several minutes. When he opened the driver's side door, the car's interior light came on, and she recognized Mark. He hesitated for a moment before striding toward her front door, his white coat highlighted by the light from the street lamp.

He paused on her doorstep, and she could almost hear the thoughts going through his head. It was late. There were no lights on in the house. Should he wake her? What would she say?

Kelly examined her own feelings. Should she remain quiet? If he knocked, would she answer it? Or would she let her inaction turn him away?

Almost without making a conscious decision, she moved a few steps to the end table in the living room and turned on the lamp there. Apparently that was enough encouragement for Mark.

He tapped lightly on the door. "Kelly, it's Mark," he called softy. "I know it's late, but I need to talk to you. May I come in?"

Kelly cinched her robe more tightly closed, then opened the door. She gestured him inside, still unsure of what to say, then locked the door behind him.

They stood awkwardly for a moment, then each reached out for the other, and the embrace that followed seemed to last forever. Kelly found there was a lump in her throat that made speaking difficult. "I'm... I'm so glad you're okay," she said.

"I know it's late, but I'm having a hard time unwinding, and I wondered if you were, too."

"I was trying, but without much success," Kelly admitted.

"I knew I couldn't sleep until I talked this out with someone."

Kelly's heart thudded in her chest. Would the things Mark wanted to say be the same ones that had kept her awake tonight? She motioned him to the sofa and eased down beside him. "Then why don't you tell me?" Kelly looked into his eyes and held her breath.

3

Mark sat on the side of his bed, groggy with lack of sleep after thrashing about for most of the night, unable to rest and emotionally wrung out. He'd left Kelly's house about a quarter to two. Right now she'd be getting ready for church, but she'd promised to call him after the services. Until then, he was on his own.

After the shooting, Eric had offered to take Mark's Sunday evening shift in the ER, and Mark readily accepted the offer. At that point, he felt like he never wanted to see the inside of a hospital again. Now, less than twelve hours later, he wondered what he'd do to occupy himself if he didn't go to work tonight. There was a time when his life revolved around his shifts in the ER: sleep, eat, go to work, come home, eat, sleep, repeat the cycle. Since he'd started dating Kelly, the pattern had expanded to include time with her, plus an occasional dinner with Anna for variety. One of those relationships might eventually demand more of his time. He knew which one, but he didn't want to think about that right now.

Last night had changed a lot of things. Mark's thoughts seemed to be stuck on the shooting—and his emotions while it was going down. He hung his head, closed his eyes, and wondered why he hadn't confessed to Kelly. Maybe today…

The buzzing of his cell phone startled him. He picked it up and frowned when the caller ID showed "anonymous caller." Could it be a reporter? None had managed to find him last night, but he had no doubt they'd remedy that today. Surely a telephone solicitor wouldn't be calling at eight o'clock on a Sunday morning.

Oh, well. He had nothing better to do. Might as well answer it. "Dr. Baker."

"Doctor, this is Detective Jackson."

Mark wished he could clear the cobwebs from his brain. Like slogging through mud, the synapses slowly clicked. Jackson was the lead detective investigating the shooting. Mark had met him and his partner, Detective Ames, last night—or, more accurately, early this morning. His mental picture of Jackson was of a short, stocky African-American in a wrinkled suit, the almost laser-like intensity behind his dark eyes a warning not to mistake a disheveled appearance for carelessness. Mark had decided to walk carefully around Jackson.

"Doctor, are you there?"

Mark sat up and swiveled around to perch on the bedside. "Uh, yeah. What can I do for you?"

"I thought you might want to know that we've ID'd the two victims of last night's shooting."

ID'd the victims? He already knew who the chief victim was: Sergeant Purvis. Then Mark realized the detective was talking about the gunman and the man—didn't he call him his brother?—the man who'd been essentially dead on arrival in the ER. "Okay."

"They were brothers," Detective Jackson said. "The older was Hector Garcia. The gunman was his younger brother, Ignacio, aka 'Nacho.'"

The names meant nothing to Mark. "Who?"

"Yeah, I'm sure the names aren't familiar," Jackson said, "but this may help you. They were members of the Zeta drug cartel."

That information opened Mark's eyes like a cup of strong coffee. Generally, his newspaper reading was confined to the sports section, but almost everyone in Texas knew that the Zetas were the most feared drug cartel in Mexico. Even the Mexican police and military walked carefully around the Zetas. He'd heard they were operating in the state, but he figured it would be further south, near the border. On the contrary, these men had been in Drayton, right in the heart of north Texas.

"I wanted to let you know," Jackson went on. "Since Ed Purvis shot Nacho, we're going to give some protection to the Purvis family for a while. We can't do that for everyone involved in the incident, but I thought I should at least warn you. The Zetas have a strong sense of revenge, and you might want to be extra careful yourself."

"What about Kelly?"

"Who? Oh, the nurse who first interacted with Nacho." There was a rustle of paper. "She's next on my list to contact."

"I'll do it," Mark said. "We're supposed to talk later today." He paused. "I don't guess the people in the OR attending to Sergeant Purvis are at risk, though."

"We don't think so, but you can never tell what kind of twisted logic these people have about getting even," Jackson said. "Anyway, I've got to get going. I'll call if we need anything more from you."

"Detective, one thing before you go. I know you generally keep information like this confidential, but would you give me Sergeant Purvis's address? I want to go by later today and personally express my condolences to the family."

"Did you talk with them last night?"

"Only briefly, and frankly after Mrs. Purvis heard about her husband's death, I don't think she took in anything I or the other surgeon had to say."

It took a good bit of cajoling, but eventually Jackson gave Mark the information he needed. "But be sensitive," the detective cautioned.

"I will be." Mark remembered how it was when his brother died. There were a slew of people in and out of the house. Most were well-meaning and helpful, but some just wanted to focus on assigning blame. To Mark and his family, it didn't matter that the other driver was drunk, was driving with an invalid license. Joe was still dead, and his family needed sympathy and support. Mark figured the Purvis family was in the same situation.

After ending the call, Mark shuffled into the kitchen and put on a pot of extra-strong coffee. He had a hunch he'd need it—it promised to be a long day.

"Shouldn't you be home?" Tracy Orton asked.

"Why? To worry about what's already happened?" Kelly said. "No, it's Sunday, and I wanted to be in church this morning. Actually, I needed to be here."

The two women stood in a relatively quiet corner of the Drayton Community Church, out of the traffic pattern of people exiting after the Sunday morning service. Tracy's dark hair was pulled back in a ponytail. Her makeup was understated. She wore very little jewelry. Her dress was a simple white sheath. But, as always, what most people noticed first was the hint of mischief that gleamed in the eyes of Kelly's best friend.

"Well, how about some lunch?" Tracy asked. "We can lust over the menu items we can't have because they're fattening, and you can tell me about last night."

Despite her somber mood, Kelly smiled. "I'm not sure about the lusting, but... yes, I think I'd like to talk to somebody about what happened." She paused, considering her next words carefully. "And there's something else I'd like to run by you."

"Want to ride with me?"

"No, I'd better go in my car. I'll meet you there," Kelly said.

They turned to go, but stopped when a voice behind them said, "Kelly. Surprised to see you here today, but I'm glad you've come. I've been praying for you and Mark."

Kelly turned slowly to face the pastor. "I'm glad I came. The sermon was just what I needed to hear this morning. And thank you for your prayers."

"Is Mark okay?" the pastor asked.

"We talked late last night. He was pretty shaken, but I think he'll be okay." No need to go into details with the pastor beyond what she'd shared with him last night.

"Well, keep me posted on developments." He smiled and moved away.

Kelly nodded. *I will... with some of them. But not all of them. Not right now.*

Kelly was already seated in a booth at the back of their favorite little cafe when Tracy walked in. "I ordered iced tea for both of us."

"Great." Tracy sat down opposite Kelly and dropped her purse on the seat beside her.

They made small talk until after the waitress took their order. Then Tracy said, "So, the account in the paper was pretty sketchy, and the TV reports didn't tell me much more. I want to hear all about what happened."

Kelly was surprised that it took so little time to relate last evening's sequence of events. "Mark got the gunman to back up toward the door of the trauma room," she said in conclusion. "Sergeant Purvis burst through, knocking the man off balance, ordering him to drop the gun. Instead he fired, and we ducked. When we looked up, the gunman was dead, and Mark was calling for a gurney to take Purvis to the OR, where he died."

"Wow!" Tracy reached across and covered her friend's hand with her own. "What was going through your mind when all this was happening?"

"I tried to be calm, tell myself that if he pulled the trigger I'd end up in a better place. Of course, I'm not sure the same could be said for Mark, and I didn't have any idea where the aide stood."

"So you prayed for them?"

Kelly bit her lip. "Actually, no. Instead, I found myself thinking, 'Mark can't die not knowing.'"

"Not knowing what?"

"Not knowing that I'm falling in love with him."

Mark hadn't been to visit a family in mourning since a college friend died years ago. At that time, he and three of his fraternity brothers had driven almost an hour each way to pay their respects. He didn't remember much about the experience, except that he was glad he had someone with him. The sickly-sweet scent of flowers, the people conversing in hushed tones, all made him wish he could hurry and get out of the house.

A year later, his own brother had been killed in an auto accident, his life snuffed out by a drunk driver. Mark had virtually sleepwalked through that experience, letting his parents deal with the people who came by. A few of Joe's friends wanted to talk, but Mark tried to avoid them. He didn't want to talk about what had happened to his brother. He wanted it all to be a bad dream, and if that wasn't possible, he just wanted to get through the experience.

Since that time, the closest Mark had come to death was in the emergency room. Visiting the bereaved and attending funerals weren't on his list. Nevertheless, for reasons he couldn't explain, Mark felt the need to express his sympathy to Sergeant Purvis's family in person. He figured that most people there would be dressed informally, but after he'd donned khakis and an open neck knit shirt, Mark decided that felt wrong. He wasn't the average person coming to say, "Sorry for your loss." No, Mark was there to say, "I'm responsible for your husband getting shot." Somehow, it seemed that called for him to wear something different.

He pulled his dark suit from the closet. He found a clean white shirt in his dresser drawer. His stock of ties was laughably small, but he finally found a muted maroon-and-gold striped one that should be solemn enough. Mark looked in the mirror and decided that he was as dressed for the occasion as possible. If he ended up going to the funeral—and that was a very big "if"—he'd wear the same thing. He doubted that the Purvis family was going to notice much about his attire, either today or later. No, they had other things on their mind.

As Mark turned the key in the ignition of his white Toyota Camry, he wondered if he really should make this visit. Would Purvis's widow even talk with him? Would the family be in church this morning? No, it was more likely that if they weren't home they'd be at the funeral home, making final arrangements.

Mark decided that if he didn't do it now, he'd worry about it until the visit was behind him. He punched the address he'd wheedled from Detective Jackson into his car's GPS and pulled away from the curb. Suddenly, his collar was too tight. His throat was dry. He adjusted the car's climate control, but still he felt rivulets of perspiration running down his back.

Mark wished he could believe that praying would help. No, it had been too long since he'd even tried. Instead, he called on a meditation exercise he'd learned from a med school classmate. In a few moments, he decided that it—like so many other things in his life—wasn't working.

As soon as her declaration that she was falling in love with Mark was out of Kelly's mouth, the waitress served their lunches. Tracy was almost beside herself by the time the dishes were on the table and the waitress gone. She ignored her food, leaning forward toward Kelly and dropping her voice. "You're in love with him? Are you sure?"

Kelly picked up a half of her tuna sandwich, then returned it to the plate. "Pretty sure."

"And you suddenly decided this last night while a man was holding you and Mark at gunpoint?"

"I know," Kelly said. "It sounds crazy. Mark and I have been dating for several months. I knew I was growing fond of him, but finally, last night, when our lives were in danger,

I discovered..." She grimaced. "This is hard to say out loud, to hear myself admit it."

Tracy met her gaze but remained silent.

"I couldn't imagine life without him."

"Does he—?"

"No. I haven't said anything to him yet. Last night, he came by my house sometime after one. He was having a hard time coming down from the experience, and frankly, so was I. We talked for almost an hour about what we'd gone through, just letting our feelings out. Mainly we kept on rehashing the situation, saying the same things again and again until we finally ran down like a train engine out of steam. A couple of times he seemed as though he wanted to say something more, but each time it was like he hit an emotional wall and clammed up. And I couldn't bring myself to tell him what I was feeling, either."

"I see." Tracy shoved her salad aside. "Well, do you want some advice?"

Kelly shook her head. "Not really. I just had to share this with someone I could trust to keep my secret."

"Well, I'll give you my advice, whether you want it or not." Tracy paused to drink deeply from her iced tea. "Tell Mark how you feel."

Kelly felt her stomach twisting. She didn't want to hear this. "But what if he doesn't feel the same way?"

Tracy shrugged. "Only one way to find out. You know what your feelings are. Dollars to donuts, Mark hasn't examined his own. The only way to help him do this is to tell him what you discovered last night."

"But—"

"I know. He may not feel the same way. But you need to let him know where you stand, so he can figure out how he feels. You've got to make this a two-way street."

Kelly looked down at the almost-untouched sandwich on her plate. She knew Tracy was right. But another factor that no one had mentioned—the elephant in the room, so to speak—was Mark's dating Dr. Anna King. How serious was that? How foolish would Kelly feel if she told Mark how she felt, only to have him say that he had feelings for Anna.

Maybe Kelly did need to make this a two-way street, but what if she discovered that she'd missed a directional sign and was on her way to a head-on collision?

Ripped-From-The-Headlines Action
Enjoy these fast-paced reads from Abingdon Fiction

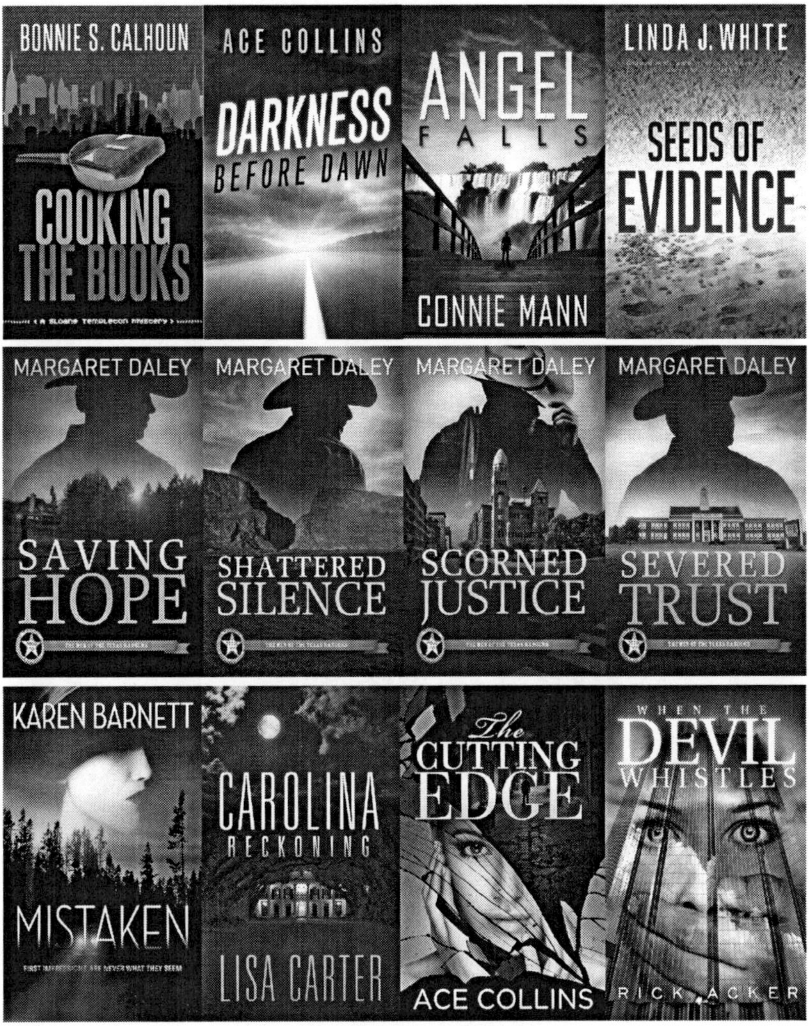

www.AbingdonFiction.com

 **Find us on Facebook**
Abingdon Press | Fiction

 **Follow us on Twitter**
@AbingdonFiction

A Novel Approach To Faith
Enjoy these entertaining reads from Abingdon Fiction

www.AbingdonFiction.com

 Find us on Facebook
Abingdon Press | Fiction

 Follow us on Twitter
@AbingdonFiction

Abingdon fiction™

Travel Back In Time
Enjoy these historical novels from Abingdon Fiction

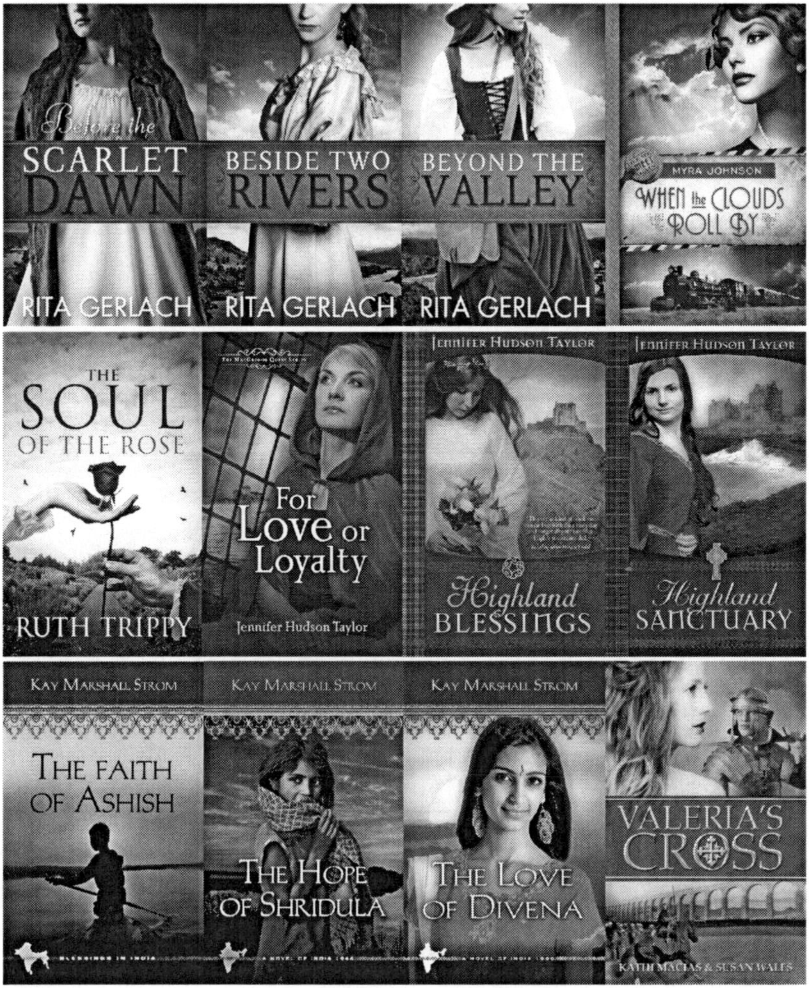

www.AbingdonFiction.com

 Find us on Facebook
Abingdon Press | Fiction

 **Follow us on Twitter**
@AbingdonFiction

Fall In Love With A Good Book
Enjoy these romantic reads from Abingdon Fiction

www.AbingdonFiction.com

 **Find us on Facebook**
Abingdon Press | Fiction

 **Follow us on Twitter**
@AbingdonFiction

Abingdon fiction™

Escape To A Simple Life

Enjoy these Amish and Mennonite novels from Abingdon Fiction

www.AbingdonFiction.com

Find us on Facebook
Abingdon Press | Fiction

Follow us on Twitter
@AbingdonFiction

CPSIA information can be obtained at www.ICGtesting.com
Printed in the USA
BVOW05*1407200516
448785BV00002B/2/P

9 781501 816307